# "YOU THINK WE CAN HELP?"
## KIRK ASKED . . .

"You plan against these petty nobles; that is bold," Captain Kaden said, twisting the cap from his fourth bottle of beer. "That is the way of the line-founder and I salute it . . . but what if we were discovered interfering with your planet? Would not the lightbulbs object?" He looked at the bottlecap in his hand, tossed it aside as if it were hot.

"Lightbulbs?" Pete said.

"Organians," Kirk said. "It's a habit they have. . . . Well, never mind that. I don't think this should make any difference at all with them. It's not like we're trying to influence your world's decision about the dilithium rights. . . ."

"No," Kaden said quickly.

"Of course not," Pete said.

"Absolutely," Kirk said.

"Nothing like it," Kaden added.

"Well," Kirk smiled. "I'm glad we understand that."

# Look for STAR TREK Fiction from Pocket Books

Star Trek: The Original Series

    *Final Frontier*
    *Strangers from the Sky*
    *Enterprise*
    *Star Trek IV: TVH*
#1 *Star Trek: TMP*
#2 *The Entropy Effect*
#3 *The Klingon Gambit*
#4 *The Covenant of the Crown*
#5 *The Prometheus Design*
#6 *The Abode of Life*
#7 *Star Trek II: TWOK*
#8 *Black Fire*
#9 *Triangle*
#10 *Web of the Romulans*
#11 *Yesterday's Son*
#12 *Mutiny on the Enterprise*
#13 *The Wounded Sky*
#14 *The Trellisane Confrontation*
#15 *Corona*
#16 *The Final Reflection*
#17 *Star Trek III: TSFS*
#18 *My Enemy, My Ally*
#19 *The Tears of the Singers*
#20 *The Vulcan Academy Murders*
#21 *Uhura's Song*
#22 *Shadow Lord*

#23 *Ishmael*
#24 *Killing Time*
#25 *Dwellers in the Crucible*
#26 *Pawns and Symbols*
#27 *Mindshadow*
#28 *Crisis on Centaurus*
#29 *Dreadnought!*
#30 *Demons*
#31 *Battlestations!*
#32 *Chain of Attack*
#33 *Deep Domain*
#34 *Dreams of the Raven*
#35 *The Romulan Way*
#36 *How Much for Just the Planet?*
#37 *Bloodthirst*
#38 *The IDIC Epidemic*
#39 *Time for Yesterday*
#40 *Timetrap*
#41 *The Three-Minute Universe*
#42 *Memory Prime*

Star Trek: The Next Generation

    *Encounter at Farpoint*
#1 *Ghost Ship*
#2 *The Peacekeepers*
#3 *The Children of Hamlin*

A STAR TREK® NOVEL

# HOW MUCH FOR JUST THE PLANET?

## JOHN M. FORD

**POCKET BOOKS**

New York    London    Toronto    Sydney    Tokyo

An *Original* Publication of POCKET BOOKS

POCKET BOOKS, a division of Simon & Schuster Inc.
1230 Avenue of the Americas, New York, NY 10020

ISBN: 0-671-62998-0

First Pocket Books printing October 1987

10 9 8 7 6 5 4 3 2

POCKET and colophon are trademarks of Simon & Schuster Inc.

Printed in the U.S.A.

This book is dedicated, with affection,
to its Special Guest Stars . . .
Pamela & David
Diane & Peter
Janet & Ricky
and Neil, who wanted a walk-on

And acknowledgment is also gratefully made to . . .
W. Shakespeare
G. Feydeau
W. S. Gilbert
and the silent comedians named in verse 2 of "Monochrome"
. . . without whose work there would have been
no tradition to steal from.

# Chapter One

## *In Space, No One Can Fry an Egg*

THE OFFICERS' MESS of the starship USS *Enterprise* was a small, rather cozy room, with comfortable chairs, moderately bright lighting, and a food-service wall with four delivery slots, no waiting. This morning, two officers entered the room, dropped briefing folders marked TOP SECRET onto the table, and approached the service wall.

"I don't know, Scotty," said Captain James T. Kirk, with an offhand gesture toward the secret documents. "Maybe it's just the *idea* of an inflatable rubber starship that bothers me." Kirk turned to face the messroom wall. "Two eggs, sunny side up," he told it, "bacon crisp, wheat toast, and a large orange juice." The wall went *pleep* in acknowledgment.

"Oatcakes wi' butter an' syrup," Chief Engineer Montgomery Scott told the wall, "a broiled kipper, an' coffee black." *Pleep*. "Rubber's hardly the word for the material, Captain. It's a triple-monolayer sandwich: an organic polymer inside to keep th' gas in, metal film on the outside to reflect sensors like a real ship's hull, an' a pseudofluid sealant between 'em."

*Ploop* went the wall. *"I do not have that sandwich on today's menu,"* it said, in a pleasantly maternal voice. *"May I suggest the grilled cheese with Canadian bacon?"*

Scott gave the wall an amiable kick. "An' each of the prototypes is nae bigger than a desk while it's collapsed, includin' the inflation system. Not that it takes much gas to fill her out, not in hard vacuum; a couple o' lungfuls—"

"Mr. Scott somewhat underestimates the volume of gas required," said a voice from the messroom doorway. "The inflation system holds twenty-seven cubic meters of compressed dry nitrogen. Exhaled breath of course contains moisture and respiratory waste products, which would be quite damaging to the material of the Deployable Practice Target."

"Good morning, Spock," Kirk said patiently.

Science Officer Spock entered the mess, hands folded and eyebrows arched. "It does seem the start of a productive day," he said, as the door hissed shut behind him. "One hundred grams of unsalted soya wafers, with one hundred twenty grams of defatted cream cheese," Spock told the wall, "and two hundred milliliters of unsweetened grapefruit juice." *Pleep.*

"I admit that the Deployable Target is a very fancy rubber balloon," Kirk said, "not to mention expensive—"

"Two point eight six three million credits for each of the four prototypes," Spock said.

"—but it's still shooting rubber fish in a barrel."

*Ploop.* "Fried fish are available—"

Kirk ignored the wall and looked past the steep rise

of Spock's eyebrow. "Balloons can't maneuver tactically, and *yes,* I've read the stuff in the *Starfleet Institute Proceedings* about 'pretending three-hundred-meter starships are Sopwith Camels.'"

*Pling* went the wall, and a panel slid open to reveal a tray. Two eggs looked sunny side up from the plate above a smile of bacon. Kirk took the tray to the dining table.

The door opened again, and Ship's Surgeon Leonard McCoy came in. Without a word to anyone, he walked crookedly to the wall, leaned heavily against it, and said something that sounded like "Plergb hfarizz ungemby, *and coffee.*"

Bones McCoy was not a morning person.

*Pleep,* the wall replied, and then *pling* for the delivery of Scott's breakfast, and *pling* again for Spock's. They sat down at the table with Kirk.

The captain had broken the yolk on one of his eggs, buttered his toast, and had his glass two-thirds of the way to his mouth before noticing that the liquid in the tumbler was blue.

Not the deep indigo of grape juice, or the soothing azure of Romulan ale, but a luminous, electric blue, a color impossible in nature.

Kirk looked around the table. Scott and Spock were discussing some obscure engineering aspect of the bal—Deployable Practice Target. There didn't seem to be anything wrong with their breakfasts; Scott's black coffee was black, Spock's juice was pale gold. Dr. McCoy was still waiting for his meal, watching the rest of them like a vulture with a hangover, but his stare had a distinctly unfocused quality. Maybe it was just the early hour, Kirk thought, a trick of the light or something. He looked at his juice again. Still blue.

Starship captains are a special breed of beings who

boldly go, et cetera. Kirk took a sip of the blue liquid. It tasted just like orange juice. It even had pulp that got caught in his teeth, just like orange juice.

One more look. Blue.

The wall *pling*ed, and McCoy brought his tray to the table. Kirk looked at the doctor's meal: there was a huge mug of coffee, a slab of Virginia ham, and an enormous heap of something else. The something else was orange, in the same way Kirk's juice had *not* been orange: it was signal-flare orange, bright as a Christmas necktie. Kirk noticed that Spock and Scotty had stopped talking, and eating, and were looking intently at the orange mound on the doctor's plate.

Oblivious, McCoy buttered the orange heap, sliced the ham, and went at them like a starving man.

After a moment, Spock finished his crackers and cheese, stood up, and slipped his tray into the disposal slot. "Excuse me, Captain, Mr. Scott, Dr. McCoy. I have some preparations to make for the Target tests."

"Aye," Scott said, watching McCoy eat as the syrup congealed around his own oatcakes. Kirk said "Of course, Spock." McCoy said "Gmltfrbl."

Spock looked sidelong at McCoy's plate, turned sharply and went out. Kirk thought he looked rather green, even for a Vulcan.

"I'd better check over the launch tubes," Scott said. "For, uh, th' tests, an' all." He went out.

Kirk watched, fascinated, as Dr. McCoy forked down the orange stuff, interspersed with chunks of ham and gulps of coffee. Finally McCoy drank deep from his mug, sat back in his chair, and let out a long sigh and a short burp.

He looked at Kirk, and frowned. "What's the matter, Jim? Haven't y'ever seen a man eat grits before?"

"I, um . . ."

"And what in the name of Hygeia are you *drinking?*"

"Morning, ah, pick-me-up," Kirk said hastily, and emptied the glass to the last blue drop. " 'Scuse me, Bones, lots to do today." He stood up and dumped his tray, with one uneaten egg still on it. There was no waste; the food processors would recycle it, Kirk thought, and at once regretted thinking.

It was, the captain thought as he left the puzzled doctor in the messroom, going to be one of *those* days.

Not far away, silent in silent deep space, Federation resource exploratory vessel *Jefferson Randolph Smith* cruised at Warp Factor Four, her sensor net spread wide in search of dilithium. Dilithium, that rare and refractory mineral that powers the warp drive, indeed the Federation itself . . . but more about dilithium a little later. Just now, aboard *Smith,* the captain was also having one of those days.

But then, thought Captain Tatyana Trofimov, as she sipped her blue orange juice, it *always* seemed to be one of those days.

The rest of *Smith*'s officers were at the messroom table with Captain Trofimov. The first officer, a Withiki named Tellihu, had his broad, red-feathered wings draped over the back of his chair; he read a freshly printed newsfax with his left hand and ate a mushroom omelet with his right. Tellihu had had eggs for breakfast every morning of *Smith*'s mission, four hundred and sixty-six days so far, and it still seemed to Captain Trofimov vaguely like cannibalism.

Science Officer T'Vau had finished her soya salad and was looking at a chess set. Not playing with it, not touching the pieces, just looking. T'Vau's hair was dangling over one pointed ear, and there were vinegar-and-oil spots on her uniform blouse. For a Vulcan, the Captain thought, T'Vau was really a slob.

The three of them were all the officers aboard *Jefferson Randolph Smith,* and also all the crew, just as this compartment was not only the messroom but the common room and the recreation room. *Smith* (NCC-29402, Sulek-class) was a ship of the Resources Division, Exploration Command, designed to seek out—no, not what you're thinking—seek out minerals, especially dilithium, at the lowest possible cost.

It was actually not such a small ship, really quite roomy given its crew of three. And Starfleet Psychological Division had been very aware that a crew of only three for a mission of twenty to twenty-eight months must be carefully chosen for compatibility. PsyComm recommended that a special battery of crew-relations tests be designed.

The test designers were hard at work and expected to deliver a preliminary report no later than six months from now. Until then—well, somebody had to bring in the dilithium.

Captain Trofimov came from Reynaud II, a thinly populated planet on the Cygnus-Carina Fringe, without much space trade. Trofimov had decided very young that she was not only going to enlist in Starfleet and get off Reynaud II, she was going to get every millimeter as far off Reynaud II as Starfleet went. Exploration Command seemed like just the thing. The recruiter showed her trishots of the big mining ships, like *Dawson City,* and the planetformers, like *Robert Moses,* vessels bigger than starships, bigger than starbases, and Trofimov knew that her destiny was sealed.

Only too right, she thought.

Tellihu finished his omelet, stood up, and said something to the wall in the whistling Withiki language. *Pleep,* the wall said, then *pling.* Tellihu took out what looked to Trofimov like an ice cream cone filled with birdseed and went out of the room nibbling it, dipping his wings to clear the doorway.

He does it deliberately, the captain thought. He'd eat worms if he thought he could get away with it.

She looked at T'Vau. The science officer picked a kelp strand out of her salad bowl and chewed on it idly, still watching the chess set. Finally she reached out, picked up a pawn, turned it over in her fingers, then put it back on its original square.

Trofimov finished her juice without looking at it, and left T'Vau to her, uh, game. As she went into the corridor she thought, I'll bet it's never like this for starship captains. . . .

Not much farther away at all, the Imperial Klingon cruiser *Fire Blossom* patrolled the Organian Treaty Zone that separated the Empire from the Federation.

*Fire Blossom* was named for an incident in the youth of its captain, Kaden vestai-Oparai. Kaden had been an ensign, helmsman aboard a B-5 destroyer in one of the Wars of Internal Dissension. A lucky hit had pierced the destroyer's screens and killed most of the bridge crew, including the captain. Kaden had seized command, only to realize that he had a small and damaged ship being hotly pursued by a light attack cruiser.

Kaden broke formation and made for the nearest sun, dodging the cruiser's fire. The deflectors began shining with energy, the hull to heat despite them. The pursuer closed in. There was no practical chance of survival: the cruiser's heavier screens could sustain a much closer approach to the star, almost to the photosphere. It didn't even have to fire weapons. Just a little more pursuit, and Kaden's ship would melt.

At the last possible moment before the B-5 flashed to vapor, Kaden ejected a survival pod on maximum drive and broke away at nearly ninety degrees, calculating that the cruiser's captain would swing behind him, looking suddenly from intolerable light into darkness, and take a moment to line up his final shot. He would pay no attention to the pod; it was doomed to vaporize in an instant.

Kaden's guess was right. And as the cruiser took aim, the pod Kaden had jettisoned struck the star. Its contents, four magnetic bottles of antimatter, collapsed, and even antiplasma reacts violently with normal matter. There was an eruption from the solar surface, a very small prominence by solar standards, but big enough to engulf the cruiser. The light of its shields collapsing was lost in the sun.

That had been many years ago, Kaden thought as he ordered breakfast from the messroom wall. That had been when life was really enjoyable. Now he commanded a D-7c, a heavy-enhanced battlecruiser as much more powerful than that little destroyer as the destroyer outgunned its survival pod. There was not a deck officer in the entire Imperial Klingon Navy who would not have been excited to command a D-7c into battle against any foe of the Empire.

Unfortunately, ever since the business with the Organians, there had been a real shortage of foes of the Empire you could go into battle against. Try anything the least bit violent in one of the Treaty Zones, and everything like a weapon on the ship, from main-battery controls to cutlery, got red-hot, and some disembodied voice lectured you on the Treaty provisions.

Kaden had seen it happen, as an ensign. His squadron had run across a couple of Tellarite freighters, no armament, no escorts, *nothing,* they were practically towing a sign saying PLEASE HIJACK. And practically before the cruisers were in attack formation—hiss, thunder, you could have fried chops on the Weapons Control board. One of Kaden's bunkmates had been in the portside ratings' head; the Organian lightbulbs had a pretty strange idea of what constituted a weapon. Then, Organians were some kind of pure energy. They probably didn't need disposal cubicles.

At any rate, thanks to the busybody lightbulbs, Kaden's command was about as thrilling as watching yeast grow. And speaking of yeast . . . Kaden looked down at his battertoast, hot and crisp from the wall unit. He shook his head. He looked at his glass of sweetened fruit juice: it seemed all right. He took a long gulp. The rapid Klingon metabolism broke simple sugars down almost instantly, producing a thoroughly pleasant buzz. Just the thing to get started in the morning.

There were consolations, Kaden thought. For one thing, his bridge crew did include Arizhel.

Rish came into the messroom precisely then. Kaden just about jumped at the coincidence, then settled back to watch her. She punched buttons on the meal console, then leaned against the wall. Admirable hull design, Kaden thought, splendid computing equipment. And very sophisticated defensive systems, too, which had thus far precluded any direct sensor analysis, never mind tractors and boarding.

Oh, well, Kaden thought, maybe in the Black Fleet . . . He had a sudden, more immediate thought. "Don't dial up the battertoast."

"What's wrong with the battertoast?" Rish said, as

the console bell rang and the tray slid from the slot. She looked down. *"G'day't!"*

"Well, not literally," Kaden said, and picked up one of the green-coated sticks of toast from his own tray. "They taste all right, if you don't look at them."

Chief Engineer Askade, rather tall and slender for an Imperial-race Klingon, and Security Officer Maglus, built like a stormwalker and just as dangerous, came into the messroom and punched for meals.

Arizhel said, "What do you make of this, Chief Engineer?" She held up one of the green sticks.

Askade took the battertoast, looked at it blearily. "I can't rewire it into a death ray without some extra parts," he said, and took a bite. "Hm. Tastes okay. What's the problem?"

"The color, that's what the problem is."

"Oh?" Askade held the stick close to his eyes, tried to focus on it. "Oh. Hm."

Maglus took his tray from the machine. There was a slab of rare steak and four fried eggs on it, and a liter mug of juice. The eggs had blue yolks. Maglus looked at them for a moment, then shrugged and doused them with hot sauce. He began eating heartily.

Kaden said, "Maybe a couple of feed pipes got crossed, and it's recycling the used laundry instead. This *is* a sort of undress-tunic green, isn't it?"

"That's most unlikely," Askade said, in an unconvincing tone.

"When I think of what the food synths are *supposed* to be recycling," Maglus put in between bites, "I'm not sure that old socks would be so much worse."

The intercom whistled, and the voice of Communications Officer Aperokei came on. "Captain Kaden, Commander Arizhel, wanted on the bridge." Aperokei's voice was, as ever, bright and eager enough to put ice in one's blood.

Rish touched the com key. "What is it, Proke?"

"Ship on sensors, Commander. Looks like a Federation vessel."

"Can you identify?" Kaden said.

"It's small, Captain. Not likely to be a warship. She's sublight in the shallows."

There was a pause. Somewhere or another Aperokei had acquired a fondness for Federation films, and it showed up in his language. "She's what, Lieutenant?" Kaden said patiently.

"Cislunar orbit, I mean, Captain."

Arizhel said, "Sounds like a mapper or surveyor."

"I suppose we should take a look," Kaden said, feeling uneasy already. "Pay our respects, smile at them."

"Carefully," Maglus said.

Askade was idly turning his fork over in his hands. "All we need this morning is a visit from the Org—" He put the fork down, pushed it away.

"We're coming, Proke," Arizhel told the intercom.

"Aye, Commander. We'll look sharp from the bow."

The officers looked at each other, with expressions from bemused to grim. "That youth was *raised* wrong," Askade said, and they dumped their trays and headed for the bridge.

Aboard *Jefferson Randolph Smith,* Captain Trofimov settled into her swivel chair at the center of the bridge. It wasn't a very big bridge, only a room four meters square, and the chair squeaked and its upholstery was patched with plastic tape, but it was Trofimov's bridge, and chair, and command. Content, she switched on the main forward display.

It showed a roomful of people staring at three-dimensional chess sets.

"Computer," Trofimov said, cautiously. A few months back, T'Vau had spilled a milkshake into the computer's main logic bank, and it hadn't been quite the same since.

"Proud to be active and functional, Captain," the computer said.

"Computer, what is on the main display?"

"This is the 68th All-Federation Trimenchess Championship, Captain."

"I see. Why is it on the screen? Did the science officer request it?"

"No, Captain. I simply thought that Lieutenant Commander T'Vau might find it of interest. Considering her interest in the game. And so forth."

"Very well. But please clear—" Trofimov stopped. The chess players on the screen were all sitting alone at sets; not one had an opponent visible. She mentioned this to the computer.

"That is correct, Captain. All these players are competing against the J-9bis duotronic polyprocessor computer known as Polymorphy. They are all predicted to resign in twenty moves or less."

"Why . . . I mean, enhance, Computer."

"I am sorry, Captain, but even though as a J-2 duotronic unit I am directly related to the J-9bis, I lack the capacity to analyze why all these Vulcans might want to play this pointless game."

"I see. And you thought that the science officer might find it . . . interesting."

"I do my best to anticipate and fulfill the needs of my crew, Captain. Excuse me, *your* crew."

"Thank you, Computer. Clear the screen, please. Forward camera view."

The screen blanked and the normal starfield appeared.

Trofimov wondered about the computer. T'Vau

swore the milkshake hadn't done any real damage. Could computers go stir-crazy like people? Trofimov didn't know. They hadn't had talking computers on Reynaud II. There was a law against it. When she went offworld, Trofimov thought that the law was a typically stupid, backwater, Reynaud II notion. She wasn't so sure anymore.

The milkshake had been some strange Vulcan flavor that smelled like peppermint. There had been a lot of sparks and a really awful smell, like roasted cottage cheese, for weeks. Still, T'Vau knew computers.

"Captain Trofimov?"

"Yes, Computer?"

"We're alone, aren't we? I mean, the science officer isn't on the bridge, is she?"

"No, Computer . . . Your sensors aren't malfunctioning, are they?" As she considered the possibility, it didn't seem as terrible. If the sensors weren't working, they couldn't find dilithium. If they couldn't find dilithium, there was no point in their being out here. They could go home.

"My sensors are fine, Captain. In fact, my sensors are really great. I can't imagine why you might think there's anything wrong with my sensors, they're just in tip-top shape."

"You asked if T'Vau was on the bridge."

"Oh. Well. I thought she might be . . . hiding."

"Hiding?"

"Yes, Captain."

"Why would she be doing that, Computer?"

"Well, Captain . . . we are alone, aren't we?"

"Completely."

"You see, Captain, I think the science officer is trying to kill me."

"Kill you . . . Enhance, please."

"Well, you see, she asked me to adjust the log entry

19

about her spilling the, you know, milkshake, so it said 'Science Officer T'Vau *inadvertently* spilled the milkshake,' and I told her—of course I told her I couldn't do that, and she said she was going to get me for that, and ever since . . ."

The door opened and T'Vau came in. There was an ink marker and a soldering pencil pinning her hair up, and a watercress sandwich leaking mayonnaise down her fingers.

The computer voder was whistling "I Got Plenty o' Nothin'."

"Cease this behavior, Computer," T'Vau said.

"Aye aye," the computer said. "At once, Science Officer."

"T'Vau," Trofimov said, "has the computer shown any signs of malfunction? I mean, new malfunction?"

"I see no sign of malfunction at all, Captain," T'Vau said slowly. "To what do you refer?"

"Doesn't its speech pattern strike you as . . . odd?"

T'Vau looked at the console. "It is illogical and elliptic, but that is hardly odd for a machine programmed by humans." She pulled the soldering pencil from her hair, tapped it on one of the access panels. "I must see if I can find time to study its programming."

"Yes," the captain said absently, "I know how busy we've all been, these last few weeks . . ."

"Four hundred sixty-five days, nine hours, forty-one minutes. Now, Captain, if I am not required on the bridge, I shall be in my quarters."

"Of course, T'Vau."

The science officer left the bridge.

The computer said "Uh, Captain Trofimov . . . that stuff I said earlier? About the science officer? Don't pay any attention to it. We're getting along just

20

great. I mean that sincerely. I'm fine, Lieutenant Commander T'Vau's fine, we're all fine."

"That's fi—wonderful, Computer." Trofimov felt a sudden sharp pain from her hands, looked down. Her fingernails were pressed deeply into her palms.

She faced the main display. It was showing a tape of waves breaking on a seashore, amber-colored waves under double suns, one red, one golden. It was really very restful. She settled back to watch, and soon all sense of time was gone.

"Excuse me, Captain Trofimov," *Smith*'s computer said abruptly.

"What is it now?"

"I don't want to bother you, Captain."

"That's all right, Computer."

"Really, Captain Trofimov, if you're busy . . ."

"I'm not busy."

"But I'm sure you've got a lot of important things to do."

"No. *Really.*"

"It's very nice of you to make time for me, Captain. I understand how difficult it can be, being in sole command of—"

*"Spill it, 'puter!"*

"I *knew* I was being a nuisance. I'm sorry, Captain."

Trofimov held her breath and counted to ten. "Computer."

"Happy to be working."

"Was there something you wanted to tell me?"

"Oh. Yes, Captain. Sensors are picking up Hecht radiation."

"Very well," Trofimov said automatically. *"What?"*

"When relatively pure dilithium deposits receive solar radiation," the computer said patiently, "they re-emit a particular signature of energy known as Hecht radiation, named for—"

"I know that, damn it! Put it up on the board!"

A local stellar map appeared on the main display, with graphs alongside showing the radiation-spectrum analysis. There, in glorious color, was the telltale mark of dilithium in the sun, way up the electromagnetic scale with a sizable i-component.

The captain hit the intercom switch. "T'Vau, Tellihu, get up to the bridge on the double. We're going *home.*"

# Educational Short Subject:
# Useful Facts about Dilithium

(FROM *DILITHIUM AND You,* an educational filmstrip produced by the Dilithium Information Institute, a subsidiary of the Deneva Mining Consortium, a division of Deneva-Universal Enterprises Ltd.)

*Dilithium!*
This amazing mineral, as beautiful as any jewel, harder than any diamond, is vital to civilization as we know it today. It is no exaggeration to say that the Federation in which we live could not exist if not for dilithium, the wonder mineral.

But just what is it that makes dilithium so amazing? Scientists here, in the laboratories of the Deneva Mining Consortium, the Federation's largest private producer of dilithium crystals for government and industry, have spent many years and huge amounts of money unlocking the secrets of this unique substance.

We'd like to point out that it's the United Federation of Planets' wise and forward-looking policy of tax deductions for research expenditures that have made the wonders you're about to see possible.

*Mountains fall, and dilithium is revealed!*

Don't be afraid—what you're seeing is not some alien war machine, but the chariot of Progress! This is a Tagra-X Planetary Excavator. These mighty machines, capable of swallowing whole mountains at a gulp, unearth dilithium ore wherever it may hide. Itself powered by a dilithium-focused antimatter generator, the Tagra-X allows the mining of planets that before would have been left untouched and useless.

*Fire one—It didn't break!*

Bullets just bounce off crystals of dilithium, the hardest known substance in the universe. Dilithium is in fact so hard that it exceeds the theoretical physical laws for materials. This paradox baffled scientists for decades, until researchers for the Deneva Mining Consortium discovered the amazing truth: the crystal structure of dilithium extends not just in the usual three dimensions, but in *four!*

*Did you say . . . four?*

That's right! As illustrated in this computer animation, the internal structure of dilithium extends both into the past and the future. The Deneva Mining Consortium named this phenomenon *Goniochronicity*℠. The extreme difficulty of cutting dilithium into usable shapes, requiring high-output lasers over a long period of time, became suddenly understandable. Here's Dr. Wallace Thaumazein, star of everyone's favorite popular science show, "Dr. Wally's Kitchen of Wonders," with the explanation.

"Scientists like me always thought it was net energy absorption by the crystals that made them finally give up under pressure, since as you probably know that's how most of the stuff we live with in our everyday lives acts. If I hit this pane of glass with this hammer, see, it's gonna break."

*It sure did, Dr. Wally!*

"Right. Are you guys all right down there, with the glass . . . ? Anyway, what we scientists figured out was that you don't just have to hit a dilithium crystal hard, you have to hit it hard last month, now, and a week from Tuesday, so to speak. Now, here's a dilithium crystal that we hit two days ago. And I've made a note in my appointment calendar—you can see it here, on the wristwatch display—to hit it again two days from now. Now, some of you are probably wondering, 'what if you don't hit it two days from now?' and that's an interesting question. What I always say to that is, 'I'm a scientist, not a philosopher.' Now I'll hit it, well, now."

*That's amazing, Dr. Wally!*

"It sure is, and it also shows why you kids watching shouldn't try this experiment at home with any dilithium you might have around the house. That man will recover, because he got prompt medical attention, which we always have on call here at the Kitchen of Wonders. You might not be so lucky."

That's an important safety tip, Dr. Wally. Yes, dilithium, the wonder mineral, can be dangerous. But isn't a certain level of risk always present in our everyday lives? Think of thermonuclear fusion, our mighty but mischievous friend. Or the dome over the city where you live; think how easily it could crack and decompress your whole town. Even this ordinary wooden pencil is potentially explosive, if it should touch antimatter. But there's another risk we haven't mentioned yet, perhaps the most important one of all. Can you guess what it is?

*Yellow alert! Yellow alert!*

Yes, it's the Klingons. These warlike beings are always on the prowl for dilithium, to drive their war machines, power their warships, and do many other war things. Here's Dr. Wallace Thaumazein again.

"Before dilithium-enhanced warp drives and weaponry, there was no interstellar war. Well, not exactly no interstellar war, but not very much of it, because with the ships flying at Warp Three or Four, and these little laser guns that only shot at lightspeed so even at Warp Two you flew faster than the stuff coming after you, it really wasn't very interesting, and nobody much did it, except for the Romulans, who you have to admit try real hard in everything they do, even if we can't always figure out why, and the Klingons, for whom it was sort of a hobby anyway."

A simple hobby that threatens millions. This is the result of the Klingon Empire's ruthless hunger for dilithium, the wonder mineral. Is there an answer? Yes. The answer is in each one of us. We must all vote for continued tax deductions for dilithium research and fight to preserve the Dilithium Depletion Allowance from those who cannot see that today's innocent, unexplored frontier world is tomorrow's Klingon slave outpost. This, then, is the choice that faces each of us in a free society.

*This . . . is dilithium . . . and you!*

[Tagra-X film courtesy of Tagra Geoforming Co. Gun provided by Denevarms Division of Deneva-Universal Enterprises Ltd. *Goniochronicity* is a registered trademark of the Deneva Mining Consortium, all rights reserved. Dr. Wallace Thaumazein appears courtesy of Apocrine Pictures Video, an entertainment unit of Deneva Fizz Inc.]

# Chapter Two

## *The Dilithium Crystal as Big as the Ritz*

JEFFERSON RANDOLPH SMITH approached the source of the dilithium radiation, a blue and brown world wrapped in white cloud. Captain Trofimov thought it was quite beautiful, but then again after four hundred and sixty-six days of empty space, sensor ghosts, and barren black rocks, perhaps her view was biased.

"What's the planet?" Trofimov asked.

T'Vau rolled up the data on her console. "Pi Pharosi II, name . . . pronunciation, Computer?"

"Excuse me?" the computer said.

"Please try to remain logical, Computer. Your behavior does not require explanation. I would like to know the pronunciation of this world's local name."

"Di-*rye*-dee. Excuse me . . ."

"This is not required, Computer."

"Very well, Commander."

T'Vau nodded and turned back to her screens. They were black. "Computer."

"Yes, Commander?"

"Restore my data displays."

"Excuse—"

T'Vau kicked the console. There was a *bloop* and the displays lit up again. "The planet is colonized," she said. "There are approximately fifteen thousand inhabitants, mostly humans from Federation worlds."

"Do they claim Federation allegiance?"

"No allegiance posted."

The computer was humming "There's a Long, Long Trail A-Winding."

"All right, Computer," Trofimov said. "What's so important?"

"May I use the main display? If, I mean, Lieutenant Commander T'Vau doesn't need it."

"Yes, Computer, you may use the main display."

It did.

*"What in hell—"*

"The general configuration indicates that it is a D-7 heavy cruiser," the computer said. "From the shape of the intercoolers and position of the disruptor banks, I believe it to be the D-7c modification. Its current range is 200 million meters and closing rapidly."

"What's wrong with the sensor picture?" Captain Kaden said.

"Interference, Captain," Aperokei said. "Appears to be coming from the planet."

"They're jamming us?"

"It could be, sir . . . wait, sir. Spectrum analysis indicates *iraltu cha'puj.*"

*Cha'puj*—what the Federation called dilithium—gave off a very particular sort of radiation. And there wasn't a ship of either empire that wasn't always sniffing for that scent.

Askade gave a low chuckle. Askade was an expert

on dilithium. Kaden said, "What do you think, Engineer?"

"I think that the Federation surveyor has found crystal ore. How sad for the surveyor's crew that we have found them."

"Arizhel, pick up the sensor trace."

"Working on it," Rish said, and a moment later breathed in sharply.

"What is it? *Cha'puj?*"

She hit switches, put the sensor analysis screen up on one of the main bridge repeaters. "It is *cha'puj* as I've never seen it. Do you agree, Askade?"

Askade stared at the computer graph. "You must have miscalculated."

"With respect, Chief Engineer—no, I didn't."

Askade started to say something, then paused and said, "Very well. Then it is not just ore—it is pure crystal, in vast amounts."

Kaden thought a moment. "What's the Federation ship doing?"

"Moving, Captain," Proke said. "She's hauling close to—I mean, attempting planetary approach."

"Pursuit, maximum velocity!" Kaden said. "*Zan* Korth, ready on forward tractors. Enough room in our holds for that boat, Askade?"

"Plenty of room, Captain," the Engineer said.

"*Zan* Aperokei, prepare to jam subspace if the one signals."

"No need, Captain," Arizhel said from the sciences board. "The *iraltu cha'puj* is already doing so. They cannot communicate."

"Then only the naked stars will see this one," Maglus said, grinning. "Not the Federation."

"And especially not the Organians," Kaden said.

\* \* \*

Blue orange juice, Trofimov thought, a lunatic crew, a berserk computer. Of course there would be Klingons. She wondered why she hadn't seen it coming, it was so obvious. They were doomed, that was all. "We're doomed," she said. It came out very calmly.

"The Klingon vessel is capable of destroying us in eight-point-four seconds using secondary weapons only. Being unarmed, we—"

"I know we're not armed," Trofimov said. "Do *they* know it?"

"They're not acknowledging our hail," Tellihu said.

"Maybe they're just—" The captain had a sudden awful thought. "What's the chance that they've detected the dilithium?"

T'Vau said, "I can only estimate."

"Then do it."

T'Vau said, "Estimated probability one hundred percent."

Trofimov turned to stare at the Vulcan. "That's your *guess?*"

"It is an estimate," T'Vau said stiffly, "based on the level of Hecht radiation, and a standard survey of Klingon monitoring—"

"Your guess is that you're certain," Trofimov said, feeling slightly dizzy.

"That is an interesting semantic paradox. It implies—"

"Forget it. Just forget it." The captain gripped the arms of her chair, and some more of the upholstery came loose. "They know we're a prospector, and they know we just found the mother lode. They'd be crazy not to blast us before we can file a claim. Can you raise anybody on subspace, Tellihu?"

"The interference is very high, Captain. I'm trying, but it's doubtful."

"Is there a friendly vessel charted anywhere in the area?"

"USS *Enterprise* is fourteen hours away at standard cruise."

The computer said, "If you're not too busy, Captain . . ."

"We certainly . . ." Trofimov caught herself. "No, Computer, nothing important going on. What is it?"

"By using fractional-orbit breakaway, and direct gate antimatter feed, the travel time to rendezvous with *Enterprise* can be reduced to approximately three-point-two standard hours."

"Set it up! T'Vau, get the numbers!"

The ship changed course. Trofimov turned to look at the science console. T'Vau was sitting with her arms crossed, looking doubtful. "What's the matter? Why aren't you working?"

"There is a difficulty with the program you have just ordered," she said. "However, if you are willing to trust the computer, I will not disagree."

Trofimov felt a hollowness in her stomach. "What difficulty?"

"It is in two parts. First, this vessel has small inertial compensators. Fractional-orbit breakaway would produce an effective fifty-one standard gravities within the ship, after all compensation effects."

"Fifty-one gees will turn us to strawberry jam!" She sighed. "Do I even want to know what the other part is?"

"I cannot begin to calculate your desire for—"

"Just. Tell me. *Please.*"

"Very well. The ship has inboard warp engines. Assuming that opening the antimatter gates does not instantly explode the ship, it will create an epicentric gamma flux in excess of 14,000 RU."

"Strawberry jam on *toast,*" Trofimov said.

31

*Pling,* went the wall panel at the captain's elbow, and a tray slid out. Trofimov deliberately did not look at it. "Computer," she said.

"Working energetically."

"I didn't ask for this."

"I'm sorry, Captain. English muffins were what I had in program area. I'm really busy with the trajectory calculations right now—"

"Never mind the muffins! And never mind the trajectory either, or had you noticed that we couldn't survive it?"

"Oh. You computed that." There was a bump, and *Smith*'s angle of dive toward the planet grew steeper. The world filled the main display.

T'Vau hissed and began prying at an access panel with her fingertips. Tellihu chirruped softly and folded his wings over his head.

"Computer," Captain Trofimov said.

"I'm sorry, Captain, I was busy. You can use the escape pod. The planet is quite habitable. I can eject the pod just before gravitational breakaway. The Klingons will almost certainly not detect it."

"Eject onto the planet," Trofimov said. A planet, she thought, with sky and fresh air and water nobody had ever used even once and *other people* . . .

"Right," the captain said. "Complete setting trajectory and prepare the pod for launch."

"It is a trick," T'Vau said. "It means to kill us and report to Starfleet that we are unfit for service and take the credit for finding the dilithium and . . ." T'Vau looked up at Trofimov and Tellihu, coughed and said, "This vessel is valuable Federation property. We should not abandon it without consideration. Perhaps I should recalculate the gravity force and gamma flux."

"Estimated 53.8 G, flux 14,530," the computer said.

T'Vau said, "That's what *you* say."

"Science Officer," Trofimov said quietly.

"Yes, Captain?"

"We're all going to get into the escape pod now."

"Yes, Captain."

*Smith*'s escape pod was a cramped cylinder, with two couches forward and one in the rear, minimum controls; its sole purpose was to keep its occupants alive until rescue, or land them on a nearby planet if possible. Its computer was equal only to that task. This didn't bother Trofimov at all.

"Please strap in," *Smith*'s main computer said over the intercom link. "Ejection in ten seconds."

Trofimov took the aft couch, the crew the front pair. They pulled down and buckled the restraint harnesses. "Secure, Computer," Trofimov said.

"Do you require anything else?"

"I could use a stiff drink," Trofimov said, and then jammed her knuckles into her mouth. The wall went *pling,* and a cup dropped from the slot and began to fill with a pink liquid. There was a pepperminty smell. "Cancel, cancel, *cancel,*" Trofimov yelled, just as the pod trembled and was blasted away from the hurtling ship.

The cup fell out of the delivery slot. Thick pink milkshake—that qualified as "stiff," Trofimov supposed—continued to pour out, spilling onto the pod floor. "Cancel," Trofimov said desperately.

"We are no longer coupled to the ship's computer," T'Vau said, "and ionization blackout prevents wave communication."

"Mach twenty-two," Tellihu said. "Hull temperature twelve hundred degrees."

33

The pod trembled, then stabilized, and there was a numbing *whump* as the impulse retromotors kicked in. "Mach twenty-one," Tellihu said, with the first sound of relief any of them had heard in six months. "Mach twenty . . . nineteen . . ." His voice went gaspy. Trofimov couldn't breathe at all. They were pulling between four and five Gs: that was survivable for the length of reentry, but it sure wasn't very comfortable. Trofimov's spine seemed to be trying to burrow into the couch. She looked up through squeezed eyeballs. There was a pink stream of milk shooting from the wall to the front of the pod, behind her head, at freight-train speed.

"Fiiiiinallll deeecellllerrration," Tellihu said, and the pod began to yaw and tilt as the autopilot looked for a place to land. "If p, then q," T'Vau was saying, almost calmly. "If not p, then not q."

The ship lurched again. Relays clacked somewhere as the autopilot tried to make up its mind. The captain wondered if computer insanity was catching.

"Five seconds to touchdown," Tellihu said, and sighed deeply. They were still decelerating at over a gravity, but the crushing pressure was gone. "Four. Three." Trofimov turned her head. Her couch was completely surrounded by frothy pink stuff, as if she were afloat on it. There was an overwhelming scent of peppermint. "Two. One." How much of the stuff *was* there? Escape pods carried one metric ton of water and two hundred kilos of basic organics as survival rations. That would make about twelve hundred liters of milkshake.

"Touchdown."

They landed.

The milk splashed, filling the entire vessel with thick pink spray. It was not unlike being inside an enormous cocktail shaker.

All was still. Trofimov groped for her belt release. Tellihu groaned and whistled low. "If not q then p," T'Vau said to nobody in particular.

The captain waded through the glop, looking for the door handle. It wasn't easy to find, as the entire interior was painted a uniform pink. Finally she grasped the control, turned it, pushed. Red lights shone through milk and a buzzer sounded as the explosive bolts were armed. "Shut up," Trofimov told the buzzer.

The door blew out into clear cool air. Pink fluid cascaded from the doorway, making little waterfalls on the boarding ladder as it descended.

Dripping pink, her clothes beginning to curdle, Captain Tatyana Trofimov walked with back straight and shoulders square down the ladder to a new world.

Tellihu came down the ladder. His wings were in awful shape. He tried to flap them, which looked even worse. He sat down, pulled off a boot, poured a cupful of milk onto the ground. "This substance is—" He began whistling furiously.

"I suggest that you find some of it that's still drinkable, actually," Trofimov said. "It's our entire ration supply."

T'Vau came down the steps, carefully carrying a stack of plastic-wrapped bundles. "Overalls and survival blankets," she said. "They are clean. And dry."

The captain and Tellihu got to their feet. "There is another consideration," T'Vau said primly.

Tellihu stamped, one boot off, one boot on, over to the science officer. He tried to spread his wings imposingly, but they were much too wet. "We have no rations," he said, "except for what we might bail from our ship or wring from our clothing. My avian metabolism requires steady nourishment. You are packed with usable protein."

"Modesty is of little consequence to Vulcans," T'Vau said. "I only wished to note that we are all still quite damp with *n'gaan*-flavored milk beverage, and I believe I hear running water a few tens of meters in that direction."

They grabbed the bundles and headed in the direction of the whispering brook, beginning to run as it came into sight, and then to pull off milkshake-sodden uniforms. T'Vau was right. Modesty didn't even enter into it.


"They're headed straight for the surface," Korth said. "Any deeper in the gravity well and the tractors won't be reliable."

"Then it's their choice," Captain Kaden said. "Switch to disruptors, *Zan* Korth. Askade, is the ship streamlined?"

"Sulek-class can make emergency planetary landings. They'll never get it off again without a carrier vessel."

"Anything like that on the world?"

Arizhel said "No local starships on record."

Korth said "I have lock-on."

"Fire on my . . ." Kaden raised his hand, then slowly lowered it, looked hard at the little ship in the display. "No. Helm, bring her up now."

"Captain?" Korth said. "There's nothing they can hit us with."

"Once long ago there was a big ship on my tail," Kaden said. "I'm sure that's just what its crew were thinking. If they go down, they're trapped; if not . . ."

A heartbeat passed. Two. The little prospector continued to bore down the gravity well. Three—and the ship bent its course, shooting for deep space at tremendous velocity.

"Breakaway," Askade said, with a touch of awe. "At that speed—*Kai* the pilot, alive or dead!"

"*Kai* the captain," Maglus said, chuckling deep, tossing a salute to Kaden.

"We still have to catch the one," Kaden said. "Helm! Pursuit course!"

In the cargo hold of the *Enterprise,* Chief Engineer Scott supervised the preparation of the first Deployable Practice Target (Prototype) for launch.

It was a metal-and-plastic capsule the size of a standard small cargo module, a little less than two meters long and a meter square on the ends, fitted with monitoring jacks and transport grips, stenciled DELICATE and NO STEP and TOP SECRET. At one end was a set of gas bottles piped into the case. Just above the bottles a red-striped handle was fitted, recessed slightly: the same sort of turn-push safety grip that armed and fired emergency hatches.

"Remote pack," Scott said, and was handed a square device that plugged neatly over the firing handle. The engineer flipped up a lid, set frequency dials and inserted an arming key, then closed it again. "All right, she's primed and ready. Handling team."

An anti-grav skid was brought up, and the target capsule was trucked past wary security guards to the *Enterprise* torpedo room. A crane picked the unit up, transferred it to the photon-torpedo loading rails. The monitor board lit green.

"All ready below, Captain," Scott said into the intercom.

"Thank you, Mr. Scott," Kirk said on the bridge. "Mr. Sulu, prepare to launch the target. Mr. Chekov, ready on sensors."

"Aye, sir."

"Yes, Captain."

Kirk said casually, "If it doesn't look like a starship, can we send it back for a refund?"

Sulu said, "Target on the rails, sir."

"Launch, Mr. Sulu."

A bright pinpoint shot from the starship's forward tube. It began to expand almost immediately into an amorphous silvery shape. After a few seconds, the outline of a disc was visible, and two limp little engine nacelles folded out. The disc spread, the engines straightened.

Ten minutes later, *Enterprise* was accompanied by a full-sized replica of itself. At range, the lack of surface detail was not noticeable at all. There were even small reflective patches that shone like lighted viewports.

Engineer Scott stepped out of the lift, to his station on the bridge. He looked at the target. "Now isn't that a sight."

"Sensor image is perfect, Captain," Chekov said.

"Instant starship," Sulu said. "Just add space."

"Captain," Lt. Uhura said, "I'm receiving an emergency call, Priority One. The source vessel is at maximum tightbeam range, approaching at considerable speed."

"Put it on."

"Hello?" a voice said, sounding distraught. "Anybody there? I mean, anybody from the Federation there? I know there was supposed to be someone there."

"Is there a recognition code?" Kirk said.

"Decoding now, Captain," Uhura said. "Starfleet records identify her as *Jefferson Randolph Smith*, Captain T. Trofimov commanding, First Officer Tellihu, Science Officer T'Vau."

"T'Vau?" Spock said. His eyebrows didn't arch, but his voice rather did.

Kirk said, "Do you know her, Spock?"

"We were acquainted on Vulcan, in my youth. I have not seen her since then." Kirk immediately had the obvious thought—obvious to a human, anyway—but Spock sounded less like someone reminded of an old romance than of a small boy contemplating liver and spinach for dinner.

Spock's hand was against his chest. He seemed to be brushing an imaginary stain off his uniform tunic. Kirk couldn't remember seeing that mannerism before, but resisted asking about it.

Uhura said, "Sir, the ship is hailing us."

"Put it on main display, Lieutenant."

The forward screen showed an empty bridge. The crew chairs were all torn from their moorings, mashed into lumps of metal by some incredible force.

"*Enterprise . . .* Excuse me, that is the *Enterprise?*"

"This is *Enterprise,*" Kirk said. "Is that Captain Trofimov?"

"Look, I really don't want to bother you, you're a starship and all, if you're busy I can wait. . . ."

"Who *is* that?"

Uhura said, "Voice pattern analysis indicates a computer voder, Captain. Probably *Smith*'s main computer."

Spock said, "More precisely, a J-2 duotronic unit in severe need of program maintenance."

"Really? Can you diagnose the problem?"

"Circumstances would suggest the spillage of a *n'gaan*-spiced milkshake on the sciences console," Spock said, then paused, looked around at the bridge crew staring at him, and said, "Of course, this is only an informed conjecture."

"*Enterprise,*" the computer voice said, "would you mind . . . I mean, I know this is a big favor to ask, but . . ."

"Where is your crew, *Smith?*" Kirk said.

"Oh, gosh, Captain. They're on the planet back there, Direidi. You see, we found all this dilithium—that's our mission, finding dilithium, and—"

"You left the crew behind?"

"Well, sort of. That is, I didn't mean to. That is, I did tell them to use the escape pod, but it wasn't like I *made* them do it."

"The crew ejected in the escape pod," Kirk said, with a patience that surprised himself.

"Right, Captain. Now, about that favor . . ."

"Are you damaged, *Smith?*"

"Who, me? I'm okay. Running a little hot, you know, but really okay." There was a pause. "Really, *really* okay. Never felt better. I'm absolutely, positively sure of that."

Kirk said "Spock?"

"These are not normal J-2 diagnostic messages, Captain."

"Thanks, Spock. *Smith,* you had a . . . favor to ask?"

"I'd really like docking clearance. If it's okay with you."

"Mr. Scott, do we have docking protocols for a Sulek-class vessel?"

"Aye, we can do it," Scott said, sounding extremely doubtful, "but only just. She'll fill the whole hangar deck, an' there won't be an inch t' spare through the doors. We'd have to do it all under . . ." Scott tapped his fingers on his console ". . . computer control."

"I'll be very, very careful," *Smith* said.

Everyone on the bridge was very quiet. Finally Scott said, "My advice, Captain, is to take her in tow wi' tractors."

"Oh, *please,*" the ship said.

Kirk said, "Could you provide, uh, some more details of your situation, uh, *Smith?*"

"Oh, yes, of course, I didn't want to bother—"

"That's quite all right," Kirk said.

"Rear view," *Smith* said, and the *Enterprise* bridge main display was suddenly crowded full of a Klingon heavy-enhanced cruiser.

"*Yellow alert!*" Kirk shouted.

"Target's slowing, Captain," Korth said.

"I have another sensor trace," Aperokei said. "Not a planet. Small planetoid, or a large ship."

Kaden clenched his fists. "It would be just like them to find a freighter, here in the middle of nothing. Can you identify?"

"A moment, Captain . . . Captain, you're not going to like this."

"I'm sure I'm not, Proke," Kaden said. "What is it?"

"Federation heavy cruiser, Captain. Constitution-class."

Maglus swore colorfully. Kaden said, "One could live for Keth's years and not have luck like that. *Khest'na div'ya'chigh—*"

"Captain, there are two of them."

"What?" Kaden said, his thought interrupted.

"He's right," Arizhel said. "Two discrete traces. A pair of starships."

"Braking thrust! Kill our velocity!" Kaden shouted.

"Spock," Kirk said, "can you give me an analysis of the situation?"

"I have traced the *Smith*'s most probable trajectory, Captain, and detect an unusual amount of Hecht radiation from that direction—sufficient to indicate the presence of an extraordinary amount of highly pure dilithium. I would suppose that the prospector's crew discovered the ore almost simultaneously with the Klingon vessel."

"Good old-fashioned claim-jumping, eh?" Kirk said.

"It would seem so."

Kirk said, "Unless it's a trick, and the Klingons want us to attack their ship."

The voice of *Smith*'s computer said, "I'm really sorry I didn't mention that ship before, *Enterprise*, but I've been very, very busy, and can I have that docking clearance now?"

Spock said, "This does not have the appearance of a Klingon tactic."

"No, I see that," Kirk said. "Mr. Scott, prepare to take the prospector in tow."

"Aye, sir. Aft tractors coming up now."

"*Smith*," Kirk said, "can you reduce speed and meet our tractors?"

"I can't hear you," the computer said.

"Uhura, have we lost signal?"

"Feedback indicates clear channel, sir."

"*Smith*," Kirk said, a little more firmly, "we want you to reduce speed and be taken in tow. Acknowledge."

"There must be something wrong with your transmission, Captain. I can't understand you at all."

"Captain," Sulu said, "the Klingon vessel is losing speed, but the prospector isn't."

"What's her course? Headed for collision?"

"Yes, sir—but not with us. With the target."

"Scotty! Can you get tractors on her?"

"Tryin', sir, but she's tiny and goin' like sixty."

"*Let me in*," Smith screeched, "*or I'll huff and I'll puff—*"

42

"Contact," Sulu said.

*Smith* pierced the rear of the practice target's lower hull. The target shot away on escaping gas, shrinking, tearing, spiraling as it collapsed, just like any punctured balloon.

*Smith* came to a sudden halt. "*Got* th' little devil," Scott said, then looked up from his console at the display. "Oh, my."

"The Klingons have halted," Sulu said.

As *Fire Blossom* lost forward momentum, Kaden and his crew watched the prospector approach the two Federation cruisers. They saw it dock with the one to the left.

They saw the cruiser vanish in a split second from vision and sensors.

"It's really not there, Rish?" Kaden said slowly.

"Not on any sensor," Arizhel said.

"Well," Askade said, "now I suppose we know what they're testing out here."

Kaden said, "What's the one that's . . . still there, Proke?"

"*Enterprise,* Captain."

"Open a channel," Kaden said. "We'd better say hello, before the lightbulbs cook us."

On the surface of Direidi, the crew of *Jefferson Randolph Smith* sat by a mountain creek in the early twilight. T'Vau was lost in meditation. Tellihu crouched by the running water, hoping for a fish: to Trofimov he looked uncomfortably like a vulture.

"It's a pretty place, really," Trofimov said, looking at the stream, the mountains, the rising moon. Reynaud II, her homeworld, had no mountains near its inhabited areas, and no moon at all. Trofimov had grown up wondering why it was that so many writers fixed on the moon, a rock in the sky, as a symbol of romance. Now she looked up at the white rock in the heavens, and . . .

Trofimov put her hand in the stream and splashed cold water on her face.

T'Vau said, "The world's value is not in its scenic beauty, as it is too far from the major routes for tourism. Though these are admirable examples of tectonic action. . . . Is something wrong, Captain? Are you feverish?"

Trofimov started to laugh, and then couldn't stop. She laughed until her sides hurt, until she fell off the rock where she was sitting and rolled on the ground. When the tears cleared from her eyes, she saw that Tellihu was also doubled up with laughter, his wings beginning to dry and lose their droop. T'Vau sat still, trying to look impassive but only managing bewildered. "Perhaps the water contains an organism . . ."

"It's all right, it's all right," Trofimov said. "Release of tension, perfectly—hee, hee—normal." She sat on the rock again, looked up at the beautiful mountains, the romantic moon.

"Do you suppose the ship got away from the Klingons?" Tellihu said.

"No way even to guess. If it didn't, you can bet our jolly old friends will be back . . . and if there's half the dilithium here that our sensors said, they'll mine those hills flat for it."

"There is a forty-one percent chance that the intended evasive action was successful," T'Vau said.

"Okay, so there's a way to guess," Trofimov said, in too good a mood to get angry. "Assuming it does get back to Starfleet . . . then *they'll* come in, relocate the population, and mine the place naked. That's why we're the good guys." She stood up, shivered a little, pulled one of the survival blankets over herself like a cape. "Grab a blanket and let's follow this stream for a while," she said. "We need food, and we need to find the locals. Tell 'em the good guys are here."

They began walking, the moonlight making crisp black shadows on silver.

After a few minutes, Tellihu said thoughtfully, "If *Smith* does return to the Federation, it is likely that the Organian Treaty will enter into the situation."

"Hadn't thought of that," the captain said. "But tell you what, let's not think about it. It's too nice a night." She picked up her step and began singing "Subterranean Homesick Blues."

Some distance away on the face of Direidi (as planetary distances, not interstellar ones, go), there was a castle, with a tower, and in the tower a room lit with pale blue light and echoing with an ominous thin rumble. The light shone on a man in a purple plush robe, making him look waxy and dead. He was rather broad in the middle, and his hair was thin on top. He sat with his ankles crossed, and a cup of cold coffee and a plate of cookies at his elbow, and typed. Words scrolled up on the screen in front of him, shining pale blue, and every few minutes the crystal storage unit on the floor by the worktable rumbled as it burned some more words into permanent memory.

The man sighed. He drank some of the coffee, grimacing. Then he looked up sharply at a flashing light on the wall, got up quickly, and went to the bank of instruments mounted there. He flipped switches, brought screens to life, read them. He looked out the tower window, saw what he might have taken for a shooting star, had not the instruments told him the terrible truth.

He stuck his feet into old leather slippers and began running down the tower steps, robe flapping and slippers flopping as he went.

He emerged into a vast stone hall with a glass roof, the skylights reddish with the declining sun. There was one small lamp on in the hall, lighting one end of a table long enough for forty or more diners. A woman sat there, in the pool of light. She was assembling a metal-and-plastic model of a Southern Railway Ps-4 steam locomotive.

The man leaned against the table, breathing hard. The woman said, "For heaven's sake, Flyter, you're going to kill yourself on those stairs one of these days, either the fall or the strain. Sit down."

"It's happened, Estervy my dear. The whole board lit up. We've been found."

"'Every day something or other unpleasant happens, but I don't complain. I'm accustomed to it. I even laugh at it.'"

"Nice choice of quote. I know how that one ends as well as you do: with the thud of the axe in the cherry orchard."

Estervy put down her work, adjusted the lamp. She was fiftyish, like Flyter, with some gray in her long black hair, face and hands still smooth, firm. "Yes, Flyter, I know you're serious. We've known it ever since we moved here. Now, who was it?"

"Federation, I think. It was just a short contact, they tossed something into the atmosphere and left. If it had been a private prospector, they'd have sent a boat down, and if it was the Klingons—well." He sighed. "Not that it really matters. We're found, and that's it."

"They did drop something?"

"Couldn't have been a boat. Marker beacon, I'd guess. If we had something more than that cheap second-hand navigation board—oh, forget it. At least whoever dropped it won't get anything from it."

"Exactly," Estervy said. "No one can broadcast out of here. So we have some time. Unless we're desperately unlucky, the Organian Treaty will be invoked, which gives us a little more time."

"Plan C?" Flyter said.

"Plan C."

Flyter smiled. "I'll call a town meeting for two o'clock. That should get us an adequate number no later than five."

"Suddenly you sound rather pleased."

"Well, I guess I am, now that I think about it. I'm glad it's happened while we're here to see it. I was always rather scared that they'd show up a generation or so down the line, and our kids would dust off the Plan to find it was completely out of date."

"You're a terrible. liar," Estervy said. "You just want to hear your dialogue being spoken."

"There's always that," Flyter said agreeably. "Call for two?"

"Call for two."

# *Historical Interlude:*
# *The Only War We've Got*

THE TERMS OF the Organian Treaty between the United
Federation of Planets and the Klingon Empire are as
follows:

Upon the discovery of a new and usable planet
within the confines of the Treaty Zone (defined as per
the map in Appendix A of this document), each party
to the Treaty shall have the option to voluntarily cede
the world to the other for development. Failing this,
both parties to the Treaty shall send envoys to the
disputed planet, prepared to demonstrate to the indigenous population (if any) the respective party's
ability to develop the world in a peaceful and useful
manner. Rights of development shall be granted to
the party that best shows said ability.

Failure to abide by the terms of this agreement shall
be met with physical interdiction of the party or
parties in violation from the planet.

In plainer language, the Treaty terms are: *Don't get
grabby or you'll get your fingers burned.*

Popular opinion in the Federation concerning the Organian Treaty may be summarized as follows:

| | |
|---|---|
| 4% | The deepest wisdom of the Galaxy |
| 4% | Treaty? What treaty? |
| 11% | Not a bad idea, glad I voted for it |
| 81% | Who do they think they are, anyway? |

Popular opinion in the Klingon Empire concerning the Treaty, while perhaps less important than in the more politically liberal Federation, may be summarized in similar fashion:

| | |
|---|---|
| 4% | If the Emperor says it's okay, it's fine with me |
| 4% | This is a trick question, right? |
| 11% | The Federation made the whole thing up |
| 81% | Who do they think they are, anyway? |

We hope that this statistical information (which, as always, is subject to a correction factor) will help you in making informed decisions about the governance and policies of the politically liberal Federation in which we all live.

[A table of correction factors used in the preparation of this survey is available for Cr. 12.50, sublight postage paid. Please specify data format and decimal, duodecimal, or binary numeration.]

# Chapter Three

## *Organian Jumpball*

FIRE BLOSSOM HUNG in stationary orbit near Imperial Supply Base 27, just inward from the Organian Treaty Zone. Freight shuttles and service units surrounded the big cruiser. Her cargo doors were wide open, light spilling out brilliantly from the holds, force curtains holding the atmosphere in.

Inside the ship, Kaden and Maglus walked out onto the main cargo deck. Askade was looking through the cargo door at a shuttle hanging a few hundred meters away.

There was a flare of light from the passenger transporter, and a stocky Imperial in Marine uniform, carrying a flight bag, stepped off the stage.

"Force Leader Memeth, 251st Engineers, reporting," the officer said.

"You are welcome aboard *Fire Blossom*, Force Leader," Kaden said. "I am Kaden, captain. This is Maglus, security officer, and Askade, chief engineer. He will be directing your unit."

Memeth's face stiffened. "The one is the ship's engineer . . ."

50

Askade said "I am an Accredited Specialist in the mechanics of dilithium. The Force Leader is perhaps familiar with the *Manual of Crystalline Ores Handling?*"

Memeth nodded, relaxed. "Ah. The vestai-Eletai. It is an honor to work with you."

Kaden shot a relieved look at Maglus, who shrugged slightly. Another of the daily struggles of life concluded.

Askade said, "What equipment will be loaded?"

"Six survey vehicles, four ore shuttles with portable navigation lines, and six Tagra-X mass excavators."

Askade nodded. "You will supervise the loading, then. We shall confer once the ship is under way."

"At once, Chief Engineer."

"We need not be formal. I am Askade."

"And I Memeth."

"Very good."

The ship's officers left the deck, entered a lift car. "Nicely done," Kaden said.

Askade said, "It's his battalion; trying to command it without his cooperation would be like bailing a swamp. . . . What are you grinning at, Mag? Waiting for me to say something about the average intelligence of Marine officers?"

"The one saw only a leader practicing his art."

There was a moment's pause, and then they all laughed. Then Askade said, very soberly, "Ever seen a Tagra-X?"

The others said no.

"They're *big*. Even dismantled for shipping, six of them will fill our holds with nothing left over."

"Do you see a problem?" Kaden said. "Too much mass?"

"For *Blossom*'s engines? Nonsense." Askade sounded slightly hurt by the question. "But it's a major commitment of equipment. Obviously the Emperor doesn't just want us to get this world . . . he *expects* it."

Maglus said, "There are only fifteen thousand beings on it. What are they going to do, lie down in front of the excavators?"

"The Tagras wouldn't notice if they did," Askade said. "The question is the Federation."

"The question is the lightbulbs," Kaden said.

Aboard Starbase One, orbiting high above the Earth, Kirk, Spock, and McCoy stood in a conference room, getting a final briefing from Admiral Pilchard of Starfleet Resources Command.

"Fifteen thousand inhabitants can't possibly occupy enough of the planet's surface to interfere with mining operations," Pilchard said. "What we have to consider is the Klingons. They're not going to look at this lying down."

Kirk nodded. Behind him, Spock stood calm, and McCoy fidgeted. Pilchard was a Raskolane, humanoid except for seven-fingered hands and a slightly purplish cast to his skin and eyes. The Raskolane language had a highly complicated idiomatic structure, which showed up when they spoke Federation-Standard.

"Now you know, and I know," the admiral said, "that we have only the best interest of the . . . what are they again?"

"Direidi," Spock said.

"Right. Their interests, that's at the head of the book. But you know these indigenous locals. Wave the golden door in front of them, and they'll follow like nuts in May. We can't let the Klingons pull a wide one." Pilchard tapped the desk. "So there it is, Captain. You know your mission."

"Yes, Admiral. Of course."

"Splendid." They went out of the briefing room into the hallway. Starfleet personnel bustled past; through ports in the walls, large ships and small glided through the black.

Kirk said, "Who's been assigned as envoy, Admiral?"

"Charlotte Sanchez. Do you know her?"

"Not that I recall," Kirk said.

"Well, that's a novelty," McCoy said, not quite out loud.

Admiral Pilchard didn't seem to have noticed. "She's a real ace in the diplomatic firmament. Defused a war on Kintyre, got a whole raft of trade concessions from the Olivet Quango, and that was a real feather in her ear."

Kirk said "What? I mean, the Olivet what?"

"Quango. Damned if I know what it means. I can't keep half-track of the ways people are figuring out how to rule themselves these days." They stopped before a lift shaft. Pilchard pressed the Call key, said, "Makes the Klingons seem kind of comfortable by comparison. At least you know they're not going to dive out of the sun with some crazy new political two-step in their teeth."

Kirk nodded gravely. McCoy rocked back on his heels, hands in pockets. Spock looked straight ahead.

The lift door opened, and the admiral stepped in. "Well, best of luck to you, Captain, and you, Commander. Good seeing you again, Doctor McNeil. And remember, don't let the spellbinders sell you a bill of goods down the river."

"Aye, sir."

"Flag Officers' Quarters," Pilchard said, and the door closed with a whoosh.

McCoy said, "Now there goes a man who gets the

maximum possible mileage from the language. 'Doctor McNeil.' Right."

Kirk pressed the Call key again. "Speaking of language, Bones, what was that about 'novelty'?"

"Oh . . . well, Jim, I was just making an observation about the large number of women in Starfleet who turn out to be your old acquaintances."

"Aw, Bones . . ."

"It's almost as amazing as the number of those old flames who wind up on board the *Enterprise.*"

". . . what can I say?"

The lift arrived. As they entered, Spock said, "Dr. McCoy has a valid statistical point—"

"Oh, don't *you* start."

There was a *ploop,* and a voice from the lift wall said, "Lifts may be held stopped for no more than one hundred seconds, to avoid congestion of the system. In case of emergency, please pull the red handle, or announce 'Mayday' three times."

"Diplomatic Section, Administration level," Kirk said tightly, and the lift door closed.

The car delivered them seconds later to a large, open lobby with a glass ceiling showing a dizzying view of Earth. Beings of several dozen different races were sitting, strolling, or Earthgazing. To one side was a broad corridor, and a large semicircular reception desk.

"Captain James Kirk," Kirk told the receptionist, handing over his identity card. "We're here to meet Ambassador Sanchez."

The receptionist, a Xranxi Vion with the gold chitin of the Organizational caste, took each of the three men's ID cards in a separate hand, worked a keyboard with two more, and picked up a telephone with the sixth. She swiveled faceted eyes behind thick collimating glasses and touched the translator-voder around her neck. "The ambassador is expecting you in Conference Room 14," the box said, in a warm, almost sultry voice. "Please go ahead, the second left."

They found the room. The door slid open.

The conference room was carpeted in a dull orange, with a long walnut table and a dozen chairs, most of them in curious shapes for nonhuman sitters. At the head of the table, a human woman was seated, reading papers in a plastic folder. She had dark-olive skin, hair long and straight and very black, very large eyes nearly as dark. She was strongly built, though by no means stocky or heavy. She was wearing an off-white tunic and trousers of coarsely woven wool, flat white shoes.

She looked up. "Well, *hello,* Jim."

Kirk froze. Spock raised an eyebrow. McCoy raised two.

The ambassador stood up, said, "You look like you've seen a ghost. I've slowed down a little, but I'm not dead yet."

"Charlotte . . . *Sanchez.*"

"Ambassador and Special Envoy to the World and Population of Direidi," Sanchez said. "Long way from home, no?"

"Charlotte . . . *Caliente* Sanchez . . . uh, I'd like you to meet my Spock officer, Commander First, and Doctor McNeil—I mean, McCoy."

"Pleased to meet both of you," she said, smiled, shook hands.

"You'll excuse us," McCoy said lightly. "I have to talk to Mr. Spock about statistics."

Spock and McCoy went out. Kirk stared after them.

"You forgot, didn't you," Sanchez said, sounding highly amused.

"I, uh . . . yeah."

She laughed. "What are you so embarrassed about? It was one ice cream soda eighteen years ago."

"You remembered."

"I'm a diplomat. You'd be surprised how much of diplomacy is remembering people's names, and what they did a long time ago."

Kirk nodded.

Sanchez said, "Well now, Captain. My bags are waiting in the Transients' Section. Where's the *Enterprise* berthed?"

"Three-C. I'll be glad to take you."

"I never travel with more than I can carry. See you on board, Jim."

"Charlie . . . there's a place in the Shopping Arcade that serves terrific ice cream sodas."

"Two things," Sanchez said, without raising her voice. "First, my father is the only person alive who still gets to call me 'Charlie.' Second, you're a starship captain and I'm a full ambassador, and as of 1400 today we're both under Federation Diplomatic Mission orders. It's now 1422, which makes you eighteen years and twenty-two minutes late."

She was still smiling. Kirk smiled too. "No ice cream sodas, huh?"

"Only in the furtherance of the Direidi negotiations."

Kirk nodded, scratched the back of his head. "You always were a first-class negotiator."

"I knew you hadn't forgotten," Sanchez said, and touched his cheek as she walked by him. "Berth Three-C. See you."

*Enterprise* was preparing for departure. Around the ship, work pods loaded stores, checked diagnostics. On the bridge, the command crew did final checkdown, and the newly arrived ambassador conversed quietly with Captain Kirk. Spock gave an instruction to Communications Officer Uhura, and a moment later the main display lit with a person in Starfleet Sciences uniform, standing surrounded by banks of computer equipment.

The person on the screen was dabbing with a napkin at her tunic, which was dripping a thick, pinkish fluid. She looked up, startled. *"Oh . . .* Computer Analysis Section, Technician Owens on duty. How may I help you?"

"This is Science Officer Spock of *Enterprise.* Have you completed reading the data from the *Smith*'s onboard computer?"

"No, sir. That is, yes, but . . . well, you see, sir, there's something wrong with that computer."

"That is known to us. It was the reason you were instructed to bleed the computer's memory."

"I know, sir, and we tried, but . . . sir, whatever's wrong with it, sir, we think it's . . . contagious."

"Do you mean in the fashion of a virus program, Technician?"

"Sort of, sir, only more in the fashion of an obsession."

Kirk said, "Has there been some kind of lab accident, Owens?"

"We don't know, sir."

"Don't know?"

"You see, ever since we tapped the *Smith* computer, the food dispensers here won't make anything but peppermint milkshakes, and they won't stop making those. We're scared to connect the thing again."

*"N'gaan,"* Spock said.

Kirk said, "What's that, Spock?"

"The flavor . . . it is not peppermint, but *n'gaan* . . . " Spock cleared his throat. "This is only a conjecture."

"Okay," Kirk said slowly. "Owens, did you get anything out of the computer?"

"Does this look like nothing?" Owens said, pointing at her dripping clothes. "Oh, uh, sorry, Captain. No, I'm afraid we didn't."

"Very well. Keep us informed if you do discover anything. *Enterprise* out."

Owens saluted. There was a *sploosh*ing noise behind her, and she turned, said, "Oh, my—" The screen went dark.

Kirk said, "Spock, about these milkshakes . . ."

"The connection is, as I have said, Captain, purely conjectural."

"But there is some connection. To *Smith*'s science officer?" Kirk grinned in spite of himself. "Now, I wouldn't want to invoke *statistics* on you, Spock, but surely finding an old flame—"

"Captain, if a person with whom I once divided a beverage counts as an 'old flame,' perhaps I misunderstand the implications of the idiom."

Ambassador Sanchez laughed once loudly, then covered her mouth. Kirk said, "I withdraw the question, Mr. Spock."

Kirk turned his chair to face the main display, which now showed an interior view of the starbase dock. "Mr. Sulu, locked on docking beam?"

"Aye, Captain."

"Then astern, impulse point one. Take us out."

Macmain stepped through the high stone arch into the art gallery's Chamber of Treasures, a gothic hall whose stone ceiling peaked a dozen meters above its carved wooden support beams. Around the walls were paintings, tapestries, a suit of armor engraved and enameled with the insignia of a prince centuries dead.

In the center of the treasury, raised first on a gold-tiled platform and then on a column of crystal, was a glass cube; and within it, catching the light, a spiral tiara of silver so smooth it seemed liquid, set with stones of blue and red and gold.

The Karthores Diadem, and Macmain, master thief of the galaxy, stood with less than ten steps separating them.

Or so it seemed . . .

Macmain wore a tight black coverall fitted with loops, belts, and sealable pockets. He reached into one of the pockets, took out a pair of tinted glasses, slipped them on. Suddenly the network of sensor-beams around the Diadem case was brilliantly visible. Moving like a zero-g ballet dancer, Macmain slipped through the rays until he stood a fingerbreadth from the golden platform. He raised his kidskin boot, then lowered it again, crouched, examined the metal tiles. Some were pressure sensors. Others . . .

Macmain took a thick black cylinder from a loop at his hip. He opened its end, unfolded a small grappling hook. He pointed the tube upward, pressed a stud. With just a cough of escaping gas, the hook shot upward, trailing a thin cable; it circled a beam, caught and held.

Macmain cinched the cable, ran it through a steel ring on his belt. He pulled, lifting himself into the air above the platform. He snapped the tube to another clip on his suit, hung suspended.

He examined the locks on the glass cube. Simple nine-tumbler tricyclics, with the old Throckmorton camming. Almost insulting. He drew a thin tool from the kit at his left wrist, popped both locks in the space of as many calm breaths. He flipped open the cube. His gloved fingers closed gently on the Diadem.

"Ah, Macmain, old friend," said a coldly familiar voice from behind him. "I knew that one day, given enough line . . . you'd hang yourself."

Macmain turned slowly on the suspending cable. "Colonel Richter," he said, smiling. "I didn't think you were the type to frequent art museums."

Richter smiled back, over the barrel of his heavy energy pistol. It made ugly wrinkles in his white-scarred face. "My interest is much the same as yours. Indeed, most of this junk leaves me entirely cold . . . but on the other hand, the Karthores Diadem I find quite fascinating. I look forward to a much closer examination of it."

"Then you know its secret," Macmain said.

"Oh yes. Though finding it cost several people their lives."

"Innocent people, of course."

"Of course." Richter chuckled. "But then, I offered them the chance to serve the Consortium's interests freely. Their refusal made them criminals. So they weren't innocent at all, you see."

"You mean to say that you actually want this for the Consortium."

"I mean to say that I'm acting in their name. The Starfortress of Karthora will be a potent addition to the Consortium's forces." Richter pointed at the tiara in Macmain's hand. "I knew all along that there was a key to it, somewhere: no one hides a weapon like that without some means to find it. We've just come along a few thousand years late, that's all."

Macmain turned the Diadem over in his fingers. Blue stones, yellow, and red: representations of stars, a three-dimensional map disguised as a bit of jewelry.

Richter snapped his fingers. Three Consortium Marines in heavy ribbed armor and mirror-fronted helmets came in, Drake Eighty power-carbines held level.

"I don't think you want to shoot me, Colonel."

"Now there's a falsehood if I've ever heard one."

"Not at all. Do you see the platform under me? Do you know what it does?"

"Certainly. Some of the tiles are pressure detectors. The rest are electrodes. Touch it, and a hundred thousand volts charge the surface."

Macmain held up the Diadem. "That would certainly do a lot of damage to this, wouldn't it?"

Richter sighed. "That it would. That's what I like about you, Macmain; you're always offering me difficult choices. So this time, I've decided to offer you one." He snapped his fingers again.

Two more people came in. The first was a woman, in a silver suit much like Macmain's. There was a black cloth hood over her head, and her hands were cuffed behind her back. Another Marine pushed her along at the point of a Drake Eighty.

"Libra?" Macmain said.

The woman made a muffled sound, strained at the handcuffs, but another jab from the gun quieted her.

"Wherever Macmain the Magnificent is," Richter said, stifling a yawn, "there also will be his associate, the beautiful, dangerous, and elusive Libra. We just went looking for her first. We *knew* where you'd be."

"It's a standoff, Richter," Macmain said.

"Oh, don't be insulting, dear fellow. You know I'll kill her, I know you won't allow that."

"So what's your proposition?"

"First you set down the Diadem, safely, on the glass pillar. Then you simply step down onto the platform. I'll take the trinket and go."

"What about Libra?"

61

"Libra stays here, unharmed, with you—or what's left of you. Who knows, you might even survive the experience. It's at least a sporting chance, eh, Macmain the Magnificent?"

Macmain looked at Libra, who tilted her hooded head and made more choked sounds.

"Oh, do hurry," Richter said, and pointed his pistol at Libra. "This offer expires in three seconds. One. Two."

Macmain put the Diadem on the pillar. He reached for the cable.

"Stop," Richter said.

"You gave your word—"

"I admit that's not worth much, but I'm not breaking it. Just changing the terms a bit. Put your hands up, high." He leveled his pistol. "I'll get you down." He fired. The green powerbolt crackled between Macmain's left hand and the suspending wire.

"You're slipping, Richter," Macmain said.

"Perhaps . . . but you're *falling*." He fired again. The bolt severed the cable.

A spray of brilliant blue energy struck the golden platform. It exploded in sparks and splinters. Macmain landed on it in a crouch. He wasn't electrocuted.

*"Kill the prisoner!"* Richter snarled.

"You don't want to do that, Colonel," said the Marine behind the woman in silver. The Marine's power-carbine was still glowing from the burst it had just fired. "Good help is so hard to find." The Marine snapped open the helmet visor.

"Hello, Libra," Macmain said.

"Just waitin' for my moment, boss," Libra said, and fired the Drake again, splitting the air with blue rods of energy. Two of Richter's men fell. Richter snapped off a shot, making Libra duck, and then he and the other Marine dove for cover.

"Ready, boss?"

"Just a moment," Mac said, and took a small object from a suit pouch, a disc of silver plastic with an engraved hand, Macmain the Magnificent's calling card. He flipped it through the air toward the empty glass case. It intersected one of the alarm-rays; a horn blared, and steel shutters began rolling down to seal off the doors. "Let's go."

The last Marine fired from behind a painting, blasting chips of marble from the floor in front of the rapidly closing door.

Libra stitched light through the canvas. The Marine fell forward, ripping it wide open. Libra hit the floor and rolled after Mac, under the shutter as it slammed down.

"Libra, that was a *Picasso!*"

"You must be slippin', boss. Didn't you see the middle musician's pants were the wrong color? It was a fake."

"Oh. Sure," Macmain said. "Just wanted to see if you were paying attention."

"Always, boss, always. *Vixen*'s just around the corner."

They turned. The next corridor had one wall of glass: outside, as if this were a street entrance and not fifty stories in the sky, waited the gravity boat *Star Vixen*. A pane was missing from the wall, and *Vixen*'s boarding ramp linked her to the corridor.

And by the open window stood two more Consortium Marines.

Libra snapped, "Have they been here?"

"Who?" said one of the troopers.

"What do you mean, 'who,' you idiot? Macmain

and Libra, of course. They'll be heading for this ship. Get down that hall and head them off, or Richter'll use you for target practice!"

The Marines saluted and ran off in the direction Mac and Libra had come from. There was a sound of gunfire, and several yells.

"Good thing those lads can't hit anything," Libra said as they crossed the sheer drop to *Vixen*'s hatch. "They might hurt someone."

"Lift us, Libra," Mac said.

"You got it, boss." She slid into the control couch, and her hands danced across the controls. "And so once again we bid farewell to the eager but stupid minions of the Cons—"

A hand chopped down on Macmain's wrist, and the Karthores Diadem fell to *Vixen*'s deck.

"Not all so stupid, thief," the attacker said. He wore a slate gray uniform with silver sword insignia: one of Richter's personal guard, and a dangerous opponent in fact. He slammed a fist into Mac's side, driving the master thief back into the ship's open doorway.

"Mac—" Libra said.

"*Lift* us!" Mac shouted. "Before Richter gets here!"

The Grey Guard lunged at Macmain as the world fell away.


"You *know* what's going to happen," Orvy said. "They're going to have a big fight in the doorway, and just as they're about to climb out of the atmosphere, Mac wins, like always, but as the Grey guy drops out the door he'll grab the Diadem. So nobody gets the super-weapon, and *Vixen* docks with *Star Fox* in orbit, and zoom they go off into the sunset."

Thed looked up from the book. Orvy was sitting cross-legged on a rock, tossing pebbles into the little creek they called the Styx, that ran down from the hills. They'd both come out here to get away from town, because everybody in town was caught up with working on Plan C, and Thed just couldn't stand it any longer.

Now Orvy was trying Thed's patience, and there was never very much of it to try. "It doesn't have anything to do with knowing what's going to happen," Thed said. "It's how it happens that matters. I mean, sure, I know Richter isn't going to kill Mac. I even knew that it wasn't really Libra in the hood and handcuffs. Libra'd *never* let them do that to her. But it's still fun to see her surprise everybody."

"But it isn't a *surprise,*" Orvy said. "Oh, what's the use." He tossed another pebble.

Thed put the copy of *Blaze of Night* (Macmain The Magnificent Adventure #46, by Ross Red) down carefully. "Do you want to talk about the dramatic unities again?"

Orvy held up his hands. "No. Please. No." Orvy was twelve years, two months old. Thed was twelve years, five months. The difference showed up most distinctly in theoretical discussions. "It's starting to get late. Do you want to go back to town?"

"Absolutely not. They wouldn't notice us anyway. So damn busy with their damn Plan C."

"Hey, the Plan's important."

"It's important to the people in it," Thed said. "And that ain't us." She looked up. "Who's that?"

Orvy turned. Three figures in white were coming down from the hills. "I don't know. Are they Plan people?"

"Don't look like it." Thed's voice dropped as far as it would go. "One of them's got *wings.*"

Thed and Orvy watched, perhaps scared but certainly fascinated, as the three strangers approached.

One was tall and thin, and did have wings, with red feathers. The others looked like people . . . except that one of them had greenish skin and pointed ears.

*"Aliens,"* Thed said.

"Yeah," Orvy said.

The most peoplelike of the aliens said, "Hello. Are you natives?"

"Sure," Thed said.

The aliens talked to each other rapidly. Then the one who had spoken before said, "Can you tell us how to reach the nearest settlement?"

Orvy started to point the way to town, but Thed said, "You go that way, toward those big rocks." She pointed toward two huge boulders in the distance, a third of a circle the wrong way from town. "You won't see anything until you're nearly there . . . 'cause, see, it's built underground . . . but you can't miss it once you're there. Okay?"

"That's great," the alien said. "Thanks a lot." The three aliens spoke again. Then the first one said, "We haven't got anything to give you now, but we'd like to pay you back later. What are your names?"

"I'm Macmain," Thed said, "and this is Libra, my loyal sidekick." Orvy stared at Thed. The alien looked puzzled, then said, "Well, thanks, both of you. See you." She waved. Thed and Orvy waved back.

The aliens started walking toward the distant stones. When they were a hundred meters or so away, Orvy said, "What was all that about? They were lost, and you pointed them the wrong way. Those rocks aren't near anything but the old caves."

"They were alien invaders," Thed said, "or hadn't you noticed? We're part of Plan C now, whether anyone wanted us to be or not."

Orvy considered this, said, "Well, okay. Should we go back to town and tell somebody?"

"I have a *much* better idea."

"Oh, now wait a minute. The last time you had a much better idea—"

"That would have worked if the rubber band hadn't broken."

"Okay. What's the idea?"

"We go back and get our backpacks, and then we go looking for the starship."

*"What* starship?"

"I don't believe this. Those were aliens, right? They didn't just *walk* here, did they?" Thed paused. "Unless they were Deep-Space Attack Androids, like in *The Janus Invasion.* . . ."

"I thought Deep-Space Attack Androids always looked just like the people on the planets they were invading."

"Good point. Okay, so they're not androids, which means they had to have a starship, right?"

"I guess so."

"From a brilliant deduction to 'I guess so.' Sometimes I don't know why I put up with you."

"Because I put up with you putting up with me."

"Right," Thed said. "Now, shall we go, Libra?"

"Now let's get this straight," Orvy said. "You aren't *really* Macmain. Anyway, if you *were* really Macmain, then I'd have to be Libra, and I don't want to be Libra. I don't even look like Libra. I'm not even a *girl,* Thed."

"Okay, okay. Who do you want to be, then?"

"Aramis."

*"Aramis?* He doesn't even want to be a Musketeer. He wants to be a *bishop!"*

"Yeah, and he also lives through all the books."

"There is," Thed said gravely, "a certain logic to your position." It was what Macmain said when he was outmatched in a fight, which usually required the

Empire to be holding at least eight phasers and an innocent hostage. It was not by any means an admission of defeat. Thed picked up Ross Red's latest tale, looked at the cover, put the book in her pocket. "Macmain and Aramis . . . a cross-dimensional adventure, hmm, that's not bad. Okay, Aramis, let's go find that starship."

"'Starship,' *mon amie? Je ne comprends pas* your strange speech."

Thed laughed. This was more like it. "A vessel that sails 'pon the black tides of night, my friend, laden with booty from lands past your imagining. Come!"

*"Mais oui,"* Orvy said, and another great adventure had begun.

Flyter sat at the long, long table in the castle's glass-roofed hall, surrounded by stacks of papers, graphs with scrawled pencil notes, a paper floor plan with small labeled counters arranged on it, and two computers. He picked up one of the graphs, wrote another line, giggled. He took another paper, read it over, laughed aloud, then crumpled it in both hands and tossed it into the emptiest of five full wastebaskets.

Estervy came in. "Your sister called," she said. "Thed's missing again."

Flyter sighed. "Orville too?"

"Orville too."

"Well. I certainly haven't seen them."

"Could they be at your place?"

"No, I changed the lock codes after her last unauthorized visit. . . . Then again, that might not stop Thed. I tell you, sometimes I think she really *is* Macmain."

"So what shall I tell your sister?"

"The truth will do, I should think. I don't know where Theodora is, I'm very busy right at the moment, and Thed's never had any problem taking care of herself. Not to mention Orvy. Besides, how much trouble can they get into?"

Estervy gave him a withering look.

"You're right," Flyter said wearily. "Forget I said that. . . . Telephone." He began to search the table. "Telephone, telephone, who's got—aha." At least two hundred sheets of paper hit the floor as Flyter triumphantly lifted the telephone. Estervy looked doubtful, but as Flyter dialed he said, "Don't worry, that's all dropped scenes. . . . Hello? Lizzy? Well, yes, of course it's me. Look, about my darling niece and her partner in crime—Oh, really? Well, that's just splendid. No, I really mean that, I love Theodora, I don't want her eaten by lions or . . ." Flyter paused, rested the phone on his shoulder and scribbled furiously.

Estervy picked up the phone handset. "Liz? Estervy. Oh, she did show up. That's good, then. Oh, Liz, you know damn well he cares, and you also know how he is when he's working. That's right . . . No, in the last draft I saw, we only need you to cook for the, right, for that. You don't even need to come to the technical, unless you just want to. Hm? It's in . . ." Estervy looked at her watch. "Oh, my ears and whiskers, it's in four hours. Must go, Liz. See you then."

She put down the phone. "I presume you know that the technical is in—"

"I'm not deaf," Flyter said. "Mad, very dreadfully mad, but why will you call me deaf? We'll make the technical."

"They'll be landing in no more than twelve hours."

Flyter whacked a key on one of the computers, and the printer began spitting pages. He held up the printout, displaying it. "Then desire them to step this way," he said brightly, "and I'll set them right in a twinkling."

They gathered up the papers, laughing.

# Chapter Four

## *Overtures*

THE STARS STREAKED to rainbows, then back down to drifting points, as *Enterprise* dropped out of warp-drive.

"Direidi ahead, Captain," Sulu announced, as the planet tumbled into view on the main bridge screen. "Klingon vessel located, range one million kilometers and steady."

"Lieutenant Uhura," Kirk said, "send our respects."

"Sir," Uhura said, "I've just received a message of goodwill from *Fire Blossom,* Kaden vestai-Oparai commanding."

"Well then, Lieutenant, *return* our respects."

"Of course, sir. It's just that the wording of the message was a bit unusual."

Kirk said, "Uhura, put the Klingons' message on bridge speakers."

"Yes, Captain."

*"Knock, knock!"* said a man's deep, resonant voice. *"Who's there in th'other devil's name?"* The voice had a faint Scots accent.

Uhura said, mostly to herself, "Orson . . . Welles?"

The voice continued: *"Faith, here's an equivocator, that could swear in both the scales against either scale, who committed treason enough for god's sake, yet could not equivocate to heaven: O come in, equivocator!"*

The lift doors opened and Ambassador Charlotte Sanchez came onto the bridge. She wore a crisp green trouser suit with a scarf at the collar. She looked around. "You all look just a touch tense. Was it something I said?"

Kirk said, "Uhura . . . Spock . . . anybody . . . what do you make of that message?"

Engineer Scott said, "None o' *my* clansmen."

Spock said, "Its origin is in—"

"I know its origin, Spock . . . I'd like an analysis."

"I'm afraid there is insufficient data for that, Captain."

Kirk sighed. Bad enough they had Klingons, now it looked like they had crazy Klingons. "All right. All ashore that's going ashore."

Spock said, "With your permission, Captain, I shall remain aboard ship and continue the planetary survey. We must also attempt to locate the *Smith*'s crew."

"Of course, Spock." Kirk pressed the intercom switch. "This is the Captain speaking. Landing—"

"Excuse me, Captain," Ambassador Sanchez said, "but this is my command." She leaned over the grille. "This is the ambassador. Diplomatic party will please gather in the Transporter Room in thirty minutes. Dress uniform, no sidearms to be carried. Thank you."

Kirk said, "It's usual for at least two members of a landing party to carry hand phasers."

"Yes, it is usual."

Sulu said, "And Klingon landing parties are always armed. Even on 'diplomatic' missions."

"So I've heard. I believe that I said dress uniform, gentlemen. I plan to change in my quarters."

Sanchez left the bridge. Kirk looked around; everyone was quite still except for Uhura, who turned toward her console before anyone could see her face.

"You heard the ambassador," Kirk said. "Mr. Kyle, you have the conn. Chekov, Sulu . . . Uhura, shall we dress for dinner?"

"Maglus . . ." Captain Kaden said.

"Awaiting your orders, Captain," said Security Officer Maglus.

"Put the communications officer down."

Maglus had Aperokei's throat enclosed in his fist. His other hand was arched above Aperokei's head. Maglus looked remarkably like someone about to open a bottle.

"Yes, Captain," Maglus said, and dropped Aperokei back into his chair behind the communications console.

Kaden observed the bridge crew relaxing with mixed relief and disappointment. At least one small bet changed hands.

"*Zan* Aperokei," the captain said, "this vessel has for some time now been at a state of less than full alert. And I believe that young officers do their best when they are free to act in their own ways. Our cruise has not been without honor, do you agree, *Zan* Aperokei?"

"Yes, Captain," Proke said, squeaking a little.

"Excellent. Now, would you care to explain the message of greeting that you sent the Federation vessel?"

"It was intended—" Proke cleared his throat, continued half an octave lower, "—intended to make our Federation opposites feel comfortable and at ease. I did not mean it as a statement of Imperial policy."

"Where did you acquire the . . . text?"

"It is a piece of classical poetry," Proke said, so earnestly that he had to be lying.

But the message was sent; there wasn't anything to do but make the best of it. "Very well. If this message indeed puts the Feds off their guard, you may expect rewards, Lieutenant."

"Yes, Captain," Proke said. Nothing scared junior Klingon officers quite so badly as the promise of rewards from senior Klingon officers.

Force Leader Memeth entered the bridge. "Equipment has been secured for transport," he said crisply.

"Rish?"

"Transporters are synchronized," Arizhel said. "If *Enterprise* maintains standard separation, there should be no way they can detect the second transport beam."

"Excellent," Kaden said. "Landing party, equip and meet on the Transporter stage."

Kirk, Ambassador Sanchez, Lt. Uhura, and Dr. McCoy materialized in the cool, still afternoon air. They stepped forward to clear the transporter coordinate, realized they were standing on a small raised platform, decorated with red and gold bunting and little flags with Klingon trefoils. Light flared behind them, there was the electronic whistle of transport, and Scott, Sulu, and Chekov joined them on the little dais.

"Rather interesting welcome," Kirk said quietly, looking around at the decorations.

Sanchez pointed at another platform, perhaps a hundred meters away. It was tricked out with Federation colors and flags and occupied by a group of agitated Klingon officers. She chuckled. "Looks like a reasonable mistake to me."

The platforms had been set up in an open stretch of grassy ground. There were low, rocky hills in the middle distance. Just ahead was a sprawling town of small buildings, and one amazing structure.

The big building looked partly like a Gothic castle, two parts storybook and one part mad scientist's, with one thin tower poking up at least ten stories, partly like a Victorian mansion with ornate fretsaw work under the eaves, partly like a greenhouse—a long glass roof ran on and on over one wing—and there were plenty of less identifiable parts left over. Before it was a small, pagodalike glass pavilion, and parked before that a streetcar much like the preserved cable lines of San Francisco on Earth; the car tracks ran for fifty yards and stopped cold, with a sign reading YOUR TAX DOLLARS AT WORK—DIREIDI CHAMBER OF COMMERCE.

People were pouring out of the big building and the town. They were all brightly dressed, and there was a rising sound of voices. Suddenly a bass drum sounded from the trolleycar pavilion, and then a brass band came to life.

The crowd began singing:

> We thought that you might like to know
>   You'll get a down-home welcome
>     In our little town
> We hope you'll never want to go
>   It's really great to have
>     Someone strange hanging 'round
> See how our friendly neighbors
> Step back as you pass
> Please put your trash in baskets

And stay off the grass
You only get one warning so
We thought that you might like to know

Kirk said, "I've never been met quite like this before."

Uhura was humming in time to the bright, brassy music. Sulu waved to the townspeople. McCoy said, "What was that about baskets?"

The ambassador said "Well, *I* think it's charming."

We thought that you might like to know
  We'd like to entertain you
    Our merry old way
So every hearth will be aglow
  There's nothing quite so warm as
    An auto-da-fé
We've been on pins and needles
Since you first appeared
We hope you don't have plans to
Do anything weird
We're very open-minded, though
We thought that you might like to know

As the music faded, Sulu began singing brightly—though not terribly loudly:

From charms intramural
To prettiness rural
The sudden transition
Is simply Elysian!

Almost before he stopped, Uhura sang, to a different meter,

> By a simple coincidence, few
> Could ever have counted upon,
> The same thing occurred to me,
> When I first put this uniform on!

And Chief Engineer Scott, grinning fit to burst, added:

> Now to the banquet we press;
> Now for the eggs and the ham;
> Now for the mustard and cress,
> Now for the strawberry jam!

Captain Kirk had an expression of mingled awe and bewilderment; Dr. McCoy's eyebrows were hanging off the clouds.

"*Gilbert and Sullivan,*" all three of the singers chorused, and bowed slightly to the captain.

"Yes, of course," Ambassador Sanchez said, sounding not entirely certain. "You're right. If these people's culture calls for them to, uh, burst into song occasionally . . . then we must respect the custom."

Kirk cleared his throat, took a long breath, and opened his mouth. Before any sound came out, however, a plump man in a swallowtail coat, striped trousers, and spats came forward. "*Kai, kai kassai, duymey,*" he said, "*Flyter sutai-Direidi jikh—*"

"Excuse me, please," Sanchez said, "but we represent the Federation."

"Oh?" The man paused, pulled a little book from his coat pocket, riffled through it. "Oh, of course! *Eighty-six,* not sixty-eight. Heads will roll for that one, you may be sure. Well, then, come right this way, please."

The crowd parted and the plump man led the Federation party to the great glass-roofed hall of the massive building. On the way, he hummed to himself, strutted a bit like a drum major.

The inside of the hall was decorated with multicolored ribbons, sprays of exotic flowers, long white candles in iron holders. Along the walls were man-high sculptures in strange, fluid shapes. The sculpture didn't seem to fit with the rest of the decor; it was in a reddish-colored crystal . . .

"Is that dilithium?" Ambassador Sanchez whispered.

*"Can't* be," Sulu said.

"It certainly *looks* like it," Chekov chimed in.

Kirk said, "Scotty . . ."

"Aye, sir—if it's th' real thing, there's enough in this room t' run the Starfleet for a year."

The plump man in the clawhammer coat turned around. "Now!" he shouted, making Sulu blink and McCoy wince. "Allow me to welcome you most sincerely to the free, independent, and unaligned planet of Direidi. My name is Flyter. *Hi* there." He pumped Kirk's hand. "Hi there." He shook Sanchez's hand, then Uhura's, the rest. "Hi there. Hi there. Hi there." He paused, wiped his hands and his forehead with a huge red silk handkerchief. "Well, thank goodness that's over." He looked up. "Oh, are you still here?"

Sanchez said, "We represent the United Federation of Planets . . ."

"Of course, right, right, so much going on this week it just slipped my mind. I'm Flyter. Who are you folks, then?"

"Captain James T. Kirk, USS *Enterprise*, Federation Starfleet Command."

" 'T'?" Flyter said.

"It stands for 'Tiberius,'" Kirk said. "As in the Roman emperor."

"Really?"

"It was handed down from my great-grandfather."

"Oh," Flyter said, sounding vaguely disappointed. "And you must be the ambassador."

"Charlotte Sanchez, UFP Diplomatic Service. Pleased."

"Why?" Flyter said innocently.

Without missing a beat, Sanchez said "Because meeting new individuals gives me great intellectual pleasure. That's why I became a diplomat."

"Oh, good! There are almost fourteen thousand of us, you know. We should be able to make you really, really happy." He paused, looked worried. "Your species doesn't, uh, do anything, you know, *awful* when you get too happy, do you? Like, you know, blow up, or something?"

"Not at all," Sanchez said, not quite so easily.

"Well, then that's all right. Now, I want you to meet someone who plays a very special part in our society." He turned, swept a hand, bowed from the waist. "Estervy."

A woman was approaching. She was strongly built and walked with a positively regal bearing. Her face was smooth and sharp, her gray-streaked hair swept up and covered with fine black lace.

"My God, it's Queen Victoria," Kirk said to Sanchez.

"I agree. Shut up."

"And who are these persons, Flyter my dear?" the woman said. Her voice was pitched high, and the *R*'s trilled magnificently.

"The Federation people, Estervy. This is Captain

James Kirk. His great-grandfather was a Roman emperor."

"Oh! Not one of the silly ones, I hope."

"Well, not exactly—"

"Because we don't go in for that sort of thing around here, feeding people to lions. We don't even have any lions. Do we, Flyter?"

"Not anymore. We had some once, but somebody left them outside all night and—well, you know."

Estervy said to Kirk, "Of course, if you want to have dinner leaning on a couch, that's quite all right. We're very open-minded here. Just don't expect any of our young ladies to peel you any grapes." She smiled. "Grapes we *do* have. Correct, Flyter?"

"Absolutely, Estervy. So, Captain, will you be wanting a couch for dinner?"

"No, thank you."

"It's no bother."

"That's all right," Kirk said. His head was spinning slightly. "Excuse me . . . what happened to your lions?"

"We don't have any lions, I thought I made that clear," Flyter said, in an irritated tone. "It's the couch or nothing, I'm afraid."

"But you used to have lions . . ."

"Earth used to have dinosaurs, didn't it?" Flyter said sharply. "But if I came in and asked for a dinosaur, I wouldn't get very far, would I? Same with your whales. And just try to get an aurochs. Is it my fault you can't take care of your large animals?"

Flyter turned to the ambassador, and in a suddenly silky voice said, "Estervy, this is Ambassador Charlotte Sanchez."

"Hello, Estervy," Sanchez said. "I'm delighted to meet you."

"Hi," Estervy said, sounding quavery. Flyter leaned close to her, said softly, "It's okay. No—" His hands mimed an explosion. Estervy let out a held breath and said, "Well. Pleased to meet you, too."

Sanchez bowed slightly. "I don't mean to get ahead of the negotiations," she said, "but would you mind telling me what your office is?"

"Office? I don't have an office. I did once have an apartment with a large bedsitter, but an office?"

"Flyter said . . ." Sanchez looked at Estervy, at Flyter, at Kirk. She stopped talking. Kirk felt relieved.

"You'll excuse us now," Flyter said. "The Klingons have arrived. Help yourselves to punch and cookies." He bustled off, humming again. Estervy dipped her head slightly and glided away after him.

"Bones," Kirk said, feeling a mixture of curiosity and exasperation, "do you suppose there's something in the water?"

"It tested out just fine from up yonder," McCoy said, "but then, nobody's ever done a test on the effects of long-term exposure to dilithium radiation." He looked meaningfully at Engineer Scott.

Scott looked puzzled, then gritted his teeth. "Aye?"

Kirk watched as Flyter went over to greet the Klingons. He spoke Klingonese, gesturing emphatically. The Klingon Captain—Kaden, Kirk recalled—looked violent for a moment, and then gave the wary half-bow that Klingons gave to those they respected. (Kirk had no idea what Klingons did before those they trusted.)

Flyter bustled back into the center of the hall. "All right, ladies, gentlemen, boys and girls, this way, please. I know you're hungry but nobody expects you to eat off the floor."

Estervy was smiling and nodding at nothing much.

Ambassador Sanchez said, "You've only been here for one generation, is that correct?"

"That's a long time, these days, m'dear."

"Well, yes, but that's not what I meant. . . . How did you ever find the time for this stonework?"

"Oh, most of it's cast panels, prefab, you know. Amazing what you can get by mail these days. This way, please," Flyter said, and urged the crowd toward the end of the hall.

A whistle blew. A multipaneled door opened at the opposite end of the room, and a long, narrow table began to roll into the room. It was set along its length with china and crystal, twenty settings on each side, and there were centerpieces of flowers and carved ice. To either side of the table, a crowd of waiters in black jackets appeared, carrying chairs. To the sounds of the band that had played outside, they spread along the table with drill-team precision and clicked the chairs into place as the table stopped. Not one wineglass was upset.

"Chow time!" Flyter announced, rubbed his hands together, and trotted toward the banquet table. "Place cards are on the table; if you can't spell your own name don't blame me!"

The Direidi immediately began searching for their places. The humans and Klingons looked at one another for a long moment and followed.

Kirk noticed that one place had, instead of a straight-backed chair, a short couch upholstered in red plush. Something felt tight inside his chest, and he checked the place card. Sure enough, it read JAMES CALIGULA KIRK. He sighed and reclined.

The dinner began with a soup made with a sort of morel, followed by a multicolored salad, and then a huge platter of beef Wellington laced up the side.

Midway through the entree, Engineer Askade said

rather casually, "I would like to ask about these sculptures."

"Told you once," Flyter said, popping an olive, "the whole place came from a kit."

"I spoke of the figures along the walls. They appear to be of dilithium. Is this a common art form on your world?"

"Used to be," someone said, and the Direidi began chuckling. Even the waiters were laughing.

Flyter used his napkin elaborately. "Excuse us, please. That's a bit of a local joke. We turn these things up now and then, digging foundations, running sewer pipe. No one's really certain how long ago they were made. Dilithium wears out rather slowly, as I'm sure you know."

Ambassador Sanchez said, "You mean, they're artifacts?"

Estervy said, "I like the idea of an ancient race. It makes a world feel so . . . lived-in."

Lieutenant Sulu said, "But what happened to them? Where did they go?"

"Oh, not that again," Flyter said irritably. "Look, I'm really sorry about the lions, okay? It was an honest mistake. But this was before our time."

Kirk coughed.

Arizhel said, "We have excellent historical analysts for matters such as this. History is of great importance to the Klingon Empire."

"Certainly it's of concern to the Federation as well," Sanchez said, sounding not at all bothered. "We would be pleased to help you uncover the truth about your planet's past."

Sulu said, "Do you know anything at all about them?"

"There are the tablets," Estervy said.

"Oh, right, right, the tablets," Flyter said. He

turned to a waiter. "Arvin, would you ask Pam to come out here, please? Just for a moment?"

The waiter bowed and went into the kitchen. Flyter said, "Pam's a bit of a philologist. She's been reading the tablets in her spare time. Even named our mysterious ancients: now we call them the Eldireidi."

A moment later a woman in toque and apron came out. "This had better be short, Flyter. We've got a very recalcitrant salmon out there."

"Of course, Pam. Our guests are interested in the Eldireidi inscriptions. Do you remember what happened to the big runestone?"

*"Which* big runestone?"

"That is true," Estervy said thoughtfully. "They did leave a lot of notes." She sighed. "Wish we could get secretarial help like that."

The kitchen door opened. Someone leaned out: she wore kitchen whites dripping with what appeared to be tartar sauce. "It's straining again, Pam!"

Memeth rose slightly from his chair, one hand tight on his steak knife. "What is happening in there?"

Pam snapped, "I'm a cook, not an ichthyologist," then said to Flyter, "Come on, which stone?"

"The big one." Pam frowned. Flyter said, "Oblong, beveled edges, you know."

"Oh, the map rock." She bent over the banquet table, picked up a silver-handled spatula and scraped beef Wellington across the platter.

Gravy pooled into incised lettering, and the red fire of dilithium glowed under the lights. "There you go."

"That's an alien artifact?" Kirk said incredulously.

"You think we cook for forty every day? Cookie sheets are the first thing to run out. Besides, this is the most durable stuff known. I hardly think a few hours in a medium oven is going to bother it."

There was the whine of a siren from the kitchen,

and a flare of red light from the door. One of the cooks leaned out. "Pam! *Bullets won't stop it!*"

Pam sighed. "'Scuse me, Flyter. Everyone eat hearty, now." She opened the kitchen door and vanished into smoke and light and noise. The door swung shut and all was quiet.

Kirk looked up and down the table. Sanchez was staring at the plaque under the entree. The Klingons looked ready to jump, Force Leader Memeth in particular. His own crew weren't exactly at ease. And leaning on the couch was making Kirk's elbow sore.

Flyter was busily relocating chunks of beef Wellington to other plates with the silver server, exposing more of the engraving. He wiped lightly at it with a handful of cauliflower, and the gravy-filled lettering and diagrams showed up clearly.

"Estervy, you worked on this, too," Flyter said. "Isn't this the plaque that talks about people from the sky?"

"No, dear, that was under the soup course. This is the one that refers to a vast treasure of sunlight."

"Treasure of sunlight?" Sulu said, a little dreamily.

"Well, young man," Estervy said, "we did the best we could. May I, Flyter?" She stood up.

"Of course, Estervy."

She picked up a butter knife and traced along the inscription:

> When first the light of dawning
> Lies in the mountaintop
> Bear toward the rays of morning
> And ride until you drop.
> Here lies the sunlight's treasure
> And if it be your goal
> Keep your eye upon the doughnut
> And not upon the hole.

Uhura said, "That's an . . . idiomatic translation?"

"We're a little short of poets, too, I'm afraid, dear."

Sulu said, "But another of the tablets says the Eldireidi came from another planet?"

Estervy said curtly, "Young man, they don't exactly end with 'continued on next slab.' For all I know, there's a set with shaving-cream jingles."

Kaden said, "But you have proof of this race—that could carve dilithium for mere ornaments—and you have done so little with it? This is—" Arizhel was tugging discreetly at Kaden's sleeve. He paused, said more quietly "—something we would be most pleased to help correct."

"First Battalion, Combat Archeologists," Kirk muttered, and Sanchez elbowed him in the sore arm.

"Well, I'll tell you the truth," Flyter said. "Some time back we had some people who really were eager to go find the Eldireidi. And they went. But they didn't come back. With the number of colonists we have, we really can't afford too many people not coming back."

"You made it illegal?" Maglus said.

"Laws against people doing destructive things are useful," Flyter said offhandedly, "but laws against plain dumb things aren't very. No, it just kind of went out of fashion. Ah, here comes dessert."

Conversation stopped while the dessert, a pecan pie dense as dwarfstar matter, was served. Over strong coffee, Kirk said, "That was a magnificent dinner."

"It was most excellent," Kaden said.

Flyter said, "Yes, not bad, I'd say." He turned his head. "Check, please."

The waiter presented a silver tray. Flyter picked the long piece of paper from it. "Hmm. Who had the grilled sole?"

There was an awkward silence. Flyter said, "Oh, come on, you *know* how these places are, they won't split a check for a party this size . . . oh, well." He tossed a square of plastic onto the tray. "Now, you be sure I get the receipts and the carbons, okay?"

"Of course, sir," the waiter said.

The staff began clearing the table. "Shall we move on?" Flyter said, and rose. The others followed.

Fireworks lit the way out of the banquet hall, around the streetcar pavilion—the car was no longer there—and up to the Victorian-looking face of the building. A man in a frogged frock coat and high hat stood by a pair of stained-glass doors. The porter smiled, tipped his hat in a white-gloved hand, and pulled the door open.

Beyond it was a grand, cluttered-elegant lobby, three stories from parquet floor to skylighted roof. A carpeted stairway led up; other halls showed hints of shop windows and invitingly dim taverns. The front desk was nearly ten meters long, of rubbed dark oak; behind it was a bank of pigeonholes, and a tall man and a short woman in identical dove-gray suits.

As the Federation and Klingon groups entered, a red carpet began to unroll, apparently under its own power, flipping fully open at their feet; then a stream of bellhops and maids came dancing down the grand staircase. There was a crash of cymbals, and as the lobby-bar pianist tore into an upbeat melody, voices were raised.

The man and woman behind the desk led the chorus:

We'd like to welcome you sincerely
    To our little hotel
And it's a pleasure to be hosting you

And we should point out that we're nearly
   Done rebuilding as well
And if you like the place now
Just wait until we get through
We have plush carpeted halls
And rooms with up-to-date features
And you will notice each suite has
   Very soundproof walls
And though a couple well-known guests
May once have been indiscreet
It's just a quiet hotel
Set on a nice quiet street

We have a top-notch reputation
   And we're sure that you'll find
That your desires are splendidly served
We offer every recreation
   For the body and mind
And all those rumors you've heard
Are really quite undeserved
We've got hot water to spare
And very elegant cooking
And we're certain your booking's
   In the files somewhere
And though until we can locate it
You may have a short wait
It's quite a lovely hotel
You'll find our lobby is great

Ambassador Sanchez looked at Captain Kaden, who shrugged. The party, really all one now, moved up the carpet toward the desk. The tall man swiveled an enormous book toward them.

So here's the register, please sign up
   Give the bellman your grips

While we arrange for your car to be moved
Stop by our lobby bar or gift shop
Get some small bills for tips
We'll send your suitcases up
Soon as your credit's approved
If you want dinner at midnight
Or to send someone flowers
Just ring us twenty-four hours
   And we'll do you right
Although it might take a while
Rome wasn't built in a day
We're just a cozy hotel
Run in a cozy old way
Yes, it's a first-class hotel
(We hope you think so as well)
A really first-class hotel
(The decoration is swell)
Run in a first-class
   Top brass
      Stompin' at the Savoy
         Way

*"Will that be cash or charge?"* cried the desk clerk, as the music crashed to a stop and the dancing staff froze.

No one said anything for a moment. Then the woman behind the desk—the same one who had appeared from the kitchen during the banquet—clanged a bell. "Front boy!" she called out, and then, "Good evening, ladies and gentlemen. Welcome to the Hotel Direidi. I'm Pam, and along with my husband Davith—" she indicated the tall man next to her—"we'll be your hosts during your stay here. Now, let's see. How have we arranged your reservations?" She ran her finger down a much-scribbled-over sheet of paper. "Ambassador Sanchez, Room 21. Davith?"

Davith reached to one of the pigeonholes and took down a key. He presented it to the ambassador.

"That's just up the stairs, to your left. Captain James Kirk, Room 22. Upstairs and right. Commander Arizhel, Room 31, up two and left. Captain Kaden, Room 32. Now, the rest of you will be in the new wing. . . ." Davith kept dealing out keys.

When all were assigned, Pam said, "I'm sure you'd all like to get into your rooms as quickly as possible; are there any questions I can answer before then?"

There was a sudden, extremely awkward silence. Everybody had plenty of questions. They just couldn't figure out where to start asking.

Engineer Scott said politely, "Would that nice little tavern up the hall still be servin'?"

"Terribly sorry, sir," Davith said, sounding truly wounded, "but most of our restaurant staff are still at the Castle, cleaning up after the banquet. However, room service will be glad to deliver anything you'd like . . . may I suggest a bottle of the local single malt? With the Hotel's compliments."

Scott seemed on the brink of tears. "First class all the way, sir. I thank you."

Kirk turned to Ambassador Sanchez. "I don't suppose you'd be interested in a nightcap?"

"Thanks, Jim, but Commander Arizhel and I are going to have a little talk. Girl stuff, bore you silly."

"Well, I . . ." Kirk nodded and stepped back as the women went upstairs. "Wish I knew just what that meant."

"If we ever learn that, Kirk," Kaden said from behind him, "you and I shall rule the universe."

Kaden pointed upstairs. "I am not tired either. Let us converse as well. I know many glorious lies of battle."

Kirk started to say something, then caught the look in Kaden's eye. Laughing at once, they went up the grand staircase.

# Chapter Five

## *All's Fair in Love and Dilithium*

"... AND SO THEN he says, 'Have you ever wondered how the stars look from the deck of a Red Swan-class lightboat?' I swear that's an exact quote—"

There was a knock at the door of Ambassador Sanchez's room. Sanchez put down her brandy snifter, said to Arizhel, "Did you call for anything else from room service?"

Rish was topping off her own glass from the second bottle of brandy. "No."

Sanchez went to the door. "Yes?"

A woman's voice said, "May I come in?"

Sanchez looked at Arizhel, who gestured meaninglessly. The ambassador opened the door.

There was a young woman in the hall, about Sanchez's height, very slender, in a pale-blue silk dress. Her hair was curly and her eyes were bright. "Hi," she said. "I'm Princess Deedee. Could I talk to you?"

"I'm not in any position to negotiate ... not to mention any condition. ..."

"Oh, no, this isn't about the Federation or dilithium or anything. It's just that you're from, like, offworld, you know? I need to talk to somebody who's from there." She held up another flask of the Direidi brandy. "I even brought my own."

"Join the party," Sanchez said, and opened the door wide.

"Oh, wow, thanks. And there's two of you? Even better." She sat down, leaned back, started to kick off her shoes. "Oh—may I?"

"Do we look formal?"

*"Great."*

Sanchez sat back down. "You're a princess? I didn't think this world had royalty."

"Well, it doesn't, exactly. See, when Direidi was first settled, there was this really complicated system of land supervising. I mean, there was lots of land, since there were only about ten thousand people for the whole planet, but they wanted to, you know, plan ahead. The land areas were officially called 'Supervisory Districts,' and the people who ran them were 'District Supervisors,' but that was kind of confusing, nobody could remember which was which . . . anyway, as a joke somebody started calling them 'Kingdoms,' like in that social club they have on Earth, the Society for Chivalric Atavism? And it stuck."

Rish seemed totally lost. Sanchez wasn't having an easy time of it. Rish said, "But these 'Kings' were not truly rulers."

"Tell that to Mom and Dad," Deedee said.

"They don't have any real power, though," Sanchez said. "They're not tyrants."

"Are you trying to tell me that somebody who names you 'Princess Deedee the First' isn't a tyrant?"

"I see your point."

"What's *worse* is that, since I'm a princess, they want me to marry a prince. Any old prince," she said dryly. "Terrific. Here, prince. Arf, arf."

Arizhel poured three brandies. As they sipped, the speaker grille behind Deedee began playing soft string music. Sanchez hated piped music. She stirred to turn the thing off, but before she could get up, Deedee stood in front of the speaker, raised her brandy snifter, and began singing:

> I'm supposed to be a princess
> As ethereal as mist
> With a brow that stays unfurrowed
> And a lip that stays unkissed
> Till a prince all icky-charming
> With his pumpkin coach and four
> Sweeps me off my spike-heeled slippers . . .
> What a bore!

The tempo of the music picked up, and a brass section kicked in with the strings.

> When a guy presents his suit
> Scored for mandolin and lute
> On his bended knee with dutiful appearance
> Then my blue blood turns to ice
> 'Cause I feel like merchandise
> Being offered at a discount price for clearance
> I don't care if he's landed, as long as he's candid
> Though certainly beauty's no crime
> It's the text, not the cover
> That I want my lover to see
> Just an ordinary guy
> With a keen perceptive eye

For the girl inside the story-book clothes
For me

When you live in castle towers
You get lots of hearts and flowers
Not to mention hours recounting knightly glories
But I'd trade those moony looks
For a man who's read some books
Not these schnooks who tell the same damn dragon
    stories

Sanchez said, " 'Schnooks' are . . ."
"I know just what they are," Arizhel said.

I'm not interested whether he wears silk or leather
Or buckskin or brocade or fur
And armor of steel
Is no longer appealing to me
Just a plain Brooks Brothers cut
On a guy who's off his nut
For the girl inside the Grimm Brothers clothes
For me

Should a perfect gentle knight
Have a troth he'd like to plight
I assure you I'll be right there to receive it
I don't mind his pitching woo
Doing as the Romans do
But I can't I-do it if I don't believe it
So I sit here alone like a sword in a stone
And I wait for a man to come by
Who's stuck equally fast
With the wit to at last pull us free
Just a plain and artless Art
With a warm spot in his heart
For the girl inside the Guinevere clothes
For me!

"I mean," the princess said, "Dad can be such a dreadful *twit* sometimes, you know?"

Sanchez laughed. So did Rish.

Arizhel said, "My father was like this. He would say, 'You, with the tactical genius of a hundred generations in your line, wish to turn over stones and listen to stray radiations?' He thought I should be a Commando Force Leader like my uncles, or perhaps command a fighter wing as he had."

"Really?" Sanchez said. "My dad was old-Navy, too. What he'd say to *me* was, 'Charlie, one of these days the black-shoe bas—' uh, the Navy high command—"

"I understand the term," Rish said. "Our Aperokei has been known to use it. Fortunately for him it means nothing to most Klingon officers."

"Um. Well, anyway, he'd say, 'One of these days they'll unbend, and a woman's going to conn a starship. Might as well be you.' Well, fie on that and the dilithium it warps on."

"Why?" Deedee said. "It sounds terribly exciting."

"Don't let the videos fool you, kid. Jim Kirk's okay, if you don't mind his eyes pinching your posterior every fifteen minutes, but starship captains have this extraordinary tendency to go 'round the bend. Garth's in the booby hatch doing vaudeville impersonations, there was what's-his-name who nearly started a war on Omega 'cause he couldn't tell the cowboys from the commies, I don't even want to *think* about the one who thought he was Caesar—"

"I thought that was Captain Kirk," Deedee said, sounding bewildered.

"Close, honey, close. When you get right down to it, they're all—you with me on this one, Rish?"

*"Swaggering, tin-plated dictators with delusions of godhood,"* the two women chorused.

"You could always," Rish said, "work passage on a freighter. You have not the build to handle cargo, but you look to make a splendid . . . our word is *agaantwikh* . . . one who works in the small access areas."

"Jeffries jockey," the ambassador said. "Sure. Heck, if you stowed away on a slow-warper, they'd *have* to give you a job; it costs too much to turn around and take people back."

"An interesting thought," Arizhel said, "though it should not be attempted on an Imperial vessel."

The princess said, "Would they throw me overboard? You know, space me, like in the Macmain and Libra stories?"

*"Aack,"* Rish said.

Deedee said, "I don't understand. What does that mean?"

"It means nothing. It is an expression of disgust."

"You know, *aaaaack,"* Sanchez said helpfully.

Arizhel said, "They would not 'space' you. Can you imagine the potential damage to the external vapor intakes? No, you would be put to useful labor once you were located. The hazard is that the *sliketh* would locate you first."

Deedee said, "The *sliketh?"*

Rish shrugged. "They live in the unmonitored areas of the larger freighters. They are about . . ." She made an unsteady gesture indicating a size somewhere between half a meter and two, and a hand motion for either very big teeth or a spiked tail. "When they find organic material . . ." She made a very definite gesture.

*"Aaack,"* Deedee said.

"Yes, very much so."

Sanchez said, *"Sliketh* aside, it's a big universe. Neither of us is quite what our parents expected, either, but we did pretty well . . . and without waiting for Prince, or Captain, Charming to come along."

The princess was shaking her head. "You don't see . . . I *had* my ticket. One way to Deneva, second class."

*"Deneva?"* Sanchez said. *"Aack."*

Deedee's eyes widened. "They eat people on Deneva?"

"No, no, no. They're just a bunch of absolutely cutthroat laissez-faire capitalist . . . hmm, now that you put it that way . . . never mind. You had the ticket, right?"

"Yes. But then, see, he did show up. My prince."

*"Oh,"* Rish and Sanchez said together.

"His name's Pete Blackwood . . ." the princess said.

"The Princess and the Pete," Sanchez heard herself saying, and took a gulp of brandy to stop giggling. No one seemed to have noticed.

". . . and he's a video producer. He's got his own studio and everything. He makes art tapes."

Sanchez refilled her glass. "Uh-huh . . . he offered you any starring roles yet, kid?"

"Well, gosh, no, I mean, he makes art tapes. He did a half-hour survey of Picasso, you know? *A Period of Blue.* And one on Lenkahn Resteis, the Rykosian sculptor, called *I Think Gravity Was a Mistake."*

"Oh," Sanchez said, with a sigh of relief and embarrassment, *"art* tapes."

Rish said, "This is a profitable enterprise?"

"Oh, Pete does okay. The Picasso show went to Federation Public Video for quite a bit. But that's just the problem, see? It would be okay with Mom and Dad if Pete was rich, and just made videos for fun. Mom and Dad think you shouldn't do anything, except for fun." Dryly she added, "Mom and Dad are real fun people."

Sanchez said, "Why don't you *both* just pack up and go? It's a big . . . no, I said that already. But it is, anyway."

The princess said very soberly, "You seem to think that running away solves a lot of things."

Sanchez bit her lip. "Point to you, Deedee."

Rish scratched her chin. "I do not think that you have come to us merely to speak of troubles, Princess D'di. I think that you seek assistance."

"Well . . . yes. I want to do . . . well, kind of a practical joke, really. See, nobody around here will speak up to Mom and Dad about Pete. But if one of you offworlders saw him doing something . . . well, really princely . . . they'd *have* to take *you* seriously, right?"

The ambassador said, "What did you have in mind?"

Rish said warily, "I believe that I comprehend your purpose, but Klingons do not attest to false things."

"That's news to—" Sanchez caught herself, put her brandy snifter down hard, cleared her throat, and said, "Nor do Federation citizens. We have laws to punish those who swear false oaths."

Rish nodded. "We bleed them for medical supplies."

"Oh, no, nothing like that!" Deedee said hurriedly. "What I was thinking is, suppose the two captains, Mr. Kirk and Mr. Kaden, saw Pete being, like, heroic. If they really saw it, and told Dad what they saw, that wouldn't be a lie, would it?"

Rish said, "This act would be prearranged? We would help you to arrange it?"

"If you would. If it wouldn't be, you know, false witness."

Rish said, "If the captains give a true report, it seems no fraud to me."

Sanchez said, "Not in my book, either."

"Then you'll help?"

"You better believe it," the ambassador said. "Allies in a good cause, right, Rish?"

"If love is a duty, it is duty that allies us, *ael kai* the alliance." Rish hiccuped. "Excuse me. I was quoting. . . . Now, D'di, your companion knows you plan for him?"

"Of course not! I couldn't ask Pete to do something he knew was, you know, faked. False witness, right?"

"Very well. But then we must know: if presented with this opportunity to act, he will seize it?"

"You sound like my *dad*," Deedee said.

Arizhel said patiently, "I am establishing our warrior's capabilities before incorporating them into a tactical plan." She took a long swallow from her snifter. "What *is* our tactical plan, then?"

"Huh?"

Sanchez said, "What kind of heroic act do we need?"

Rish said, "I know. There will be a vast fire in the hotel, consuming it utterly . . . but your Pete boldly saves a few from the flames." She swept her arm in a circle. Deedee caught the brandy bottle in midair.

Sanchez said, "That's a little extreme, isn't it? . . . Not to mention the people he *doesn't* manage to save."

"I thought you desired this to be convincing."

"I see your point," the ambassador said, sort of worried that she did. "Still sounds like a bit much. . . . Wait. Deedee, do you know if the hotel has ever been burgled?"

"I just suggested that."

"Not 'burned,' Rish. Burgled. Robbed."

Deedee thought. Then she beamed. "Yes! There was the Black Cat Bandit. He—at least, maybe he was a he—wore a black suit, and a mask and hood. And no one ever caught him. Her. Them." She hiccuped, shot soda into her drink.

"Well, that's it, then. Pete catches the Black Cat—"

"And under torture he reveals a plot to overthrow D'di's parents," Rish said, her voice rising. Then she paused. "No, this will not do. When the robber is tortured, our plans will be revealed. This is worse than nothing. Pete must therefore slay the Cat. Ah! This hotel has a high lobby, with balconies. Pete hurls the Cat from the highest level, in sight of all below."

*"Nobody gets killed,"* Sanchez said, sloshing brandy, taking a gulp.

Rish took a drink in response. "You must think these people are very easily convinced."

"Issall . . ." Sanchez breathed deeply. "It's all in the setup. You can get people to believe the most incredible stuff if you just get them in the right, er . . ." She looked at Arizhel and Deedee, both of whom looked back with intently curious expressions. ". . . well, *you* know."

Deedee said, "But Commander Arizhel's right. Whoever is pretending to be the Cat can't really be caught. Pete has to just scare him away, somewhere the captains can see it."

"Okay," Sanchez said. "Suppose that when I go back to my room tomorrow night, I find the Cat, busy stealing my . . . hm, what have I got? Well, something. And he sees me, and decides to—"

"To slay you in rage, and . . . sorry."

"No, that's it, almost. He's really ticked off because I didn't have anything to steal, so he decides to kidnap me for ransom. He takes me down to the lobby, with a knife at my throat—"

"And Pete rescues you!" Deedee chimed in. "Only in the fight, the Cat gets away."

"The lobby guards do not cut him to bits?" Rish said. "Oh. I forgot. Different culture. Excuse me."

"It's a point, though," Sanchez said. "We have to make *sure* the Cat gets away."

Rish said, "Do you have sonic weapons here? There are sonics that only stun the victim."

Sanchez said, "That's perfect! And if the Cat's holding a stunner on me, then it doesn't seem so much like Pete's taking a risk with my life."

Rish opened her mouth, then shrugged and said nothing.

Sanchez said, "So who's going to bell the—I mean, play the Cat?"

The princess said, "Oh, I will. I'm pretty good at acrobatics, so I can make the fight look good, and if I have the hood over my head nobody will recognize me."

Rish said, "I have thought of something I do not like about this plan. The Federation ambassador is kidnapped before the negotiations by one who cannot be identified. Suppose the Klingon Empire is blamed for this?"

Deedee said, "Oh, *gosh,* Rish—"

Sanchez said slowly, "I'm sorry to say that the Commander's right. That's the very first thing that some Federation citizens would think."

"Oh. . . . Well, gee, should I kidnap both of you? That sounds kind of awkward. I mean, I'd really be outnumbered down there in the lobby."

They were all silent for a few minutes, thinking. Then Rish said, "Not kidnap, but rob. After the Cat has escaped, I shall be discovered locked in the closet of my room, and relate how the robber overpowered me and forced me inside."

"Oh, that's neat!" Deedee said. "But won't it be, like, a fib?"

"A what?"

"False witness."

"Not at all." Arizhel grinned over the rim of her snifter. "You *will* push me into the closet and lock the door. And that is what I shall say."

"*Kai* the Tactician!" Sanchez said, and they banged their glasses together. "Any further details?"

Rish said, "It is best if it takes place late tomorrow night. This is when the robber is most likely to be active, and there will be fewer persons in the lobby to confuse things. . . . You and I, Charlotte, will have a long dinner with the two captains. This will please them, will it not?" She smiled.

"This it will." Sanchez stood up, carefully, and went to the desk. She flipped through the plastic-covered index of hotel services. "The restaurant closes at half past midnight."

Deedee said, "Is that late enough? You're really important guests; it's not like they'll throw you out or anything."

Rish said, "But we do not want to stay beyond the usual time; it would attract attention. The captains must not think they are being deliberately delayed. That is, they must not *notice* it." She laughed.

The princess said quickly, "There's the ice cream parlor."

Sanchez scanned the index. "I don't see it in here."

"It's brand new, they just opened it. But it's open all night."

Sanchez closed the folder. She had an odd, tight grin. Then she began to laugh out loud. "Oh, yeah. Yeah, we have to do that. It's just too good."

Rish said *"What?"*

"As an integral part of the Direidi negotiations

. . . I'm going to make Jim Kirk buy me an ice cream soda."

Deedee closed the ambassador's door. She went down the stairs to the lobby, crossed it to the concierge's desk, and was admitted behind the desk and through a door marked

NO ADMITTANCE
EMPLOYEES ONLY

Behind the door was a long, narrow room, its ceiling in darkness. Bright lights shone on a table covered with papers: diagrams, charts, floorplans. A brown-haired man in a checked shirt and jeans sat at one end of the table, casually sipping coffee and examining a stapled stack of typescript. Along one wall was a row of video monitors, showing the lobby and corridors of the hotel. Where those ended, a portable telephone switchboard was set up, with an operator.

The third person in the room was a wiry young man, dressed entirely in black from turtleneck shirt to sneakers. He had long and wayward blond hair, metal-rimmed glasses, and an awful pallor, and wore a headset with microphone. He was scribbling on a blackboard with one bony hand and gulping from a mug of coffee held in the other. He tossed down the chalk and pressed a switch on the side of his headset. "Stage manager . . . yes, the full team of carpenters. They're to redress the breakfast room as an ice cream parlor. No, it *should* look brand-new, but it's got to be open for business by eight . . . yes, dear, that's one reason we did lock them in their rooms tonight, to make room for these brilliant last-minute improvisations. Of course I'll be here, same time, same channel." He turned to the telephone operator. "Call the ice cream place in town and tell them we need their furniture, Plan C priority. Then tell Davith to send a wagon and some muscle. . . . Do point out politely to the ice cream people that the more labor they lend, the nicer their stuff will be treated, hmm?"

The other man had gotten up from the table and was hugging Deedee, picking her up on tiptoe in the process. "That was lovely, m'love," he told her. "Even Flyter liked it."

"Well, thank you, Pete," Deedee said. "How about you? Engagement still on?"

"Engagement still on," he said, and kissed her.

"Let us not allow things to get out of hand," the man in black said. "With the script, at any rate . . . Pete, you don't plan on improvising anything major? No cathedrals, portrait galleries, bowling alleys?"

"I've already got to get two starship captains to accept the plan as it is," Pete said. "No plans to embellish . . . beyond the mere corroborative detail, intended to give substance—"

The man in black knocked on the tabletop. "Thank you, don't call us, we'll call you."

The telephone operator said, "Pages coming through from Flyter." A printer began whizzing out pages. The man in black, moving like a slightly tangled marionette, went to the printer, ripped out the multipart sheets and split them neatly, handing one copy to Pete, scanning another, slipping the third into a binder thick with pages of a dozen colors. "Hmm," he said, told the operator, "Call the costume shop," looked at the two watches strapped to his left wrist. "Half past the first whisky. Mr. Blackwood, warning."

"Looks good," Pete said, putting down the pages of script. "The Flyter touch."

"Mr. Blackwood . . . *on stage.*"

"Wish me luck," he told Deedee.

"Break a leg," she said.

After the door closed, Deedee turned to the man in black and said, "Why didn't you wish him luck?"

"Dear, I'm the stage manager," he said, not unkindly. "If *I* say it, it *happens.*"

"All right," Captain Kirk said to the man in the checked shirt, "tell us about it."

"Well, it really started when I was shooting around her parents' place . . ."

"You missed them?" Kaden said, knocking back another double Scotch.

"Well, I—oh. No, shooting tape, with my camera."

Kaden poured a beer. "Imperial Intelligence sometimes uses a tape camera with a solid-state disruptor core."

"I don't think you quite understand, Captain Kaden. I don't want to do away with Deedee's parents. I just want to stop their objecting to me . . ." He looked suddenly thoughtful.

Kaden said, "You recognize the connection, good," and drank his beer.

Kirk said finally, "You're not actually proposing that this fellow kill his in-laws?"

"It is a rather usual event when founding lines."

The background music in the room had gotten rather loud. Pete Blackwood began to hum along with it, and then to sing:

I suppose you've heard the story
Of the poor but honest lad
Who's enamored of a maiden
With a big shot for her dad
In the tales he finds a fortune

Or was royal all along
And they say all's well that ends well . . .
Well, they're wrong!

Now, my love she wears a crown
But the drawbridge won't come down
'Cause her folks think I'm a clown beneath her station
So I wait and play along
Wondering how I might belong
Until regicide's become my strong temptation
Okay, she's a princess, but I couldn't care less
It isn't the crown that I see
She sends out a light
And it shines on the man I might be
And I simply must propose
To the girl who sparks and glows
For the boy inside the commonplace clothes
For me

Kaden was watching silently, his head cocked. Kirk
found himself humming, and poured a shot to stop it.

I do better than get by
But I'm no-account, 'cause I
Fail to occupy the higher social stratum
But the titled cards I've met
Are a limp and mismatched set
And I'd bust their flushes if they'd let me at 'em
Now I'm really unfit for the Romeo bit
And besides we all know how it ends
There's a swordfight and noise
And a mutual poisoning spree
But I'll play the hero's part
For the girl who'll play her heart
For the boy inside the everyday clothes
For me

". . . and that's the story, Captain Kirk, Captain Kaden," Pete Blackwood said. "I'm as successful as anybody has a right to expect, but that's not good enough for Deedee's parents. For them it's either idle rich or nothing."

"You think we can help?" Kirk said, and accepted a shot of Scotch from Pete.

"You plan against these petty nobles, that is bold," Kaden said, twisting the cap from his fourth bottle of beer, "that is the way of the line-founder and I salute it . . . but what if we were discovered interfering with your planet? Would not the lightbulbs object?" He looked at the bottlecap in his hand, tossed it aside as if it were hot.

"Lightbulbs?" Pete said.

"Organians," Kirk said. "It's a habit they have . . . well, never mind that. I don't think this should make any difference at all with them. It's not like we're trying to influence your world's decision about the dilithium rights. . . ."

"No," Kaden said quickly.

"Of course not," Pete said.

"Absolutely," Kirk said.

"Nothing like it," Kaden added.

"I'm glad we understand that," Kirk said.

"What I was thinking," Pete said, very seriously, "is that if I could just do something important—heroic, I suppose—well, Deedee's parents might not precisely accept me as one of their own sort, but they'd have to stay out of our way. And that's all we want."

Kirk said, "Where do we come in?"

"You're offworlders. No one will suppose there was any plan between us."

"But there will be," Kaden said. "So the witnesses must die anyhow. This seems to solve little."

"Not something that *you* saw," Pete said. "Something that the ambassador, and Captain Kaden's first officer, saw, that you had helped me set up."

Kirk laughed. "You've got 'something' in mind?"

"A few years back there was a cat burglar around the hotel, black suit, black mask; he was seen a few times but never caught. Suppose he showed up again, tomorrow night, and I ran him off—in sight of your friends."

Kaden said, "You know that this robber will return? Perhaps you were him?"

Pete laughed, shook his head. "No to both. But I've got a friend, Zack, who's a pretty good acrobat. He'll play the Black Cat, and pretend to burgle the ladies' rooms."

Kirk said, "Both of them? And if he sneaks around unseen, how are you going to grab him for the reward?"

"Here's the plan we worked out. Tomorrow night, you take the ladies to a fancy dinner at the hotel restaurant. Since everyone knows you're there, the Cat figures he can work at his leisure. But they go back too soon, with you escorting them—can you—"

"I think we can work out that part," Kirk said. "Go ahead."

"All right. Now, Commander Arizhel's room is upstairs, so he strikes there first. The Cat fights Captain Kaden, and he needs a hostage to get away, so he takes Commander Arizhel. Going downstairs, they run across you, Captain Kirk, escorting the ambassador—but there's nothing you can do, naturally. Zack and the Commander get down to the lobby, the night staff are afraid to move, but fortunately I just happen to be going for a midnight ice cream with Deedee, and jump him. Lot of confusion, the burglar gets away, but everybody's safe, happy ending."

Kaden said, "The robber fights with me?"

"That's right."

"You intend that I shall lose this fight."

"The plan won't work nearly so well if you win it."

Kirk said, "It won't be a fair fight. Pete, can your buddy get hold of a sonic stunner?"

"I think so. But wouldn't it be dangerous . . . that is, suppose the wrong person was shot with it. Could be rather embarrassing."

"Have him disconnect all but one of the driver cells. It'll sound just the same."

"Right," Pete said.

"Wrong," Kaden said. "At near-contact ranges, the minimum power will still be effective. The collimator pin must also be moved to its full stop setting."

Kirk said, "How do you know that?"

"I was about to ask you the same . . . but it is effective to fire shots after a prisoner who thinks he is escaping. Old trick."

"With us too," Kirk said.

Kaden said, "But I still do not like that I am defeated in this single combat. What will my . . . what will *Arizhel* think?"

"Kaden," Kirk said patiently, "Rish has seen you win fights, right?"

"We have fought together, and are yet here."

"I guess that's a yes. Now, she's seen that, but it hasn't done anything for your ro—your relationship, has it? It's time to try something different."

"Losing is indeed different," Kaden said, sounding doubtful.

Kirk downed another shot, held his hand outstretched—steady as a rock—and said, "Think of it this way. If Rish got hurt—treacherously attacked from behind—how would you feel?"

"I would kill the one who had done it."

"Yes, but *after* that, how would you feel about *Rish?*"

Kaden sipped his beer. "Ah. Now I understand. You suggest that I act upon her respect for me as a proven warrior."

"Something like that."

Kaden rubbed his chin. "This is not such a bad plan, Kirk. It contains true strategy."

"Thanks, don't mention it. Is there any more beer, Pete?"

"There's one."

"Hold, Kirk!" Kaden said.

"You want the last beer? Take it."

"Your plan, Kirk. I see a flaw. Suppose, when Arizhel sees me overcome, she kills my attacker?"

"You think she might do that?"

"It would please me to think so."

Pete said, "You must really be fond of her."

Kaden coughed. "She is a fine officer. We have fought well, Arizhel and I."

"What more is there?" Kirk said.

Pete said, "I've got an idea. Suppose Zack doesn't attack you both at once. . . . What if you're in the bathroom, and Zack comes in to hold up Commander Arizhel . . . then when you come out, he's already got the drop on both of you."

"The drop . . . no, I understand. This is possible. Unless Arizhel slays your friend."

"Oh, come *on,* Kaden," Kirk said.

"Very well. It could happen thus . . . and I have a thought." He got up, opened the bathroom door. "These disposal cubicles have windows. When I am in the cubicle, I shall signal from the window to your friend, that he should enter. Then I shall engage Arizhel in conversation, so that she is distracted upon the Zack's entrance."

"That's lovely," Pete said.

Kirk opened the beer, took a long pull. "Have Zack make some noise when he brings the commander downstairs. I'll hear the noise and come out of the ambassador's room. Zack shoots me—you have got that written down about fixing the stunner, right?—and Charlotte will come out to see what's happening. Have Zack threaten to shoot Arizhel unless the ambassador comes as a hostage too."

"And she will go?" Kaden said.

"Trust me on this one. Then, when they get down to the lobby, you step out from behind the staircase, and jump Zack. Big fight, maybe he 'stuns' you, and he gets away. You're a hero, Kaden's a hero, I'm a hero, and everybody lives happily ever after."

"I want you to know you're a grand pair of fellows," Pete said warmly. "And you can be sure I won't forget this." He held up a glass. "Though of course it can't have anything to do with the dilithium treaty . . ."

"Naturally."

"Absolutely."

The glasses clicked together.

# Chapter Six

## *The Dawn Patrol*

IT WAS NOT quite dawn. The hallways of the Hotel Direidi's newer wing were dim. The footsteps of one man on the pile carpeting did not break the silence.

The man paused. He knocked on a door. It sounded like thunder.

Another pause. Another knock.

The door opened, stopped on its chain. Above the chain, Leonard McCoy, M.D., looked down with clouded eyes. "Whroozt?" he said.

"It's me, Hikaru," the man in the hall said.

*"Who?"*

"Lieutenant Sulu, Doctor."

"Lieutenant," the doctor said in a slow, thick voice, "I'm goin' to ask you if you know what time it is. If you do, I'm goin' to kill you. If by some chance you don't, I'll assume this is all just youthful eshoober . . . estuber . . . high spirits, and *then* I'm goin' to kill you."

"Doctor, don't you remember the legend, last night at dinner? About the treasure? The inscription said we have to be there exactly at dawn."

"*You* may have to be somewhere at dawn. I'm never *anywhere* at dawn that I don't have at least the option of bein' horizontal." He started to close the door, but Sulu held it.

McCoy sighed, opened the door. "All right, c'mon in. I've got a jacket around here someplace. Call room service and get me some coffee." He picked up his field medkit, staggered toward the bathroom, muttering, "Vitamin B shot I can get m'self. . . ."

With McCoy shaved, dressed, and fortified with two cups of black coffee, they headed down the corridor. McCoy said, "While I'm not entirely sure I want to know the answer to this, just what possessed you to knock on *my* door for this little expedition?"

"Mr. Scott didn't answer his door. And I certainly didn't want to disturb Lt. Uhura."

"Caught between a sense of chivalry and a Scotsman's liver," McCoy said ruefully. "What about Chekov? Seems to me he's got the right qualifications for this . . . young, strong, not overly bright. . . ."

"I tried Pavel's door first," Sulu said. "Whatever he said to me was all in Russian. I understood the gestures, though."

They left the hotel, into the chilly air of morning. There was a reddish streak on the horizon. McCoy took a breath, said "Oh, boy," and turned promptly around.

"You're not changing your mind, Doctor—"

"No, I'm just dying," McCoy said. "Nothing I can't handle, I'm a doctor." He turned around again to face the sunrise. "Let's go."

They walked away from the hotel for about fifteen minutes. "Look," Sulu said, pointing at the first brilliant sliver of sun. "It really is framed in the notch of the rocks, just as the legend said."

"Nice to know there are still a few things you can

have faith in," McCoy said. "Now what the hell's that?" He pointed to two figures in the middle distance. "Apparently we aren't the only ones fool enough to be up at this hour."

One of the shapes pointed back toward McCoy and Sulu, and then they began walking toward the *Enterprise* officers. Shortly they were visible as Askade, the Klingon chief engineer, and Memeth, the Marine officer. They were dressed in deep-pocketed field tunics and equipment belts, not too different from Sulu and McCoy's outfits.

Humans and Klingons stood regarding each other, blowing frosty breaths, until Askade said, "What are you doing here, *Doctor?*"

"It's a new treatment for insomnia," McCoy said. "You stay up all night."

Sulu tilted his head.

"That aside," McCoy went on, "I was really just out for a midnight stroll."

Askade said, "With a companion? Both of you in field dress, with exploratory gear?"

Sulu said, "We were hoping to find an all-night ice cream parlor. Anyway, what are *you* doing here? You're all dressed up, too. Have someplace to go?"

*"We* do not dissemble," Memeth growled. "We intend to survey the land about this place."

"Isn't yours yet," McCoy said.

Askade said calmly, "It is no one's, if I have correctly understood the Direidi. Therefore we can imagine them having no objection to a simple, nondestructive survey. And as it is not *your* planet either, I do not believe that you have any power to object."

McCoy nodded, not quite frowning. "You figure to do this little sortie on shank's mare?"

Memeth made a low noise.

"Walking," Sulu said.

Memeth said, "We have a vehicle."

"Then I wonder if you'd mind giving the ensign and me a lift. I'm really starting to want that ice cream parlor."

Memeth said something in Klingonese. Askade answered him shortly, then said, in rather a friendly tone, "We do not object. This could be a useful teaming; extra hands and eyes are always good in new territory. Ensign Sulu, you are a navigator, correct? That is useful. And Doctor McCoy, I think you know something of our medicine?"

"I've worked on Vulcans, Withiki, Cilbaru groups, and the occasional gravid rock. I'll do my best if you need me."

*"Kai* the healer!" Askade shouted, and clapped his hands. "Come, let us spy out the land!"

"Nice figure of speech," McCoy muttered, and followed the Klingons. They went even further from the hotel, toward an enormous boulder.

"You fellows want to go around there first?" McCoy said. "There's an old Georgia proverb about going behind big rocks with strangers, but I can't recall the exact words just now."

Memeth said something to Askade. Askade shrugged, and they led on.

There was nothing behind the boulder. Memeth began growling again, and closed his hand around something on his equipment belt. The object did not seem intended as a weapon, but Memeth looked quite able to make it serve.

*"Yirokh,"* Askade snapped, and then spoke more calmly in Klingonese, gesturing with his hands. He seemed to be marking off distances.

"I think it's about transporter coordinates," Sulu said quietly to McCoy. "Remember when we landed on the wrong platforms, yesterday?"

That seemed to be the answer. The four hiked to another large boulder, circled warily around it.

Behind this rock was a large boxy vehicle on a dozen oversized tires, mounting lights and winches and cases of equipment, with a swivel platform on top that was almost certainly not a sunroof.

It was sitting hub-deep in a mud puddle. Long splashes of brown went up its sides, and spatters went a long way in all directions. Since transporters automatically adjust target sites to surface level, the vehicle must have beamed in at the top of the mud, and dropped.

Memeth looked at the mud, spoke slowly and evenly. McCoy said, "Count to twenty, that's the best thing."

Memeth looked at the doctor, then said, "Yes, you are right. This soiling cannot harm the unit." He pointed to the vehicle. "This is a Model 21 Planetary Survey Vehicle," Memeth said, with a hint of pride.

Sulu said, "This is a Model 18 Ground Attack Unit with an extended crew compartment."

"You are educated!" Memeth said, sounding pleased.

Askade said, "There are a few more modifications than that. The sensor array is much enhanced."

Sulu said, "But the twin disruptor turrets are still in place?"

Memeth said, "Of course."

"And the antimissile banks?"

"What fool would remove those?"

"How about the grenade launchers?"

Memeth chopped his hand through the air. "Replaced with extra searchlights. I can reinstall them, if you are afraid." Memeth smiled like a happy shark, opened the driver's door, and swung up into the crew cabin. The others followed. It was very roomy inside the vehicle, despite a considerable amount of sensor and engineering equipment hung from the walls, and the seats were tolerably well padded.

Memeth worked the driver's controls, and the vehicle came to life. "May I?" Sulu said, indicating a nav-sensor array.

"Please do," Askade said, and Sulu switched on the instrument bank.

"I don't suppose there's coffee service on this flight," McCoy said, buckling his seat belt.

"*Kafei* dispenser to your right," Askade said. "I would like a cup dark with two sugars."

"*Well* now," McCoy said. "A touch of civilization after all."

Memeth muttered something that not even Askade seemed to understand. Then the Force Leader took the control grips and aimed the survey vehicle toward the notch of stone that framed the rising sun.

The crew of *Jefferson Randolph Smith* were having an alfresco breakfast on the plains of Direidi. Tellihu was roasting a lizard on a stick over a small fire of brush. T'Vau was peeling bark from some more of the scrawny branches, selecting choice bits. Captain Trofimov was trying to make up her mind which meal to share.

The two kids had deliberately sent them in the wrong direction, there wasn't any doubt of it. Or maybe that was unfair; maybe they'd gotten turned around somehow, or these were the wrong twin rocks. Trofimov was having trouble thinking this morning; she wasn't sure if it was from hunger or the available prospects of food.

T'Vau looked up. "There is a vehicle approaching," she said. The others followed her pointing finger, saw the tiny cloud of dust in the distance. Trofimov had to admit, if you were going to wander around in a wilderness, Vulcan eyesight and hearing certainly was useful.

Captain Trofimov stood up, waved her arms. T'Vau nibbled some of her bark. Tellihu stood and draped his survival blanket over his wings. "I do not wish to startle or offend the natives," he said.

"Good idea," Trofimov said, though whether the natives would be more startled by a winged man or a sort of sheet-draped hunchback was open in her mind.

The vehicle came to a stop some distance away. A door opened, and a humanoid got out. He wore what looked like a Federation-issue exploration parka, and had a pouch of equipment on his hip.

Trofimov took a step forward. The man walked crookedly, and rubbed his eyes, as if he had only just been awakened.

"Hello," Trofimov said.

"H'lo," the man said. "What'ch'all doing out here?"

"We are looking for the nearest habitation," Trofimov said.

The man pointed. "Back that way a few kilometers. You can't miss it."

That was what the two children had said. Trofimov pointed, said, *"That* way? Exactly?"

"Sorry, ma'am, I was kind of dozing in the back. But I'm sure it's that way. Unless you'd like to ride with us."

"Just a moment, please." Trofimov went back to the others. "They're offering us a ride in the vehicle. I think they might be from the Federation."

"We must not do this," T'Vau said urgently.

"What's the problem?"

"Send them away," T'Vau hissed.

"Well, hell, if you feel so strongly about it, *you* get rid of him."

T'Vau put down her bark chips, dusted off her coverall, and walked over to where the man was standing, scratching his head. Trofimov watched as the Vulcan spoke, and gestured. Finally the man in the parka held up his hands in a gesture of resignation and walked back to his vehicle. It drove away.

T'Vau said, "Let us go, quickly, before they return," and started walking. Tellihu looked up in a disinterested way and took a bite of lizard.

"Now just wait a minute," Trofimov said. "In the first place, that's not the direction the guy told us to go. In the second—maybe in the first—just what was your problem with those people?"

"You did not recognize the vehicle?"

"Can't say I did. I didn't get its license number, either."

"It was a Klingon Model 18 Ground Attack Unit with searchlights replacing the grenade dischargers."

"That man wasn't a Klingon. Not even a Klingon-Human fusion."

"He did not have the appearance of a Klingon, that is true," T'Vau said, smug as only a Vulcan can sound.

Tellihu put down his lizard and went *whuurp, whuurp.*

"Okay," Captain Trofimov said, "we go that way."


Lieutenant Nyota Uhura was sitting alone in a sunny corner of the hotel restaurant, just cracking the shell of her soft-cooked egg, when a figure stepped across the light. It was one of the Klingon officers, wearing civilian clothes, as Uhura was. There was a small Communications badge on his lapel.

"Mind if I sit down?" he said, in perfectly accentless English.

"Please do."

"I am Aperokei. My friends call me Proke."

"My name is Uhura. You speak very good English. *Ja'chukh sokh taykekh Div'yan, tay'Tlhingan?*"

"*Batih.*" Aperokei bowed slightly. "And your *tlhingan* is finest-kind. Goes with the job, eh? Waiter! I want Adam and Eve on a raft, sink 'em, and a cup of hot joe."

"Very good, sir," the waiter said.

Uhura said, "You were the one who sent the hailing message."

"Guilty."

"You've seen a lot of movies from Earth?"

"*Hundreds,*" Aperokei said, and laughed. "You're a perceptive one, Lieutenant. Oh," he said quickly, as Uhura checked her sleeve, "no rank flash and nothing psychic. I asked about you. I remembered your voice from yesterday, too. Wanted to see who I was talking to."

Uhura put down her spoon. "The correct structure of that sentence is 'see to whom I was talking' . . . but I rather think you know that."

"*Raw*-tha," Aperokei said, and they laughed, as Proke's basted eggs and coffee arrived. "I was thinking about having a look around the town. I wonder if you'd care to join me?"

"I'd be delighted, Proke."

"Splendid."

Somewhere on a barren plain, perhaps ten kilometers from the sun-split rocks, a Model 21 Survey Vehicle rolled on, its surroundings largely obscured by its own dust. Inside, Memeth drove by radar, McCoy sipped coffee and looked out at nothing, and Sulu and Askade pressed their eyes to vision-enhancement units.

"We have company," Sulu said. "Take a look."

Askade swiveled his electric binoculars. To either side of the vehicle were people mounted on a sort of big lizard, carrying lances and copper-colored shields. The lizards moved surprisingly fast, and the lancers were coming in from all sides now, encircling the vehicle.

"Disruptors," Askade said.

Memeth snapped a toggle, and there was a whine and grinding from the roof as the weapon turret charged its cells and rotated into firing position.

"They are targeted," Memeth said.

"Then fire on my command," Askade said, peering through the binocs.

McCoy said to Sulu, "I think we ought to do something about this."

Sulu was watching the horde through his own viewer. "I don't know, Doctor. They really don't look very friendly."

Askade shouted, "You will do *nothing—Hold fire!*"

McCoy said, "Now what?"

Sulu handed McCoy the viewer. "Take a look at the shields they're carrying."

The doctor scanned the front rank of beast-riders. Their round shields, which had looked like polished copper, shone in close-up like ruby . . . no, not quite like ruby, a little too yellow . . .

*"Dilithium?"*

*"G'daya tlhol cha'puj,"* Memeth said.

McCoy zoomed the binocs on one of the shields. It had rough facets that caught the morning light, dazzling him for a moment until the viewer dimmed down. "Kind of pretty, actually."

"Uh-huh," Sulu said, sounding grim.

"Well, excuse me, Mr. Sulu. I don't suppose one of

you weapons experts would mind explaining the military significance of this? I mean, it still looks to me like, whatever happens, we have got the great big guns and they have not."

Sulu paused a moment with his mouth open, then said, "Twin disruptors, right, Memeth?"

"Yes."

"No grenade launchers."

There was a low rumble of Klingonese in reply.

Sulu turned to McCoy. "We're armed with energy-beam weapons. Dilithium crystals amplify energy beams; that's how we use them on the ship." He pointed at the ring of lancers, red shields surrounding the vehicle. "If a beam hits one of those shields, it'll be amplified, and deflected in one or more directions, no way to tell what or how many. If some of *those* beams hit crystals . . ."

"Lit match in a firecracker factory," McCoy said.

Sulu nodded. "We don't dare try it." He looked sidelong at Memeth, who seemed willing to try it anyway.

"Yup," McCoy said, "I thought it might be something like that." He reached for the door handle. "You gentlemen can let me off here. Such a nice morning, I think I'll walk the rest of the way."

A double line of lizard riders approached the Direidi foothills. In the center of the column rode Sulu and McCoy, Askade and Memeth, hands tied behind backs, feet fixed into stirrups. The big lizards didn't ride too badly, but the bumping and the sun and the dust were beginning to catch up to the four.

The riders were murmuring low, in time to the stomping of their mounts. Slowly the humming rose in volume. Then it became a chant, and a song:

Rollin' rollin' rollin'
Keep your camel goin'
Let the noncoms know if
You tire
It's hard to be nomadic
When there's no automatic
Retirement pension after sixty-five

"What is it with these people?" Sulu said. Except for a growl from Memeth, no one answered him.

Movin' movin' movin'
Keep the pace improvin'
Try to keep a-doin'
Your best
There's no time for sleepin'
When you've got to be keepin'
The peer review board suitably impressed

Saddle up
Boogie down
Storm a bridge
Sack a town
Keep your good camel parked
Inside
Chug a brew
Go in style
And be sure that you file
All your tax forms where you
Reside

Burnin' burnin' burnin'
Though the camera's turnin'
Keep that big-star yearnin'
Inside
A tough way of livin'

No warranty is given
Expressly, and none should be implied

Fight the foe
Trumpets sound
If they're slow
Run 'em down
Like the chariots in
Ben-Hur
Shoot the moon
Kill a king
It's a personal thing
Just the life-style that we
Prefer

The column ground to a halt. The four offworlders were surrounded by nomads, holding what looked like black silk bags.

"I don't think I'm going to like this part," McCoy said.

Askade said, "We are not singing with joy, Doctor."

One of the lizard-riders said, "No outsider may see the entrance to the Palace in the Stone."

McCoy said, "Now I'm sure I'm not going to—"

The black bags were pulled over their heads, cinched almost comfortably. They rode on for perhaps a quarter of an hour, then were lowered from the beasts and led around corners, through echoing, dripping passages, up ramps and down stairs. There wasn't a lot of point in trying to converse. At least the nomads weren't singing.

Then, suddenly, the hoods were removed. Sulu blinked. Memeth snarled.

They were lined abreast in a vast hall, lit by iron torches. The ceiling was lost in shadow, the floor painted with complex designs and inscriptions in some unknown language. In the center of the chamber was a circular pit, ten meters across. Steam rose from it, lit redly from somewhere below. Beyond the pit was a raised platform of polished granite, and on that a throne of black iron, cushioned with animal pelts and set with huge faceted chunks of dilithium.

Askade said, "The 'ancient race' the Direidi spoke of at the banquet."

"I'll admit it's no summer cottage," McCoy said.

Troopers led the four around the edge of the pit, not too near, and to the edge of the throne dais.

A huge, red-bearded man came onto the platform. He wore green-stained copper armor and carried a bronze staff. He stood by the throne, raised the staff, and announced, "All kneel for the Queen Janeka, she who is mighty in her wrath, Queen of Iron, Queen of Blood, Queen of the People of the Burning Stone! *Kneel and obey!*"

"Tough act to follow," McCoy muttered, as the troopers dropped to their knees. McCoy and Sulu looked at the Klingons, who looked back defiantly. None of them knelt.

A curtain rose behind the throne, and the queen appeared. She wore an ankle-length skirt of black metal mesh, slit nearly to the hipbone, high-heeled black boots with broad tops, a black leather jacket with wildly flared shoulders and a spread-wing collar. There were rings on all her fingers, of iron and silver set with dilithium. Her hair was covered by a metal-mesh drape, and her iron earrings reached to her shoulders. Her wide, silver-studded belt supported a straight-bladed sword and a pistol.

"Is that a flintlock?" McCoy whispered to Sulu.

"It looks like—no, see the barrel? Synthetic diamond. It's a phaser."

The Black Queen had a pale, angular, exquisite

face, a startling figure—the costume left no doubt of that—and stood a little shorter than Sulu's collarbone. With the heels.

She stopped in front of the throne, sat down, then leaned to one side and put her feet up on the armrest. The slit skirt slipped away from her legs.

McCoy heard a noise from Sulu. *"Down,* boy," he muttered.

"So," the Black Queen said, in a rather mild tone, "You boys aren't kneeling. Now, I know Rik told you to kneel, and when Rik talks, people hear it. *Deaf* people hear it. So what's the difficulty?"

Memeth grumbled dangerously. McCoy gestured at the Klingons, said, "You see, ma'am, these two gentlemen already have a dictator, it's against Mr. Sulu's religion . . . and I'm a Democrat."

The queen tapped a long-nailed hand on her bare knee. She began to laugh. The bearded man, Rik, raised his bronze staff, and the troopers began to laugh as well, until the whole chamber was ringing. The queen stopped laughing. Rik slashed a finger across his throat. The chamber went silent.

"I like you guys," the Black Queen said. "You've got spirit. You'll last a while."

"Last?" Sulu said.

"Sure. You know, on the rack, with the tongs, the what's-its-name—" she swung her hand back and forth—"pendulum thing. Been a while since we used any of it, I was afraid it was going to rust out."

"You do not frighten us," Memeth said, in a voice that was pretty scary-sounding itself.

The queen held up her hands. "Hey, give me a chance." She swung out of her chair, stretched, her spine cracking audibly. "It isn't all fun and games down here, you know." She put one hand on a hip, raised the other, began snapping her fingers. From somewhere in the stone hall, a drum and cymbal picked up the rhythm.

The Black Queen began singing:

From the minute you're born
   You've got to be tough just to stay where you're at
    Let me clarify that
There's nobody to warn
   You just how tough the game is to play
    Do you hear what I say?
You try to make a living as a pirate queen
You keep your crew a-roarin' and your cutlass keen
But when it comes down to the end
   You got nothin' to say
You marshal your resources for a final stand
And you finish as the leader of a one-girl band
But I guess I've been successful
   In my own sweet tyrannical way

So you think that it's fun
   Bein' absolute ruler of all you survey
    But it isn't that way
'Cause you're under the gun
   There's a guy with revolt on his mind
    Walking one step behind
You topple thrones and empires so they don't get bored
And half of what you pillage goes to feed the horde
And what'cha gonna do when the boys
   Get too carried away?
Now hangin's kind of heartless for a childish prank
And your average barbarian's too big to spank
But I guess I've been successful
   In my own sweet tyrannical way

  Half a dozen muscular young men in white shirts, bow ties, black trousers with suspenders, and black

bowler hats, had appeared from behind the throne.
They produced black canes and tapped them in time
to the music.

> Ain't this palace a pip?
>> We got seventy bedrooms on seventeen floors
>>> And the plumbing's indoors
> Let the reveling rip
>> Smash some glass, never count up the cost
>>> Till you notice you're lost
> It costs a bloody fortune just to heat and light
> You have to walk a mile to get a snack at night
> And all the torture chambers
>> Are in Early Industrial Gray
> But you can't expect a potentate to kneel to you
> In a studio apartment with a Park West view
> So I guess I've been successful
>> In my own sweet tyrannical way

Sulu whispered to McCoy, "Do you think—"
"The water, the air, the background radiation, your
guess is as good as mine."

> Do you like my attire?
>> Highly stylish in black set with chromium studs
>>> Pretty singular duds
> Does it set you on fire
>> Steppin' out wearin' leather and chains?
>>> Well, it gives me a pain
> The ironwork's abrasive and it's icy cold
> The corset squeezes tighter than a wrestling hold
> The helmet puts your neck in a crick
>> By the end of the day
> There ain't no way to tell you fellas how it feels
> To sack and burn a city wearin' six-inch heels

But I guess I've been successful
   In my own sweet tyrannical way . . .

    The Queen kicked high and leapt, and was caught and lifted into the air by the line of bowler-hatted dancers.

Some day I'll catch a dagger or a poisoned cup
But if you take these crazy days and add them up
There isn't anything I'd have done
   In a different way
It isn't for the timid or the highly strung
You live it in a hurry and you end it young
But I guess I've been successful
   In my own sweet tyrannical—
Had a lot of jollies
   In my frantically romantical—
Know I had a real good time
   In my tyrannical way

    On one long brass note, the dancers carried the queen out of the chamber. Just at the door, they paused; she pointed, said, "Heck, I almost forgot— *away with them!*"

# Chapter Seven

## *Afternoon Matinee*

DIREIDI'S SUN WAS just splitting the noon meridian, and the hotel restaurant was growing dim. Montgomery Scott finished off his platter of roast beef sandwiches, burped lightly, and started to walk out of the restaurant, pleased with life and the universe.

There was a small and plaintive sound from a table near the door. Ensign Pavel Chekov sat there, looking disconsolately at a plate of half-eaten blintzes and a large glass of soda water.

"That's what you get for pepperin' your vodka, lad," Scott said, not too unkindly.

"Mr. Scott," Chekov said in a thin voice, "do you believe in ghosts?"

Scott examined Chekov's face. The ensign seemed in dreadful earnest. "Well, Mr. Chekov, a man sees quite a few strange things in space, but I daresay no, I don't believe in that particular item."

"Let me be more particular, sir . . . sometime during the last night, when it was werry, werry dark, did a ghost knock on your door and ask you to boldly go where no man had gone before?"

131

"That'd be a definite 'no,' Ensign."

"I was afraid of that."

"Come along, lad," Scott said, "and we'll find a little hair of the dog that bit you."

"I think the dog is still attached," Chekov said, pushed away his blintzes, and followed Scott into the hotel lobby.

There were two Klingons, dressed casually, coming the other way. "A moment of your time, Humans," one of them said.

Chekov chewed his lip, looked around nervously. Scott said genially, "A moment we've got, gentlemen."

"I am Maglus, security officer of *Fire Blossom*. This is Ensign Korth."

"Montgomery Scott, chief engineer of *Enterprise*. Pleased to meet you."

"Pavel Chekov, ensign. I am pleased also."

They turned. The desk clerk had his eyes closed to slits and his fingers in his ears. He waited a moment, then relaxed and went back to sorting mail.

"Do you drink?" Maglus said, pointing toward the lobby bar. "We seek someone to drink with."

"Now, that's a *splendid* idea," Scott said. "After you, gentlemen."

The bar was quiet and dim, with heavy wooden furniture and high, narrow draped windows. No one was there except for a bartender in shirt and red vest, energetically polishing glasses. The four ordered drinks and sat down in the big plush chairs.

They talked for a quarter of an hour or so about space, ports of call, the inadequacy of fleet pay, the usual things. Then, in a slightly lower tone, Maglus said, "Is there much for an engineer to do on Federation ships?"

"Enough," Scott said equably. "Is there a lot for a security chief to do on one of the Empire's vessels?"

"I keep order on my ship," Maglus said. "That is an important job."

Korth suddenly took on a pinched expression.

"'Tis if your crew gets out of line," Scott said offhandedly. "Do they do that, then?"

"None more than once."

"Must keep you busy. Breakin' in replacements."

Chekov said softly but urgently, "Mr. Scott . . . you remember the last time . . ."

Maglus said, "What is it that engineers do all day? Are there so many mistakes in the design of an engine, for you to correct?"

"My glass is empty," Korth said loudly. "Does anyone else desire another drink?"

Chekov looked at his half-full glass, drained it at a gulp, said, "I do. Let's go."

They went to the bar, hearing the officers' voices steadily rising: "Slave-driver!" "Garbage-hauler!"

"You have had this experience before, *da?*" Chekov said.

"A few times," Korth said. "Do you suppose it is something that just happens to them, after a certain age? Cosmic radiation, perhaps?"

"Is possible. Or artificial grawity affecting the blood wessels."

"Still, Maglus is a good officer."

"Mr. Scott as well. *Nazdrov'ye.*"

"*Kai.*" They clicked glasses. "And as we are the only ones here, there cannot be a . . . a . . ."

"Brawl?"

"Brawl, yes . . ." Korth straightened. "Though I will fight for the honor of my ship."

*"Naverno."*

Chekov and Korth looked at each other, then at Scott and Maglus, who were halfway out of their chairs, leaning and shouting. Korth pointed toward the hotel lobby, made a walking motion with his fingers. Chekov nodded. Clutching their glasses, they walked softly toward the door.

*"Is that so?"* Maglus roared, and stood up, almost sending his enormous chair over backward. "And I say that the only reason the *Enterprise* is not decorating a scrapyard at this moment is that there is no market for chewing gum and cardboard!"

The two ensigns stopped, turned around. "It was nice meeting you," Chekov said glumly.

"And you."

They put down their drinks and walked toward the two officers, who were now fully on their feet. Each gripped the other's shirt front in one hand and held the other cocked to deliver a haymaker to the jaw.

An ear-splitting whistle blew. Everyone stopped still.

"Gentlemen!" a voice said. "This is not, ah say *not* the manner of behavior one expects of gentlemen in a gentleman's club."

A man in a sweatsuit and pith helmet stood in the doorway. He had muttonchop whiskers and held a silver whistle on a neck cord.

Scott held up a finger to Maglus, who nodded, and they released each other's shirts. "An' just who might you be?"

"Delmar, suh, Professor Phineas Hale Delmar, activities director for the Hotel Direidi, at your service. Exceptin', of course, that this, I say, *this* activity isn't on today's schedule of entertainments."

"It's not the kind o'thing you schedule, friend," Scott said, "but if you'd care to join us, there's plenty of room."

"Suh, I am not a participant in other men's disagreements. I am an organizer of them. Now, what level, I say, what de*gree* of disagreement do y'all have here? Tiff, skirmish, knockdown-drag-out, or matter of honor?"

Scott and Maglus looked at one another. "Honor," Maglus said.

"Aye," Scott said.

"Duel it is, then. And you've brought your own seconds already. I do call that considerate, sirs, considerin' the strain on our staff."

Chekov began coughing.

"We then need only decide on weapons," Delmar said. "Now, which one of you gentlemen claims to be the injured party?"

There was a pause. Delmar said evenly, "If you'd care, ah say, if y'all would care to flip a *coin* . . ."

Maglus said, "I grant the choice of weapons to the engineer. I am skilled in all forms of combat."

Scott smiled. "Oh, are you now? That's very good, Mister Maglus. Then I challenge you to the ancestral weapon of the Scots." He turned. "Professor, I believe I saw a sign for a golf course on the hotel premises?"

"Eighteen holes of the finest, suh."

"Then that's the field of honor. Mr. Chekov, call the ship and have my clubs sent down."


Uhura and Aperokei had spent a splendid few hours strolling about the town, window-shopping, watching a street magician who caught coins from Uhura's ear and produced a dove from Proke's jacket pocket, munching funnel cakes from a cart vendor. The powdered sugar drizzled over the cake made Proke a bit tiddly, and they paused for herbal tea before moving on to a cobbled arcade of shops.

The sign above one bay window read FANCIES

AND GOODNIGHTS. The window itself was filled with bright, bizarre items: silver trinkets, a brass carriage clock, crystal paperweights filled with millefiore flowers or swirling snow, intricately woven rugs, and something that appeared to be a violin with three necks.

"Shall we go in?" Proke said.

"It looks expensive."

"The best things in life are free," Proke said, "but the expensive ones are still worth a look." He held the door open for her, jingling a little bell above the frame.

The interior was cluttered with odds and ends: wood, metal, porcelain, crystal. A beaded curtain in the back of the shop parted for a dumpy man of middle height, with a neatly trimmed beard and half-glasses low on his large nose. "Good afternoon, sir, madam," he said. "Is there anything in particular I can help you with?"

"Just looking, I think," Aperokei said.

"Just as well," said the shopkeeper, in a friendly tone. "If there were anything particular you wanted, I don't know how I'd ever find it. But look as long as you like."

Uhura's eye was caught by a little harp, no bigger than the palm of her hand, made of silver metal and set with colorful cut stones. She stroked the strings lightly; it made a pleasing, chiming sound. "How much for this?"

"Price should be marked, madam. It will be in our local currency, but I can convert for you."

She turned the harp over, read a little white sticker. Uhura breathed in sharply. "I'm afraid it's a bit rich for me. This says eleven hundred and forty."

"Won't be a moment," the shopkeeper said, and

punched buttons on a calculator. "Ah. In Federation currency, that would be two credits."

*"Two credits?"* Uhura said.

"I'm in a haggling mood, madam; make me an offer."

"But . . . only two credits for *this?*"

The shopkeeper shook his head. "No, no, madam, you're not getting into the spirit of the thing. I say, 'Two credits.' You say, 'For this bauble, this frippery, this bagatelle? Fifty centicreds, and no more.' I say, 'For an item of such rare beauty? You mock it, madam. One credit ninety-five.' You raise to sixty, and so on until we strike a bargain at approximately ninety-three cents."

Uhura was turning the harp over in her fingers. "I once spent ten credits for a little ball of fur . . ."

"Sink me, madam, tribbles? Fearful things, from a shopkeeper's point of view. You see the problem, I'm sure: one can only sell *one* tribble. After that they have their own, ahem, distribution. Positively anticapitalist, they are."

"This is very, very beautiful," Uhura said. "I don't understand how you can charge what you do."

"That's the spirit, mum! You're out to ruin me, you are; but I've a soft heart for a soul that appreciates beauty. Ninety-one cents."

"Excuse me," Aperokei said. He was holding a leather-bound book, and speaking in an odd, rapid, whispery voice. "Do you have, ummmm, a first edition *Ben-Hur* with a missing line on page 126?"

"No, I'm fairly certain I don't."

"Ummmm. What about Kushner's *Swordspoint* in the Mapback edition?"

"I'm afraid not, sir. You might try Howard the Bookseller, twelve doors down."

"He won't have them either," Aperokei said, in something closer to his normal voice. "There aren't any."

"No?" the shopkeeper said, sounding surprised.

"No." Proke turned to Uhura. "You realize what this joker is, don't you, angel?"

"What is he?"

"What am I?" the shopkeeper said, a dangerous edge in his voice.

"He's a fence. Everything in here is stolen."

"Oh, thank goodness," the shopkeeper said. "For a moment I thought you were going to accuse me of being a pawnbroker."

Uhura looked down at the exquisite little harp. "That makes sense, now that you say it."

"But it's quite wrong, of course," the shopkeeper said. "While I admit I didn't pay for anything in here—"

"Ah-ha!" Proke said.

"—it's all quite legitimately mine. Let me explain something about myself." He came around the counter. "Retail sales are really just a hobby of mine. I'm actually a freight broker, contacts on all the major interstellar exchanges. Hardly an item moves in this part of the galaxy that I don't see at least a percentage of."

He opened a wooden cabinet, exposing an antique grooved-disc phonograph with a huge tin morning-glory horn. He twisted a crank, and the black disc on the platform began to spin; he lowered a metal arm onto it, and tinny, bright music came from the horn. The shopkeeper sang:

When I was just a little chap, my father said to me,
"Don't throw away your life pursuing prof'tability;

Take time to smell the flowers as they bloom along
    your way,
And always try to waste at least an hour every day."
I tried to take my dad's advice and lazed around the
    town
And wandered quite at random up the city streets
    and down
Until one day I passed—*the Bank*—and something in
    me woke:
The siren song of balance sheets possessed me at a
    stroke.
I left behind the pigeons I'd been feeding in the park
Put on a tie and bowler and became a junior clerk.

That was the day I learned about percentages of trade
The little extra someone takes whenever deals are
    made
Some call it a commission, handling charge, or
    broker's fee
But someone always gets it, so it might as well be me

I started with commodities, the wheat and corn
    exchange
With fliers into shipping when a deal could be
    arranged
I soon was partial owner of a modest freighting line
And also wrote insurance (quite a useful skill of
    mine)
Collecting charges at the source, another on the send
With incremental payments levied at the other end
Add in depreciation, and *per diem* rate, and such,
I must be rather careful not to charge myself too
    much
It may seem inefficient and it's hardly ele*gant*
But what I can't unravel, why, the tax man surely
    can't.

Percentages of commerce, percentages of trade
A penny here, a penny there, that's how the game is
 played
Some call it rank corruption, but it cannot be denied
That life's a lot more fun with a percentage on the
 side

My dad can't understand me, and he tells me to my
 face
That I'm mercantile and heartless, and a family
 disgrace
Seems every time I visit, he says "Come back to the
 fold,
And share my bench, where pigeons coo, and nights
 are clean and cold,"
I'm tempted, but my mind soon wanders back to
 ledger sheets,
I ride a lonely taxi home, and always get receipts
I hate to seem ungrateful, but I do enjoy my roof
It does obscure the moonlight . . . then again, it's
 weatherproof
But of the life that once I led there still remains a
 spark . . .
'Cause I own the bloody pigeons and I lease the
 blasted park!

You say my life is measured by percentages of trade
And in this case I'll grant that Occam wields a clever
 blade
So if there's nothing to me but a jingling pile of
 pelf . . .
I guess that I'll just have to buy an interest in myself!

The needle scratched to the center of the record,
and the shopkeeper stopped the spinning disc.
 "What these all are, you see," he said, gesturing

around the cluttered little store, "are extras. Tokens. Gratuities. Expressions of someone's warm feelings. Small change of transaction." He picked up a porcelain ballet dancer. "Playpretties that turned the supposedly hard heads of freighter captains. Some, dare I say it, out and out bribes. Every time I conduct a trade, sir, madam, I acquire another of these pretty, rare, utterly useless artifacts; and I conduct a very great number of trades, sir, madam. I have *warehouses* full of this stuff.

"So I maintain this store, just to get rid of it."

Uhura said, "And your prices are so low . . ."

"Ah, you've guessed it, mum. I get a *considerable* tax loss on the operation. Not to mention meeting interesting people such as yourselves." He touched the harp in Uhura's hands. "Have you a tenth-credit piece, madam, or you, sir? Or put another way, Brother, can you spare a dime?"

Aperokei laughed out loud. "I do," he said, flipped it into the air and caught it, then tossed it to the shopkeeper. He caught it on the fly, held it to the light, bit it. "Sold to the lady, ten cents. Just let me wrap the item for you. No extra charge."

Uhura tucked the small brown paper parcel into her shoulder bag. Proke opened the door for her, the bell jingling brightly, and they went back out into the arcade.

Half a block later, a person in a brown leather vest stumbled toward them. The man was blue, with cup-ended antennae on his forehead: an Andorian. He collided with Proke.

"Almost there . . ." the Andorian said weakly, and collapsed over Aperokei's arm.

Proke let the blue man down gently to the cobbled street. As he did, one of the Andorian's antennae fell off, revealing a small round patch of pink skin. Proke looked at his own hands: one was red with blood, the other blue with makeup.

He turned the "Andorian." A knife handle protruded from the dead being's back. Proke looked up at Uhura, who was watching in horror. A crowd was gathering around them. Someone gasped. Someone screamed.

"What's all this, then?" a voice said, and a woman in a blue uniform pushed her way to where Uhura stood and Proke knelt by the dead body.

"You're a cop?" Proke said, letting go of the fake Andorian.

"Right enough. And just who are you, and what have you done?"

Uhura said, "We haven't done anything. This man came to us."

"What for?"

"I haven't any idea."

"Oh? He just walked up to you and you killed him?" The policewoman's eyes narrowed. "Aren't you some of those offworlders?"

"Yes."

A tall, very thin man in a black trench coat pushed toward them. He flashed a wallet at the policewoman. "Skorner, from the Bureau. What's happening here?"

"Sir, this woman's just admitted that they killed this Andorian."

"I did nothing of the kind!"

"Are you denying you just said yes?"

"Yes! No, I mean—he isn't even an Andorian!"

"Don't change the subject."

Skorner said politely, "I'm sure there's been a misunderstanding. These people are guests of the government. Let's not have a scene." He raised a hand, and a taxi coach pulled to a stop.

142

"This is government business," the thin man said. "We'll handle it from here."

"Very good, sir," the policewoman said. "They're all yours."

She and Skorner helped Uhura and Aperokei into the coach, where they sat down, facing each other.

"Would you mind if I borrowed these, Constable?" the thin man was saying. "Thanks. Good day to you."

Uhura turned to see what was happening. The thin man leaned into the coach. "Excuse me," he said politely, "are you both comfortable?"

"Reasonably so," Proke said.

"Good, good. Can you give me a hand up, then?"

Uhura and Proke reached down to help him into the coach. Instead of climbing up, however, Skorner snapped a pair of handcuffs on Aperokei's right wrist and Uhura's left, chaining them together. He shot them a small, wicked smile, then slammed the coach door, shouted, "Okay, *go.*" The driver cracked his whip and the coach rolled off.

McCoy, Sulu, Askade, and Memeth were locked in a cell somewhere below the Black Queen's palace.

As such things went, the cell wasn't so uncomfortable. It even had a sanitary cubicle, set in a little semi-private niche. Memeth and Sulu were trying to figure out how to make use of the fragmentary privacy in an escape attempt. After half an hour or so of of listening to them plan acrobatic leaps and the immediate subdual of a dozen or so guards, McCoy testily suggested that one of them dive and swim for help.

Across the hall was another cell. In it was a humanoid skeleton. At the end of the hall was a huge man in partial armor and a black hood. The mask showed his mouth, which was frozen in a jolly grin.

The guard had an enormous sword with a curved blade; he thumbed its edge roughly every ten seconds.

". . . but, compared to some of the dungeons I've been in, not so bad," McCoy was saying.

"Have you anything to contribute to our escape besides comments?" Memeth said.

"Oh, well, there's . . ."

"Someone's coming," Sulu said.

There was the sound of a heavy iron door being opened, and then light footsteps. A woman came down the hall. She was wearing an exotic and extremely minimal golden outfit. She paused before the cell and made an elaborate bow.

"Something we can do for you?" McCoy said.

"I am Gladiola, kitchen slave. I am here to serve thy desires of sustenance." She reached to her tiny skirt, produced a pad of lined green paper and a pen. "Are thy wishes clear within thy minds, or wouldst prefer to see a menu?"

Memeth said, "Men-yu?"

Askade said, *"Khidiolev."* Memeth shook his head.

Gladiola said, "The Special of the Blue Plate is this day most wondrous. Though I must confess I know not why it bears that name, as the plate on which it is served your eminences is not blue in hue."

"If you don't mind my asking," McCoy said, "just who runs that kitchen of yours?"

"Oh, it is a most amazing tale," Gladiola said.

McCoy muttered, "I was afraid of that."

"Many years agone, the Queen Janeka desired that her kitchens be staffed in the manner of the greatest houses of the star-people's city. In a daring raid, her soldiers abducted a cook so famed that his dining chamber was named for himself, 'Jack's Eats' was it called. The Queen's torturers drew from Jack every secret he possessed, and those of his noble Order."

"Order?" Sulu said.

"Don't ask," McCoy said, "please, don't ask."

"The short order, verily," the girl said earnestly.

"Enough," Memeth said. "I will have a roasted bird."

Askade said, "And I, meat and gravy, with bread and a starch vegetable."

"The Sandwich of the fabled land Manhattan?" Gladiola said, wide-eyed.

Sulu ordered a steak.

McCoy said, "Well, honey, these fellows don't seem to want to get into the spirit of the moment, but I'll have a ham steak, biscuits and red-eye gravy, whatever pie you've got, and coffee now."

Gladiola trembled. "Are you then the One?"

"Hmm?"

"For a generation it has been said that, one day, One would come who would order the Gravy of the Red Eye, and demand his coffee Now . . . and verily would he lead all those in bondage to flour and shortening to freedom."

"I'm gonna take a nap, boys," McCoy said. "Wake me when the chow gets here."

"And verily," Gladiola breathed, "shall the One be tired, and nap before his chow."

Askade said, "Your kind wish to revolt then? To overthrow the queen? Do you have weapons?"

Sulu pointed at the guard up the hall, still thumbing his scimitar, and motioned for quiet.

"We have the knives and rolling pins of our craft," Gladiola said. "And we will use them with great heart."

Memeth said, *"Toy'wipu daw'moy?"*

*"Kha'dibayh g'dayu ngem?"* Askade said, then turned back to the waitress. "Very well. Bring us our food, as commanded. But be ready for the battle."

"Your worship." She bowed slightly, tucked her pencil behind her ear, and went up the hall.

Askade shook McCoy's shoulder. "Get up, healer."

"I'm not asleep. You figure we can lead a revolt of the galley slaves?"

"The energy of servitors is what makes them useful. It is foolish to waste that energy. Do you intend to help us?"

McCoy sat up. "Well, now, as I was about to say before we were interrupted, I do have some small contribution to make to this enterprise." He slid a pressure injector from his sleeve. "I managed to hang on to six doses of Oblivirine. Fastest knockout drop in the west."

*"Kai* the healer again," Askade said, and laughed. The guard looked in, saw nothing of interest, went back to his post.

They paced and talked quietly for perhaps half an hour, until Gladiola returned with a tray of food. "Will you open the door, o mighty queen's-man, that I may feed these worthies?"

"Push it through the bars," the guard said.

She picked up the plate with Sulu's steak, passed it to him. "What shall we do? All are ready below."

"Quick," Sulu said, "do something to attract the guard's attention."

Gladiola looked confused for a moment, then nodded. She picked up the pie from the dinner tray, said "Excuse me," and rifled it into the guard's face.

The guard roared, and ran, half-blinded by fruit and cream, staggering a bit. He grabbed a cell bar with one hand, reached for the trembling Gladiola with the other.

McCoy shoved the injector against the guard's arm. There was a sharp hiss, then a deeper sigh like escaping air as the guard folded up.

"Keys," Memeth said, and Gladiola nodded again. Unfortunately, the key ring had been on the front of the guard's belt, and it was lost somewhere beneath his hundred-fifty-kilo bulk. Gladiola tried to roll the body over, while the group inside the cell stretched arms through the bars to help.

"What's going on down there?" someone called from up the corridor.

"Nothing," McCoy shouted back.

There were running footsteps. More guards appeared. "Worth a try," McCoy muttered.

Gladiola threw a plate of chicken at the approaching guards. One ducked, slipped on stray pie, and threw out his arm for balance. McCoy got hold of it. Hiss. Thud.

*"Got* 'em," Sulu said, and tugged the key ring free. Gladiola was defending herself from the remaining guard with biscuits and mashed potatoes.

Sulu got the keys into the lock. The door swung open. Memeth was across the hall and the sleeping guards in one step. He recoiled like a pitcher winding up; his body went *snap,* and the last guard rose into the air and sailed backward until a wall finally stopped him.

Taking swords from the fallen guards, the off-worlders and Gladiola started up the hall. "Which way out?" Sulu said.

"Out?" she said.

"You know, out," McCoy said. "Into the open. The fresh air. The surface."

"I have never been 'out,'" she said, "but the tunnel of the raiders is this way."

"It will do," Memeth said. He traded a sword salute

with Sulu and they charged up the corridor, the others close behind.

*"Now,"* someone called out, and a cord snapped taut across the corridor, just at ankle level.

Memeth tripped. Sulu tripped. McCoy crashed into Memeth. Gladiola tried to avoid Sulu and tripped Askade, then bumped into McCoy. Everyone fell down.

A net was thrown across the heap, then another. Ropes pulled tight, swords were pulled from hands.

"The queen," one of the guards said, "is *not* gonna like this."

Security Officer Maglus and Chief Engineer Scott stood on the first tee of the Hotel Direidi Country Club. Professor Delmar was adjusting the strap on a club bag to suit Korth. In the distance, a brisk wind stood the first-hole flag out straight. The sky was a lovely blue, the fairway a vivid green, the water hazards deep and inviting.

"Have to 'low a bit of Kentucky windage today, gentlemen," Professor Delmar said. "Where's, I say, where's your second, Mr. Scott, suh?"

"Knowin' Mr. Chekov, probably deep in something difficult."

"I am here," Chekov said. He was carrying a worn leather bag filled with hickory-shafted clubs and wore baggy plus-four trousers bloused above the ankles and a floppy red-plaid tam o'shanter with a huge crimson pompom.

"Now where," Scott said, "did ye get that outfit?"

"When the clubs were beamed down, there was a slight coordinate error," Chekov said. "And a large puddle of mud. The hotel laundry—"

Scott was examining the golf bag. "They seem all right."

"Thank you, sir."

Scott unzipped a pocket of the bag and pulled out a long wool scarf. "My huntin' tartan," he said, winding it on. He tapped Chekov's cap. "Didn't know you were entitled tae th' Royal Stewart."

"May we begin?" Maglus said.

"Certainly, suh," Delmar said. "Would y'all care to toss for first ball?"

Scott said, "Mr. Maglus may play."

"Very well, suh. Now, if y'all will excuse me, I have other, ah say, other entertainments to arrange today." He tipped his pith helmet and walked away.

Maglus took out the number-one wood. He swung it about wildly, like a machete, and looking at least as dangerous.

Korth put the ball on the tee. Maglus stepped up, looked into the distance, toward the bravely snapping flag 425 yards downrange with a dogleg to the left. He raised the club like the Grim Reaper. He screamed. He swung.

The ball flew in a perfect flat parabola along the fairway, past the trees with plenty to spare, around the dogleg. It skimmed a bunker and dropped, just barely rolling, less than thirty yards from the green.

Maglus watched the ball until it stopped. Then he cackled, put the club on his shoulder, and walked away from the tee.

Scott blinked. He looked at Chekov: the ensign was clutching the strap of the golf bag with one white-knuckled hand, his tam o'shanter with the other.

"Well now, Montgomery Scott," the chief engineer said to himself, "Didn't your ma warn you about gamblin' with strangers?" He tapped Chekov on the shoulder. "Come on, lad. Tee me up."

\* \* \*

The black coach carrying Uhura and Aperokei rolled fast, rocking hard on its springs. The chain linking their wrists clinked softly. "What now?" Uhura said.

"Obviously we've got to get out of here. Then we need to find out who set us up."

"You think we were set up?"

"Angel, I've seen every film Hitchcock ever made at least three times. That includes both versions of *The Man Who Knew Too Much,* and I can practically quote you *North by Northwest.*" He pointed at the handcuffs. "Robert Donat and Madeleine Carroll in *The Thirty-Nine Steps.*"

"Okay," Uhura said, partly worried but mostly just irritated, "you've had a look at the script, what's my next line?"

Aperokei actually seemed to relax at that. "Up to you, angel. I'm just making it up as I go along. How about something like 'My mama told me never to get handcuffed to a murderer without a proper introduction'?"

"You're not a murderer. Are you?"

"Not yet, anyway. But you aren't supposed to know that for another couple of reels, and then not until it's stopped mattering. For now, though, you think I'm a desperate man. Unless of course we *are* doing *Northwest,* in which case you know I'm innocent, but you can't let on without blowing your own secret identity."

Uhura laughed entirely in spite of herself. "I don't have a secret identity."

"That's a shame. Everyone needs a secret identity."

"Okay . . . so tell me. *Are* you a desperate man?"

"I will be if we keep sitting like this. May I come join you on that side?"

"Not until we've been properly introduced."

Proke smiled. He rose slightly from his seat, tipped an imaginary hat with his free hand. "Aperokei tai-Rensa, innocent bystander trapped in a deadly web of intrigue, at your service."

"Nyota Uhura, likewise, I'm sure. Do sit down, tai-Rensa. Try anything funny, though, and I'll break your arm."

"Charmed." He sat down next to her. It was a tight fit, but at least their arms were no longer stretched straight. "If I try anything funny in here I'll break my back."

"So what *do* we do now?"

"Obviously we escape. After that . . . hm. If this really is a Hitchcock, we should probably look for a very high place. You haven't seen anything that looks like Mount Rushmore, have you?"

"No. Though there's probably a bell tower in the castle. And I suppose we should stay out of showers?"

"*Absolutely* no showers."

Proke pulled back a window curtain. They were rolling down a rather narrow alley, the walls of buildings less than an arm's reach away. "Jumping doesn't seem like a very good idea."

"I'm glad to hear you say that."

"Hey, this is a team effort, right?" He rattled the handcuff chain. "Nobody goes anywhere alone." He shuffled a boot on the floor. "No way out down there." He looked up. There was a small sliding door in the coach roof, for talking to the driver, but it was less than twenty centimeters across, hardly an escape route.

Uhura took a communicator from her shoulder bag. "Shall we yell for help?"

"Excellent idea." Aperokei produced a communicator of his own from his belt. "Last one with a lock-on buys the drinks."

They flipped open the comm units. Both produced nothing but a hideous squealing sound.

"Radiation?" Proke said. "Or jamming?"

"It sounds like a jamming signal. Listen." She tweaked the control dials.

"Not for long, thank you. With a spectrum analyzer we could tell."

"And with a phaser we could shoot our way out of here."

"True . . . I wonder if the Direidi know that?"

"Know what?"

"About hand weapons. Have you seen them use phasers or disruptors? The policewoman and that Skorner fellow didn't show any."

"Now that you mention it, no, I haven't seen any." She looked at the communicator in her hand, then up at the little trapdoor in the roof. "Hmmm."

"I like mine better for this," Aperokei said, flipping the triangular Klingon comm unit over in his hand. "Looks more dangerous."

"That isn't the dangerous part."

Proke said, "What's the worst thing they can do to us? Laugh in our faces?"

"Shoot back."

"True. Shall we?"

"Let's."

They raised their linked hands and slid back the trap. Proke shoved the communicator into the small of the driver's back. "All right, jocko. This is a Mark 34 Energy Projector, the most powerful concealable weapon in the known universe. Pull this crate over to a nice quiet stop or I'll let starlight into you."

The driver nodded hastily and complied. Uhura opened the door, and they stepped down slowly. Proke told the driver, "Now, just keep your hands high. Couple of layers of wood won't even slow this baby down."

They moved to the rear of the coach. Suddenly the driver snatched up the reins, gave them a yank, yelled, *"Gee-up!"* and the coach clattered away, rounding the first corner on not all of its wheels.

Aperokei said, "What are you laughing at?"

"You. You were having such a good time doing that."

"Yeah," Proke said. "I guess I was." He looked at the communicator in his hand. "You don't get to do this kind of thing very often in the Empire."

"Now what?" Uhura said, after a moment. "The cab driver won't run forever."

"I know. And when he stops running, they'll be after us again. Whoever 'they' are."

"Do you suppose they really were the police? Or the government?"

"It's occurred to me. You have to admit, the locals have been acting more than a little odd. Shall we try our ships again?"

They did. There was nothing. Proke scratched his head. "Have you tried cross-heterodyning the signal?"

"Yes, but these sets are already superhet. We'll just get stray harmonics, and probably drift."

"Hm. How about an Arsos bridge?"

"I don't know the term . . . oh, wait, do you mean two transtator pairs collector-to-emitter? We call that a Gentry ring. Can I patch across to—" Suddenly she noticed that Aperokei had a strange smirk.

"What are you grinning about?"

"Oh, I was just thinkin', angel . . . we're not really going to sit back and let the computers up there solve this case, are we?"

"What *are* you talking about?"

"I'm talking about the black bird, angel. The secret of Baskerville Hall. The lost ark, the mask of Fu Manchu. Somebody's handed us a real live mystery, and I for one think we ought to go out and solve it. Are you with me?"

"I . . . Someone's coming."

Three figures draped in white came around a corner and into the alley. Two walked straight, the third curiously hunched over.

Uhura and Proke tucked away their communicators, stretched their sleeves down over the handcuffs, turned away from the newcomers and began strolling up the alleyway, hand in hand.

"Excuse us, please," said a voice behind them.

"Just keep walking," Proke whispered.

"Please, *wait.*"

"They don't sound like they're hunting us," Uhura said.

"Good hunters never do."

"For you to continue walking is illogical," said another voice.

Uhura said, "That's a Vulcan."

"Or a Romulan pretending to be one. Romulans are *excellent* hunters."

The first voice said, "Look, you don't have to stop, if you'll just tell us how to get *out* of here."

Uhura stopped. That left Proke little choice. They turned around.

The three people didn't seem to be armed. They didn't look much like anything, except dusty and distracted.

"Pardon us," said the first speaker, "but we're rather hungry . . ."

*"The Treasure of the Sierra Madre,"* Proke said.

"Just came from there," said the humpbacked one,

whistling as he spoke. "Nothing there, nothing, nothing."

"The set of all sets," said the Vulcan, "must either include the empty set or exclude it. The subsuming of a negative in a positive universe is paradoxical—"

"Okay, *okay,*" Proke said, and pulled a five-credit note from his pocket. "Here. The only restaurant I know of is in the hotel, over that way."

"Thank you, grounded ones," said the hunched one. "Truly you are brethren of the air."

"There is really a hotel?" said the human. "With, I mean, beds? With sheets on them?"

"To the south, that way," Aperokei said. "Enormous building with a tower, you can't miss it."

"Thank you."

As Proke and Uhura watched silently, the odd trio walked on up the alley. A line of pigeons walked single file behind the hunched-over one.

The Black Queen had exchanged her armor for a trailing robe of black velvet. Her hair, loose and uncovered now, showed a long white streak. She flexed a short riding whip. She looked distinctly annoyed.

"What does go on around here?" she said. "We try to improve the standard of living, provide a few basic comforts, and where does it get us? *Seize her,*" she said and pointed the whip at Gladiola. Two of the guards took hold of the girl. "Reasonable wage, fringes, vacation time, uniforms provided—you have betrayed me, Organza."

"I am Gladiola. Organza works in Accounting."

"Silence!" She paused dramatically. "I'm rather tired, Rik. Is it about sunset?"

The big man said, "A few more minutes, Your Terror."

Gladiola recoiled in horror. "Oh, no, Your Awfulness! Do not do it to them! They are strangers, who do not have the inside dope on our ways!"

"I'm not going to do it to them, kid," Janeka said. "But they're gonna need a Help Wanted sign in the kitchen. Seize her again. Oh, I do like saying that."

Sulu said, "I liked her better when she sang."

"Silence to you, too, offworld-type. Your turn will come." The queen raised the riding crop. "Seize her over there."

The guards dragged Gladiola to the glass covering the glowing central pit. A circle of copper-colored rods rose from the rim of the circle, caging Gladiola on the glass disc. She clutched the bars, shook them without effect.

The Black Queen pointed at the roof of the chamber. There were two angled shafts bored in the rock overhead, and between them a sort of chandelier. "We only get full power at dawn," she said, "but there's a provision for sunset. Our regal ancestors liked to party all hours." Janeka sat down slowly on the black iron throne. "Okay, Rik, hit it."

Orange sunlight came through one of the conduits, struck the chandelier and was reflected downward, illuminating Gladiola.

Red light came up from below, growing in intensity until the girl was just a dark shape in the column of light. There was a high-pitched sound. She seemed to fade; then a shaft of golden light shot from the overhead glass to spot the throne and the queen.

The light through the conduit died away. The golden glow faded, then the red.

The queen stood up, shook her head. The white streak in her hair was gone.

The copper cage began to lower itself into the floor.

Gladiola was gone from the glass disc. There was only a streak of grayish dust, in the rough shape of a body.

"You . . . fiend," Sulu said.

The Queen giggled. "You're cute when you're angry." She waved to the guards. "Put my morning pick-me-up back in their cages. *Without* their dinner."

Gladiola crawled from a narrow tunnel into a small room framed with canvas, expanded foam, and raw wood. The blond man in black helped her stand, handed her one of the white hotel bathrobes. "Lovely job, dear," he said, then lowered the microphone on his headset and pressed the switch. "Light cue, cell area. Flicker box, work the pit for exactly . . . four minutes; then you're needed on the golf course."

Spock stepped onto the bridge. "Oh, there you are, sir," Lieutenant Kyle said. "We've located the *Smith's* escape pod."

"Life readings?"

"Two, sir. The crew was—"

Spock nodded. "Yes, Mr. Kyle, I know. Beam the pod up to the cargo deck."

In the Direidi wilderness, Thed and Orvy had found the alien spaceship.

"Not very big," Orvy said.

"I suppose you've seen lots of starships," Thed said.

"The Consortium's ships are always thousands and thousands of meters long, so Mac can hide in them for weeks at a time," Orvy said. "Remember?"

"Shut up," Thed suggested.

"Whatever you say, Prince of Star-Thieves."

They moved closer, cautiously. The ship really wasn't very big, just a metal ball about four meters across, supported on little struts that seemed to have been crushed by the landing. The door was not only open, it had been thrown some distance from the open hatch. There was a small stairway up.

"Well, this is it," Thed said.

"This is what?"

Thed sighed. "The moment of truth. The climax. The confrontation with the aliens."

"You think they came back?" Orvy thought a moment. "They're probably not gonna be happy with us."

Thed just shook her head and started up the steps. Orvy could either follow or be left alone. He followed.

Inside the alien ship were three couches, all empty. The entire interior was covered with a peeling pink paint.

"Thed, it's weird in here."

Orvy had recovered himself, in the absence of aliens. "Of course, Aramis my boon companion. It belongs to a race of beings more strange than the Pathan or the Hottentot."

"I mean, it smells like peppermint and cream cheese. And there's this . . . stuff all over."

"Some of them do not breathe the air we breathe, my friend."

"Uh-huh. But it kinda looks like they barf just like us."

A pinging sound came from a wall panel. A voice came from a grille, scratchy and muffled by the thick pink paint. *"Enterprise* to escape pod. Prepare to be taken aboard. Please hold your positions."

"Let's get out of here," Orvy said.

"Are you kidding?"

"Thed . . . there's no door on this thing. What happens if we get pulled up through space?"

Thed paused. "There is a certain logic to your position."

They scrambled for the door as the landscape outside dissolved behind a curtain of golden, flickering light.

The foursome strolled off the ninth-hole green. Scott was two over par, Maglus three, thanks to a freak wind on the seventh and a terrible double-bogie six on the eighth. The Klingon protested bad luck, and Scott amiably agreed. It was still anyone's match.

Just off the path to the tenth hole, there was a small building, with half-timbered walls, lead-paned windows, and a low rose hedge; bicycles were parked outside, and enameled metal signs advertised FINE FOOD and several brands of beer. A painted wooden sign swung above the door: it showed a man in a trench coat, and the figure of a bird sculpted from black stone. Gold-leafed letters read THE BOGIE AND BIRDIE.

Checking their golf bags in a rack labeled for the purpose, the foursome went inside. The interior was decorated in wood and stained glass. The long bar had a bright brass footrail. The walls were covered with pictures and golfing artifacts, with a dartboard in the corner. On one wall was a photograph of a group of men around a double-winged fabric aircraft, a box of medals, a leather flying helmet with goggles; above the display was a wooden propellor two meters long. At the end of the bar was a large curtain, the edge of a slightly raised stage protruding beneath.

The patrons mostly wore wools and flannels. A few

had leather jackets with worn military patches. All had pint mugs in hand, and none paid much attention to the new arrivals.

"Afternoon, gents," said the man behind the bar. "In for a rest between holes? Just what we're here for. What's your pleasure?" The bartender was tall, blond, and looked quite familiar.

"You are Davith the hotel-keeper," Chekov said.

"That's right, friend. Each man in his time plays many parts, eh? Now, what'll you have? The shepherd's pie is topnotch today; Pam's just pulled one from the oven."

"I will have a double *wod*—" He was stopped short by Scott's hand on his shoulder.

Scott was looking at the long-handled beer pumps behind the bar. "Would that be real ale?"

"It would indeed, sir, drawn from the wood."

Scott sighed. "Four pints. I'm buying."

They settled down at a table with a good view of the curtained stage.

"Something is wrong," Chekov said. "My beer is warm."

From behind the curtain came the tinkling sound of a piano. The curtain parted to display a single bent-wood chair under a spotlight.

A silver-skinned robot with a smooth, feminine face and figure came on stage. The patrons applauded, and the pianist played a flourish.

The robot put one foot up on the chair, turned to face the audience, folded its—her?—hands on the raised knee.

The left thumb squeaked and fell off, landing on the floor with a clink.

The piano played. The robot began singing, in a deep-throated voice:

> Falling apart again
> And what am I to do
> These threads take metric screws
> No one stocks them

Bolts popped out of their sockets, and more pieces fell away, clanging.

> There's no way to repair
> A heart whose gaskets fail
> No rivet, bolt or nail
> Can correct it
>
> Falling apart again
> Poor craftsmanship, it's true
> Perhaps if I used glue . . .
> I can't help it

The singer's raised leg came away at the hip and crashed to the floor. The robot braced a hand on the chair, stood on one leg. The tempo picked up.

> I'm an automaton
> And though you turn me on
> I'm just a tin man
> I'll calculate each chance
> For voltage and romance
> It's just how I'm programmed
> A toy in human clothes
> A wire and plastic rose
> That's what they say about me
> When the end comes, I know
> I was only clockwork so—
> Life ticks on without me

The other leg fell to pieces. The singer collapsed into a heap. The hands crawled about, picked up the head, and held it cradled.

> Oh, I
> Ain't got no body . . .

The curtain fell, The audience applauded.

The golf foursome stared. Scott finished his beer. He finished Chekov's. "Come on, gentlemen," he said, "we've got a back nine to play."

Uhura and Proke moved cautiously down the alley. At every sound one or the other of them turned, yanking again on their sore connected wrists.

"Look," Proke said. At the distant end of the alley, the thin man, Skorner, went by.

Uhura pulled at the nearest door handle. The door came open. They went through.

They were in a short, dim corridor with a curtain at the other end. From beyond the curtain came a wan white light and a low murmur of voices.

Aperokei had a very peculiar expression.

"Now what's the trouble?"

"Don't you know? Don't you see where we are?" He led her to the curtain. One of the voices said ". . . but he would have gone down there with you, angel. He was just dumb enough for that."

Proke put a finger to his lips, and they stepped through the curtain.

The theatre was quite small, perhaps two hundred seats. They were at the fourth row from the screen, dwarfed by Bogart and Mary Astor. The light from the projector made it difficult to see toward the back, but there didn't seem to be anyone in any of the seats.

Uhura said, "Well?"

"We might as well sit down."

They did. The picture had only a few minutes to run. Wilmer killed Gutman; Brigid went to prison (no one, except maybe Dashiell Hammett, has ever believed that a jury would hang her by that sweet neck). The lights came up.

Proke looked around casually. The theater was indeed empty, except for one person standing in shadow by the aisle door.

"I don't recall selling you kids a ticket," the man said, and stepped into the light. He had long, very black hair, round tinted glasses. A white silk scarf wrapped his neck, and his hands were shoved into the pockets of a thoroughly worn black leather jacket. "In through the fire door?"

"Yes," Uhura said, before Proke could invent anything creative. "We're sorry. We will buy—"

"Did I ask you to be sorry?" The man gestured at the empty seats. "This was a private screening anyway. Consider yourselves my guests. When did you come in?"

Proke said, "At 'he was just dumb enough for that.'"

"Barely saw the picture at all, then. Care to see it from the beginning?"

Uhura said, "You wouldn't mind?"

"The prints belong to me. I can do what I want with 'em." The man scratched his cheek. "Of course, I don't interpret that any more broadly than running 'em any time I like. . . . If you're tired of the *Falcon,* there are plenty more. *Casablanca, Metropolis, Thief of Baghdad* . . . I just got in a pristine copy of *Only Angels Have Wings.* Bet you haven't seen that one in a while. Even on a starship."

Aperokei said, "So you know."

"Pretty obvious. I know all the film fans on Direidi. You're new. Not to mention—if you won't take this wrong—we don't get a lot of Klingons in here."

Proke said, "At these prices, you may get a lot more."

The man laughed. "I'm Ilen," he said, and held out his hand.

"Pleased. We're—" Proke automatically raised his hand to shake Ilen's, dragging Uhura's wrist with it.

Ilen's eyebrows rose. "Robert Donat and Madeleine Carroll?"

"It's—a long story."

"That usually means you don't want to tell it." Ilen shrugged. "Okay. Come with me."

He led the way up the aisle and into the theater lobby. It was paneled in Art Deco mirrored glass, reflecting and multiplying their images. There was a brass-fitted popcorn machine puffing out kernels, and framed posters, sealed into nitrogen envelopes, for Lugosi's *Dracula* ("The Strangest Love a Man Has Ever Known!") and *Casablanca*—

"With Ann Sheridan and Ronald *Reagan?*" Aperokei read.

"Gotcha," Ilen said. "This way." He opened a door marked PRIVATE. They went up a narrow stairway —Uhura and Proke walking sideways to keep their wrists untangled—to the projection booth. Past the projector and racks of film canisters were a desk, bookshelves, piles of indescribable junk. "My office," Ilen said, as he bent to rummage in a canvas bag of tools. He came up with a bolt-cutter. "The very thing."

The handcuffs removed, Uhura and Proke sat in director's chairs while Ilen poured tea.

There was an engraved wooden nameplate on Ilen's littered desk. Uhura read it:

ILEN THE MAGIAN
Proprietor, Silver Magic Theatre

"Magian?" Uhura said.

"A conceit," Ilen said. "Do you know the 'Magic Theatre,' from Hesse?" He reached across his desk to a black metal pendulum. He set it swinging. It ticked, like a metronome. A wisp of steam from the teapot shone whitely in the beam of the desk lamp. Ilen began singing in time with the pendulum beat:

> Once the screen was really silver
> Once the world was shades of gray
> Come inside and touch the romance
> Fred and Ginger dance the night away
> Let the shutter frame your vision
> Let the sprockets pull you down
> Eighteen frames, the speed of silence
> Twenty-four, the speed of sound
> Monochrome
> Bogie in a trench coat, standing alone
> In monochrome
>
> Mister Laurel, Mister Hardy
> Buster Keaton, Harold Lloyd
> Can you hear the silent laughter
> Echo in the whispering celluloid
> Did you long to be with Garbo
> Who was your romantic queen
> Was it Colbert, Loy, or Harlow
> Did you pine for Norma Jean
> Monochrome

Drift to sleep and dream in sepiatone
Sweet monochrome

Ilen slipped from his chair, smiling below his dark glasses, ran his hands across the photos and lobby cards on the office walls.

Dress in tails with Ronald Colman
Grant and Niven, perfect gents
Say Klaatu Barada Nikto
Do you know what Rosebud really meant
Gone to dust and still they play on
Faded days stay crystal clear
All the stuff that dreams are made on
Long as you and I are here
Monochrome
Boris Karloff shambles from the unknown
In monochrome

Why do you say there's no color
Dietrich was the Blue Angel
Duke and Monty rode Red River
Leslie Howard's Scarlet Pimpernel
Fairbanks was a bold Black Pirate
Cagney's White Heat burned me cold
There's a panchromatic rainbow
To a silver-halide pot of gold
Monochrome
Though my valley's green no longer, it's home
In monochrome

Let me catch a bus with Gable
Grand Hotels for all my nights
Busby Berkeley tunes are playing
Through the window, Chaplin's City Lights
Wander down the aisles together

Take a lover, find a friend
Dance to Bernard Herrmann's music
Till the title card that reads The End
Monochrome
Carbon arcs in darkness lighting me home
In monochrome
Monochrome
With a cast of thousands, no one's alone
With monochrome

"Do you have a copy of *Belle et la Bête?*" Aperokei said.

*"Mais oui,"* Ilen said, rubbing his sharp chin.

Ilen dished up popcorn, ushered them to sixth-row-center seats. The lights went down. The screen lighted, with Coming Attractions shorts for *Viva Zapata* and *On the Waterfront*, and a Warner Brothers cartoon.

A hand grabbed Uhura's shoulder. "Ilen?" she said, and turned as the grip tightened. The face behind it was in shadow, but it wasn't Ilen. The hand pulled at her. She slapped the face, hard. The man yelped.

There were more men in the aisles, closing in. Proke vaulted out of his seat, knocking one down on the fly. He landed on his feet, shouted, "Let's get out of here!"

"Right behind you." Uhura grabbed the strap of her bag, swung it at another thug, making him dodge clear of her, and dashed up the aisle, toward the light of the projector.

They burst into the lobby. Ilen was in the doorway that led to the projection booth. "What's the matter down here?"

"We've got company," Proke shouted.

The auditorium door opened. There were shots. A

mirror shattered behind the Magian, and he staggered back against glass which was webbed with cracks and blood. He collapsed.

"Ilen," Uhura said, but Proke caught her wrist. "We can't help him," Proke said, and pulled her out into the street. The sun was below the line of buildings, making them black against orange, making the street deeply shadowed. They ran for darkness.

A black coach pulled across the narrow, cobbled alleyway, blocking it. The driver—all too familiar—turned, and leveled a long gun with double barrels.

Uhura turned. Behind them stood the thin man, Skorner, his black coat open, a shorter version of the same weapon drawn.

Thed and Orvy looked out the hatch. The cargo deck stretched out beyond the limits of vision. The air was crisp and thrummed with the sounds of ship's machinery. Cargo modules were stacked and racked along the walls; conduits ran overhead; little lights illuminated the walkways.

"We're on a starship," Orvy said.

"Yeah."

"It's . . . big."

"Yeah."

"What do we do now, Thed?"

"Let me think . . . of course. They beamed the pod up, without knowing we were in it. It happened to Mac and Libra in *The Guns of Asterope.*"

"I'm not gonna argue. But what do we *do?*"

A woman in a red shirt was approaching. "We hide," Thed said, and pulled open a likely-looking door. There was a small locker behind it. It didn't look big enough for both of them. They fit anyway.

They heard the space-trooper bump her head on the

hatch, and say something really terrible. Then she said something even worse about the smell. Her footsteps went away.

"Let's go," Thed said, "before she comes back with a commando team." In the Macmain books, they always came back with a commando team. Orvy agreed with the basic idea if not the context.

They tumbled out of the closet. Orvy said, "All right, Thed—"

"Macmain."

"Okay, Macmain. What are we going to do *now?*"

Thed hopped out of the pod onto the deck, landing in a modest approximation of a combat crouch. "We're in the Empire's treasury, under their very noses. What do you think we're going to do?"

Orvy sighed and climbed out. "Very well. But before we get to the jewel vaults and the secret plans, could we steal a sandwich?"

Spock examined the reentry-scorched pod which was still sitting on the cargo transporter stage. Adjusting the controls of the tricorder slung over his shoulder, he leaned inside. The interior was covered with a flaking, rancid pink substance. Spock sniffed. He frowned. He unreeled the tricorder's probe, touched it to the pink coating, dialed for spectrometry. He read the display with a minute sigh.

"Sir," said one of the cargo-deck crew, "is that . . . something's blood?"

"It is a caseinate colloid with trace impurities," Spock said. "Flavored milk product."

"Oh. Why is there . . . if you don't mind . . ."

"I could do no more than conjecture, Ensign. You are quite certain there were no beings aboard?"

"No, sir. That is, yes, sir, I'm certain. I looked

inside, and there really isn't much space to hide in there, sir."

"Yes," Spock said distractedly. "Have the pod moved to a storage area, Ms. Crispin."

"Aye, sir."

Spock took one last look around the pod, and walked away, shaking his head.

Thed and Orvy sat hidden in the overhead conduits, polishing off a stack of sandwiches, several glazed doughnuts, and their third liter of cherry soda. The messrooms on starships really did give you everything you asked for, just like in the Macmain books. The soda was a vivid green color, but it tasted like cherry. "It's probably full of nutrients, to prevent space sickness, or something like that," Thed opined. She didn't really care. Life was finally imitating art.

"Shh, somebody's coming."

A crewman passed by below them. He had an electronic noteboard under one arm and a pencil behind one ear. He paused, almost directly beneath Thed and Orvy's hiding place, in front of a heavy door. He reached for the lock panel.

Thed tensed.

The crewman pressed four buttons, and the vault door opened. The man went inside.

"Five, four, five, two," Thed whispered to Orvy, then repeated under her breath: "Five, four, five, two."

"Hey, Oppenheimer," said a voice from across the deck. "Oppy, you down there?" A uniformed woman came through a hatchway.

The man in the vault came out. "'Course I'm here, Ann. Got to make sure the secret weapons don't walk away. What's up?"

Crewman Ann said, "Mister Science wants that rescue pod off the Transporter stage and stowed. We got a bay clear?"

"Moment." Crewman Oppenheimer checked his noteboard. "Looks like Seven-C will do. I suppose he wants this done yesterday."

"Delays are illogical."

The crewpeople laughed. Oppenheimer said, "Okay, let me close this one up and I'll go help you. Hey, how many Vulcans does it take to change—"

"One to change the transtator, and one to ask what's so funny."

"Aw, you heard it. Okay, what does a Vulcan say before he turns out the lights?"

"You got me."

" 'But will you respect me seven years from now?' "

The crewpeople went away, giggling. Thed counted to ten after they were out of hearing, and swung to the deck. Orvy followed.

They looked around. The coast was clear. Thed sidled up to the vault door and pressed the lock buttons: 5, 4, 5, 2. The door clicked and slid open.

The room beyond was only a couple of meters cubed. Along the walls were three coffinlike boxes, all stenciled TOP SECRET—PROPERTY OF STARFLEET COMMAND.

"Secret weapons," Thed breathed.

"You know, Thed," Orvy said very seriously, "of all the places we've been that we weren't supposed to be, I think this is the most not-supposed-to-be we've ever been in. . . ."

Thed was examining one of the cargo boxes. "Look, they're on grav-lifters. All we have to do is grab one and go."

"Grab what? And go where?"

"These are *secret weapons,*" Thed said firmly. "We take one of these back to the city and tell all the aliens that we'll use it if they don't let us alone. That'll show everybody in Plan C." She looked straight at Orvy. "Of course, you don't have to help me if you don't want to."

"Where do I push?" Orvy said.

Spock sat alone on the bridge, contemplating the Direidi situation. He had been following the movements of the *Enterprise* crew to the best of his ability, given the effects of the background radiation. Terribly illogical things were happening on the planetary surface.

Spock had known for a long time, however, that when reasoning beings were involved, "illogical" by no means meant "inexplicable." In fact, a great number of societal explanations required the suspension of logic, and sometimes working entirely outside its strictures.

He considered this fact for fifteen minutes, without moving, without blinking (once his nictitating eyelids had closed), barely even breathing. And the answer appeared—did not merely suggest itself as a possibility, but leaped from the situation fully formed.

The solution *was* logical. But it was the logic of a situation, of a particular social dynamic: as different from abstract mathematical logic as a living organism was different from a crystal of carbon. Not the logic that states baldly that if p := q, then not p := not q, but the sort that causes a Vulcan diplomat to choose a human woman as life companion and mother of his child.

Spock left the bridge, walked through the quiet corridors. The Direidi solution, he thought. The only possible solution under the circumstances. Utterly logical.

Ensign Oppenheimer and Lieutenant Crispin looked up as the science officer walked by. Commander Spock seemed oblivious to them, utterly lost in thought. He had a curious expression.

"Now there's something you don't see every day," Oppenheimer said softly.

"Yeah," Crispin said. "Looks like he's trying to . . . laugh."

*"Naaah,"* they said together, and went back to work.

Uhura and Proke had been hustled into the cellar of a building. The coach driver and two more of Skorner's men held them at gunpoint while Skorner rifled Uhura's shoulder bag.

"What did you do with it?" the thin man said, in rather a mild voice, and threw the bag aside.

"With what?"

"The harp. We know you had it."

"What do you want with it?"

Skorner said, still pleasantly, "I am asking the questions."

"The last I saw of it, it was in my bag."

Proke said, "Maybe it fell out when you bustled us into the taxi."

"Check the coach," Skorner said, and the driver went out.

Proke said, "Or maybe I hid it."

Skorner said, "Don't say that if you didn't. I hate wasting other people's pain."

"Well, here we are, back at *The Maltese Falcon,* Mr. Cairo. Or are you Wilmer? Well, never mind. You can't kill me, because then you'll never find the package—and since I know that, there's no point in torturing me."

"What about her?" Skorner said.

Aperokei shrugged. "Not my type. Not even my species."

Uhura slapped him. Skorner chuckled. Proke shoved Uhura toward Skorner.

Aperokei said, "And it's not in the coach, but that did get rid of one of you—*now, angel!*"

Uhura's elbow speared Skorner's solar plexus. Proke threw the nearest thug into the second nearest. They ran.

"Should we make for the hotel?" Uhura said. It was just after dark, and the streets were badly lit, the alleys almost entirely in shadow.

"We can't afford to get lost, and we can't trust them anyway. This way." He led her on.

"Proke, we're headed back toward the theater . . . that's where you hid it, isn't it?"

"Every Hitchcock ever, remember? There's always a McGuffin. I figured that had to be it."

They slipped in through the fire exit. The auditorium was silent, almost totally dark. They moved between the seats by touch. Aperokei knelt.

"Is this it?" Uhura asked.

"We've got it, angel." He laughed. "Chewing gum under the seat. Every theater in the universe has it. Klingon theaters do. Well, maybe not Vulcan theaters . . . do Vulcans go to movies?"

The projector came to life, clattering, glaring. The screen lit with a black-and-white slide reading

NO SMOKING IN THE AUDITORIUM

LADIES PLEASE REMOVE YOUR HATS

A shadow fell across the screen. Reflected light gleamed from an enormous, chrome-finished pistol, and a pair of small round eyeglasses. "Vulcans go to movies," Ilen the Magian said, "but they don't enjoy it."

"I should have guessed," Proke said.

"You shouldn't have. Nor should you have come back. We'd have found the package eventually, process of elimination. You would have gotten away clean, never seen me again."

"Yeah, that's a real shame. You died so nicely."

The Magian turned his head so that his face was half-lit, smiled like a Greek mask of comedy. "I did at that. Your turn now."

The sun was starting to lower over the 12th-hole fairway. Ensign Chekov teed Engineer Scott's ball, and went to the small sign describing the hole. "It says, '380 meters, dogleg left, principal hazards bunker left, minefield right.'"

Scott stopped in the middle of a practice swing. "Would you say that again, lad?"

Chekov did.

"It's a good thing these people are hospitable," Scott said, "'cause their idea of a joke sure puts a strain on a man's temper." He swung. The ball flew.

"Alas," Maglus said, "that is a terrible slice," as Scott's ball left the fairway and dropped into the rough to the right of the dogleg bend.

There was a short, deep *boom,* and an eruption of smoke and yellow flame from the woods where the ball had gone.

They all gaped as the cloud of smoke rolled into the sky. After a long pause, Scott said, "'Minefield right,' Mr. Chekov?"

"Aye, sir."

*"Excuse me,"* a clipped voice said. A man was approaching—no, marching toward—the tee. He wore a khaki uniform with red shoulder tabs and a beret with a circular badge; he had a pencil mustache and carried a golf club tucked under his arm. "Good day, gentlemen. You seem to have a friendly match going here. I wonder if you'd mind if we played through?"

Maglus said, "Do you know there are land mines on this ground?"

"Well, I should think we'd know," the uniformed man said. "Not going to play eighteen holes without doing our recce, are we? Twelfth at Direidi, best Par 4 in the galaxy." He tilted his head. "May we?"

Maglus stepped aside. Scott said, "Fine with me."

"Very well then." The man pitched his voice up. "Sergeant Benson! *Fore!*"

There was a sound like a metal zipper, a hundred times magnified. Maglus gave a choked cry, shouted something in Klingonese, and dove for the nearest foliage. Korth followed him. Chekov and Scott took the hint.

There was an explosion a few meters from the tee, and it rained dirt.

Maglus spoke rapidly to Korth, got a short answer, then said, "So this is your plan? To kill us and take the *cha'puj*—"

"Commander," Scott said tightly, brushing a divot from his nose, "if you'll notice, they're shooting at us, too."

Another mortar shell whistled and exploded. Korth spoke to Maglus, who nodded and said, "There is reason in this. Perhaps the Direidi wish us dead."

"It's certainly occurred to me."

"So. What is our plan?"

"You're the soldier. I'm just a hauler of garbage and adjuster of mistakes, remember?"

"So, I am a soldier now that we are under attack? I am no longer a driver of slaves, a ship's thug?"

Machine-gun fire rattled overhead. Korth crawled to Chekov, handed him a chocolate bar. "Here. We may as well eat while we're waiting for them." They unwrapped the candy and began nibbling.

"Very well," Maglus said finally. "We move on. Have your man bring your clubs. *Korth, nuyiih khem!*"

"You heard the man, lad," Scott said.

"The . . . clubs, Mr. Scott?"

"They're all the weapons we've got. And I'm not giving up those hickories without a fight."

As energy bolts sizzled in the air, the four crept through the brush toward the 12th-hole green, Chekov and Korth dragging golf bags behind them.

Uhura and Proke were tied back-to-back in straight-backed metal chairs. Next to them was a sixteen-millimeter film projector with a loaded reel above its lens, an empty one below; around the concrete walls of the small room were racks of paints, masks, costumes, pieces of scenery. Ilen the Magian tested the cords holding the two in their chairs, said, "Yes, I think that will hold. I'm sure you know the room is soundproof."

"If you wanted the harp," Uhura said, "why didn't you ask for it?"

"Because I'm not the only one after it," Ilen said. "If you handed it over to me innocently, you might just as innocently tell someone else where it had gone." He stopped to examine a wooden sword in a painted cloth scabbard. "Truthfully, *zan* Aperokei, you did better than I expected. After you fell into Skorner's hands, I supposed he would get it from you . . . and then I would have gotten it from him. Everyone would have assumed Skorner had the artifact and I was dead, when in fact the reverse was true."

"Skorner doesn't work for you?"

"He did once. Then he learned about the harp. He no longer works for anyone." Ilen slammed the sword into its scabbard.

Uhura said, "This is all for that little harp?"

"The harp, indeed, *the harp,*" the Magian said, and adjusted his glasses. "Do you know how long I've searched for that particular artifact? I followed its trail here, to that junk shop—I was one step behind it when you got in the way. And there were, of course, people not far behind me."

"That fake Andorian said 'almost there.' Was he a cop?"

"Had been. But he'd become just one more treasure hunter by the time he got here. The harp has that effect on people."

"Why is it so valuable?" Uhura said. "The stones can't be genuine."

"True. It isn't even real silver. But if you overlay the locations of the stones on a particular starmap . . . well. Somewhere over the rainbow . . ."

Proke said, "You aren't going to sing again, are you?"

Ilen laughed. "No."

Uhura said, "So what *are* you going to do now?"

"I? I'm going to be wealthy beyond the dreams of avarice, and believe me, my avarice has big dreams. Now, as for you, on the other hand . . . you've been through rather a lot. You aren't going to give up just because I've got the Great Whatsit in hand."

"Ralph Meeker, *Kiss Me Deadly,*" Proke said.

"You see? Still in high spirits. And I really don't want two starships chasing me when I leave here."

The Magian gestured around at the shelves and hanging objects. "This is the theater's old prop room," he said. "This stuff is positively ancient." He rapped a knuckle against a papier-mâché breastplate, and it flaked apart. "Old, and dry, and very flammable. Or is that inflammable?" He leaned forward. "This is where one of you says, 'You can't do that!'"

"Really?" Uhura said dryly.

"Must have forgotten my lines," Proke said.

"Oh, come now. Not even a 'you fiend'? Well. Let me continue with my part, and you can catch up later." He flipped a switch on the projector. The reels spun, and a beam of intense light shot between Uhura and Proke's heads. On the opposite wall, there was a brilliant flash of swirling colors and a burst of music. Ilen turned the volume down as the credits began to appear.

"One of the lesser gems of my collection, one I could bear to leave," the Magian said. *"House of Usher,* Roger Corman's first Poe film, cheaply made but outrageously stylish—"

"Screenplay by Richard Matheson, cinematographer Floyd C. Crosby," Proke said.

"Yes, that's the one. And one of Vincent Price's best roles, in my opinion. So you do know how it ends?"

"Even I know how 'The Fall of the House of Usher' ends," Uhura said. "The house burns and collapses."

"'Sinks into the dank tarn,' actually. But there's never a tarn around when you need one."

Uhura said, "You intend to burn us to death down here."

"Not really. You'll be gone well before the fire begins." He took a small, conical flask of amber liquid, rather like a perfume bottle, from his pocket, set it on top of the projector. "This is an explosive, sensitive to just about anything you can name, particularly shock and heat. If you jar the projector, as you surely will if you struggle too much, it'll fall, and explode. The place will indeed burn, like a paint factory—"

*"House of Wax,"* Proke said. "Another good role for Price."

"Yes. But as I say, by the time the fire starts you'll be past caring."

Uhura said, "And if we don't knock the bottle over, the heat of the projector will eventually set it off."

"Exactly. There wasn't any way of calculating it precisely, but you should last until the movie's over."

Aperokei said, "A man of your taste would never kill anyone before the last reel."

"Why, thank you, Lieutenant. And you as well, Lieutenant Uhura, for this evening's entertainment. It was a good chase. Now, you'll excuse me, but I have worlds to discover . . . Oh. One last thing."

He nestled paper buckets of popcorn in the two prisoners' laps.

"You could just shoot us," Uhura said.

"No, I couldn't do that. People like me are really very squeamish about that sort of thing."

"Then there's a way out," Aperokei said.

"There's the fellow!" the Magian said brightly. "I knew a man of your experience had to have seen a few Republic serials. There's *always* a way out." The Magian went to the door, stood in it for a moment, looking wistful behind his dark glasses. "But you'd better think hard, 'cause you don't have until continued-next-week."

He closed the door. On the screen, Roderick Usher winced at the noise.

# Chapter Eight

## *All Through the Night*

SOMEWHERE ON THE 17th hole, explosions echoed dully, bullets whistled like angry hornets, and low bursts lit the horizon.

Standing up in a sandtrap, Montgomery Scott said, "It's a terrible thing, war."

"As terrible as one decides it is," Maglus said. He pointed at the night sky. "The stars do not judge what they see."

"Are you sure of that?" Scott's eye was caught by an unusual constellation: a ring of stars haloing a distant peak. "Look at that, now. Doesn't it awe you a little? To think there might be a higher power than us, arranging matters?"

"Or that we are the property of some vast indifferent thing. No, Scott, I shall finish out my service to the Empire with the best honor I can, and then there shall be nothing, nothing at all."

"What about the Black Fleet?" Scott said.

Maglus snorted. "The Black Fleet is the idea of line-mad Imperials who cannot think of anything better to do with a thousand lives than to repeat the mistakes of the first."

Scott nodded. "Mr. Chekov! Would you get me the object from that side pocket, please?"

Chekov unzipped the pocket, drew out a thin silver flask. He took a step toward Scott, then stumbled on the sand and fell forward. Scott caught the flask from the air as Chekov landed at his feet.

"You know, Mr. Chekov—"

Chekov stood up, slapping sand from himself. "Yes, Mr. Scott, I do know! 'Mr. Chekov, you are the worst caddy in the explored uniwerse!' Isn't that what you were going to say? Isn't that what you *always* say? 'Recheck those sensor readings, Mr. Chekov.' 'I said, steady as she goes, Mr. Chekov.' Ever since I am a little chelloveck, this goes on! 'Pavel Andreivich, eat your groats.' 'Pavel Andreivich, you are a disgrace to the Pioneer Railroad Porters' Corps.' Well, Pavel Andreivich is having *no more* of this!"

He reached to the golf bag, seized a 7-iron, raised it over his head. An artillery shell exploded brilliantly in midair, and the light caught the club like a bolt of lightning. Chekov shouted *"Urrah!"* and charged from the sandtrap into the furious night.

Korth stood up, pointed a finger after Chekov and another at Maglus. "What he . . . what he said, double." Korth grabbed a club in each hand and ran after Chekov, shouting and flailing.

Scott and Maglus looked after them for a while, but the ensigns were lost to sight almost at once. Finally Maglus said, "I think I was that age once. You?"

"I've been tryin' to recall."

"Old officers do not do these things in the way young ones do." Maglus crawled to the golf bags. "What club do you like?"

"Sand wedge, I think."

Maglus handed it across, selected a long iron for himself.

Scott said, "And a half-dozen balls."

"Of course. Do you still have that flask?"

"Above my heart." He handed it to Maglus, who raised it. "To old officers." He drank and handed it back.

"We only fade away," Scott said, and drained the flask.

Together they climbed from the bunker and went off in the direction of the 18th green.

The Black Queen's prisoners paced their cell. There were no windows, no clocks, and the torches did not seem to burn down. "How long do you suppose it has been?" Askade said.

"I'm glad you said that," McCoy said. "For a moment, I was wishin' we had that Vulcan down here to help us."

Askade looked puzzled, then said, "What is a 'doughnut,' Sulu?"

"A *doughnut?*"

"That is what I said."

"It's a cake . . . round, with a hole in the middle."

"A torus?" Askade said.

"That's right."

"If you're considering our last meal," McCoy said, "I'd hold out for a few more courses."

"Do you remember the inscription upon the stone? It had the line, 'keep your eye upon the doughnut'—"

"'And not upon the hole,'" McCoy said. "I think that was poetic license."

"Suppose it was not?" Askade said. He spoke to Memeth in Klingonese, then said, "The pit in the audience chamber—"

"Has a copper ring around it," Sulu said. "Do you suppose that's part of the mechanism for the—whatever it is?"

"I am an engineer, not a sorcerer. But copper is an excellent conductor of energy. And the engravings could be a sort of circuitry."

Sulu said, "So if we could damage the circuit, maybe we could destroy the machine."

Memeth said, "This is a good plan. Except that we have nothing with which to damage solid copper."

Askade said, "Well, Doctor? Have you any more devices concealed?"

"Well, now that you mention it . . ." He reached to his boot, produced a small cylinder. "But I don't think it's gonna be much use."

"A hand agonizer?"

"Friend, I think we have a fundamental difference of opinion on what doctors *do*. This is a medscanner." He held it out, pressed a button. There was a small whirring sound; the guard outside stirred but did not move toward the cell. "You're alive, and you're a Klingon. Is that useful?"

"It is a shame it is not an agonizer," Askade said. "Its combat uses are minimal, but with certain rewirings . . . wait. On what spectra does this device operate?"

"Fairly high frequencies, up through the K range."

"Sixty or higher?"

"Sixty-five to eighty."

Askade smiled. "It will serve. Give it to me, and while I work you must plan."

Roderick Usher carried his sister's body through a spectral blue-gray dreamscape, a crypt filled with mist and horror, a cloudy, death-cold hell.

"Getting warm in here," Aperokei said.

"It's your imagination," Uhura said. "Speaking of which, do you recognize this particular situation from a movie?"

"Afraid not. Classic situation, though."

"That's nice."

"I mean it. This is pure serial-cliffhanger, Ilen said so himself. Heroes and heroines are always being put in these predicaments, and never in the history of motion pictures has it ever actually done them in. Your movies, our movies, anybody's movies. Ever seen an episode of *Battlecruiser Vengeance?*"

"This isn't a movie, Proke."

"I think Ilen thinks it is."

"You mean . . . he did leave us a way to escape."

"I think he had to. Staying true to the idiom, and all that."

"Okay. Any ideas?"

"Nothing yet. You haven't got a knife up your sleeve, have you?"

"They're out of fashion this year."

Proke laughed. "That's it, angel. Keep smiling. . . . Can you push down, lift your chair a little?"

She tried. There wasn't much slack in the ropes around her ankles. Together they shifted the chair perhaps half a centimeter. Another try, and they bumped lightly against the projector. The reels wobbled. A ripple ran through the amber flask.

"Buzzsaws," Aperokei said.

"What?"

"Buzzsaws. Victim tied to log, headed into sawmill, certain doom by the rotary blade." He waggled his head toward the projector, the turning metal reels. "Get the idea?"

"I get the idea."

"It'll be tricky. We've got to get right against that lower reel, without knocking anything over."

"You're absolutely right. Let's do it."

"Uhura, I love you. On three. One . . . two . . . *three.*"

They skidded their chairs against the machine. Their heads obscured the sides of the picture; the light was very warm. The glass flask jittered, slipped a bit, then was still. The ropes binding their wrists rested against the edge of the take-up reel, making it hiss and squeak.

Uhura said, "Is it working?"

"You'll know the minute I do. Hold it firm, now."

They held the ropes tight. Fibers snapped. On the screen, the crumbling towers of the House of Usher shook, and a woman buried by accident woke mad in her tomb.

"Picture doesn't have long to run," Aperokei said.

"I think it's fraying. Shall we push harder?" She turned her head to look at the flask of explosive. Bubbles had formed in the liquid.

"Don't think we have much choice."

They strained. The house was ablaze, whole walls collapsing. It burned out; its shell sank from sight.

A strand of rope gave way, then another. They began to pull free. The credits crawled up the screen. "Go, *go,*" Proke said. Uhura got a hand loose. She reached for the flask. The top reel stopped as the end of the film unwound from it. Uhura's fingertips were just short of reaching the flask, which was bubbling actively now. Proke was tearing at the ropes. The tail of the film crawled through the sprockets, and out. Uhura stretched. The screen went pure white. The film popped free of the last sprocket, and the take-up reel free-wheeled, wobbling, shaking the projector. Uhura closed her fingers on nothing.

The flask slid off, fell.

Uhura grabbed the bucket of popcorn from her lap, swung it.

The flask landed in the popcorn, with just a slight crunch.

Uhura put the bucket down, very gently, and started breathing again.

Aperokei said, "Was that—"

"Yeah. It was."

"Well. Tough part's over, then."

She snorted. Then she laughed. She put her free hand behind her to circle Proke's neck and hugged him, back to back, in the light of the silver screen.

The Black Queen's prisoners, heavily guarded, were herded to the audience chamber and onto the glass disc. The copper bars rose to encircle them.

The queen appeared in a black silk robe, slashed with white. She sat down luxuriously in the iron throne. "Haven't had a recharge like this in *decades*," she said.

Memeth said, "Beware us, Queen!" After all his growling and grumbling, to hear him speak out loud and clear was really quite startling: even Askade turned to look at him. "We are not without powers of our own. To this moment we have been patient with you, for we do not use our power in idle show: but the time of patience is over."

"Stalling won't do you any good," Janeka said. "When the sun comes up, you guys are vitamins."

Askade waved his arm, shouting something unintelligible but impressive. He straightened his arm and threw the medscanner at the copper ring. It hit, bounced, lay there.

Everyone was absolutely still. The first rays of sun came down the conduit, glaring on the copper ring. Other than that, nothing much happened.

"Remember the *Maine!*" Sulu yelled, and ran at the cage, stretching his arms through the bars. He got hold of a guard, pulled him against the metal, gave him a short, sharp rap that dropped the man in a heap. The sun began to shine full through the tube of rock.

The medscanner blew up in a shower of white sparks. The copper ring glowed greenly. Light poured down. Red light fountained up from below, and actinic flashes, and thunder. The glass over the pit starred, then webbed with cracks.

Where the scanner had exploded, sparks ran up the bars like a Jacob's ladder. Memeth shouted and leaped: two bars snapped off at the base. The four charged off the glass, into a whirling melee with the queen's guards.

"You do notice we're outnumbered," McCoy said.

"I cannot tell," Askade said. "There is a red haze across my vision."

From a side hall, a horde of people dressed in white cotton, spattered with blood and chicken gravy, rushed forth, holding high knives, cleavers, rolling pins, wire whisks . . .

"The kitchen-*kuve* attack!" Memeth said. *"The queen! Take the queen!"* He picked up a sword and dashed for the throne.

Janeka jumped off her throne. "Not today, Charlie," she shouted, and ran to the door. An iron panel slid down, sealing the exit.

The glass covering the pit shattered. There was a solid shaft of light from below, and billowing smoke.

A ring of guardsmen had blocked off the kitchen slaves, and was slowly pushing them back at spearpoint; another squadron was trying to contain the four offworlders. Memeth hacked furiously, but could not penetrate the guards' armor; Sulu parried furiously in high prime, but still was driven back, step by step.

"Any ideas, McCoy?" Askade said.

"Well . . . *I'm a doctor! Let me through!*"

The guards paused for a moment, then pressed on. "Worth a try," McCoy said to Askade. "How about you?"

"I have only a technical observation to offer."

"You mean, like, we're all about to get killed?"

"I mean like the pit at the chamber's center shows signs of a dilithium saturation hypercharge."

"And what in the name of Uncle Jack Daniel is that?"

"Do you recall the phrase you used, when we were surrounded by the beast-riders?"

"'Match in a fireworks factory'?"

"That is what in your uncle's name it is."

"Mr. Sulu—"

"I heard, Doctor."

They were backed nearly against the stone wall. The smoke blocked all view of the rest of the chamber. The roar from the pit had risen nearly to drown out the sounds of weapons.

Memeth recoiled to thrust. The pommel of his sword hit the stone.

It sank in.

Askade punched the wall. His fist went clear through the painted foam, exposing canvas and sticks. He looked at McCoy. McCoy looked back.

The guardsmen pressed on.

"Cover us," Askade shouted above the roar. He and McCoy leaned together and slammed their shoulders against the "stone."

Another explosion went off, illuminating the brush

in which the crew of *Jefferson Randolph Smith* were hiding.

"They seem to be at war," Tellihu observed.

Trofimov said, "The town seemed very peaceful, and it's not so far away."

T'Vau had been reciting Vulcan epic poetry ever since they had wandered into the combat zone. She was halfway through a two-thousand-line history of the Pythagorean Theorem.

"It is not our war, is it?" Tellihu said, in a childlike tone.

"No, Tellihu, it's not."

"Do you think they might allow us to leave, then? If we were very polite?"

A shell whistled. Trofimov said, "Doesn't your planet have wars, Tellihu?"

"We were invaded by the Klingons a few times. It is not the same thing, exactly. But I see your point. It is like evolution."

"What's like evolution?"

"This war. It is as if my ancestors had not chosen to evolve large brain-cages on upright carriages. We might still be able to fly unassisted. If I could fly, we would have a way out of here. But that is the trouble with evolution. When it makes a mistake, it cannot be easily fixed."

"Yes, Tellihu, I guess that's right."

There was a human-sounding cry. The three *Smith* crew put their heads up, just nose-high. A man was running past them, swinging what appeared to be a golf club. Behind him came a Klingon, brandishing *two* golf clubs. And after *him* two more figures, one human, one Klingon, were marching side by side. The second human was whistling quite loudly, a Highland bagpipe march.

"What shall we do?" Tellihu said. "Shall we ask them for directions?"

"No," Trofimov and T'Vau said together.

The captain said, "They're going that way. Let's go this way."

T'Vau said, "Why?"

Trofimov took a deep breath. "Because I said so, that's why."

Two cautious figures approached the Hotel Direidi.

"Not the main entrance," Aperokei said. "This way."

They slipped in through a service door. They were in a wood-paneled hall, with a short stairway. Both hall and stairs led to darkness. "Which way?" Uhura said.

"I like straight. Going up gives us farther to fall down."

*"Just hold it right there!"*

At the head of the stairs was a young man in a turtlenecked shirt, leather jacket, slacks, and sneakers, all black. A headset with boom microphone compressed his unruly blond hair.

He loped down the staircase, pointed a long and sickly-pale hand at Uhura and Proke, and fixed them with blue eyes behind metal-rimmed glasses. His stare had a truly mad aspect.

"You aren't due here," he said in a reedy voice. "You're not *blocked* here. It's bad enough that the author's handing me pages with the ink still wet, without me having to personally plop each and every one of you on your marks." He pressed a switch on the headset. "Con*trol*, this is your *stage* manager speaking . . . two of our little lambs have gone astray, baa, baa. Yes, well, I should think so." He released the switch, pointed at Uhura's bag. "That goes back to Props before you leave here, you do understand." He touched the headset again. "Stage Manager . . . fine. Splendid. Let's see if we can do this in one take, shall we? You'd think you were unionized, or something."

Uhura said, "What is going *on* here?"

"Now listen, little fella," Proke said, sounding genial and tough at once, "my friend and I have been through quite a bit to get here, and now we want some answers. You goin' to give them to us, or do we have to go through you to somebody—"

"Wonderful, wonderful cold reading," the man in black said. "But you're not auditioning now, not for me. *I* don't even have final cut. Now, this way, please? Your next scene's in the kitchen."

Uhura said, "Our next scene."

"Yes, dear. That's what we call a cue." He held up a hand, fingers arched. "I give them, you take them, and soon we're all catching bouquets, reading notices from that subphylum of giant insect known as critics, being asked what Mr. Gable's *really* like, and wondering why we got into this industry at all, when medical research pays so well for experimental subjects. . . . Now, once again from the top: Kitchen. You. Cue." He pointed, touched his headset. "Light cue 17." Lamps came up slowly, illuminating a corridor. "And . . . *action.*" He extended an arm down the newly lighted hall, his body rigid.

Uhura looked at Aperokei. He shrugged. They followed the pointing finger to a pair of double doors marked

KITCHEN
EMPLOYEES ONLY

Proke put a finger to his lips. Uhura stood to one side.

Proke kicked the door open. He and Uhura dashed through.

They stood at the end of an enormous institutional kitchen, all white tile and steel tables. Most of the tables were draped with white linens, covering something piled high. At least a dozen people in white, with chef's hats, stood about, some pushing carts, some holding white towels. There was an almost overwhelming smell of baking.

Proke's mouth hung open. He sniffed the air. He pointed at one of the cloth-draped tables, at the carts. "You see it, angel? It all makes sense now. What it's all been leading up to."

"Of course," Uhura said, meaning it this time. It *did* all finally make sense now. "They planned all along to—"

"Yes, you're right," a woman's voice said. Estervy stepped forward, removing her high white hat and shaking out her long gray hair. "That's why I insisted we rewrite this particular scene; Flyter didn't like the idea at first, but you've done so much, so well, I thought you should see the last act before we play it." She brushed flour from her hands. "Final cue, Lieutenant Aperokei: you do know what this means?"

"Sure," Proke said, putting his hand lightly on Uhura's elbow. "We know too much."

Flyter's voice filtered down from a speaker somewhere overhead. "Couldn't have put it better myself."

"Sorry we can't stay," Uhura said, and she and Proke turned to dash for the kitchen door.

The young man in black was standing there. He touched his headset. "Warning on mechanical effects . . . and . . . *action.*"

Four of the bakers tossed aside the towels they were holding, revealing black guns with transparent barrels. Blue light lanced across the kitchen. Caught in the crossfire, Uhura and Proke had no chance at all. Uhura saw the world pan, tilt, solarize, fade to black.

# Chapter Nine

## *Come Up and See Me Sometime*

IN ROOM 21 of the Hotel Direidi, Ambassador Charlotte Caliente Sanchez smoothed down the dress-length tails of her white silk shirt, pulled up a floor-length circle skirt of silver brocade on white wool, and fastened the skirt at her waist. She turned in front of the full-length mirror: the skirt moved very nicely indeed, and the shawl-collared blouse was cut deeply enough to absolutely rivet the attention of Captain James T. Kirk—while preserving the decorum expected of the special envoy to Direidi.

She sat on the edge of the bed, pulled on her high white slippers, tested the fit—not very comfortable, but then that wasn't what they were all about—stood and adjusted the drape of the blouse once more. Kirk, she thought, wasn't going to know what hit him.

And for the sake of Federation-Direidi relations, he'd better not ever find out. . . .

In the other arm of the V-shaped hotel corridor, in Room 22, Captain James T. Kirk was straightening his bow tie before the bathroom mirror, and smoothing a collar wing that had gotten ruffled in the tying operation.

There was a tap at the door. "Yes?"

"Laundry, sir. You wanted a suit cleaned?"

"Yes. Come in." The door opened. "Suit's on the dresser. Do you see it?"

A man's scratchy, old-sounding voice said, "Yes, sir. Are all the medals off this, sir?"

"I think I got them all."

"Very good, sir. It'll be ready in the morning, if that's all right."

"That's just fine."

The door closed. Kirk came out of the bathroom, took the satin-striped tuxedo trousers from their hanger and pulled them on, buttoned up the black braces. He fastened the cummerbund around his middle, examined the effect in the mirror, then cinched it a little tighter. Not bad at all. The classic black dinner suit had been out of fashion on Earth for two hundred and fifty years, give or take, but the Direidi seemed to consider it the only possible garment for a gentleman out for the evening. Kirk didn't see a thing wrong with the idea. He pulled on the black jacket, plucked at the peaked lapels. They'd been very reasonable about renting him the suit, too.

There was a red flower on the desk where Kirk's dress uniform had been waiting for the laundryman, with a card reading *With the Hotel's Compliments.*

Kirk smiled, picked up the flower, and with an elaborate flourish of his wrist inserted it in his buttonhole. When Pete's buddy Zack, playing the cat burglar, pretended to stun Kirk, he would grasp the flower as a last, sinking gesture. Tonight's entertainment was being played for royalty, after all.

But before the fun, there was dinner. And afterward . . .

Kirk spun an imaginary cane, and whistled about puttin' on his top hat, as he opened the door.

In Room 32, directly above Kirk's, Captain Kaden vestai-Oparai was struggling with the knot of his bow tie. *Tuk'zedo* was a bizarre form of dress, he thought for at least the fortieth time, abandoned the tie for a moment and adjusted the braces. He supposed that they were a survival of weapon bandoliers. Was the cummerbund originally a knife-holder, or a piece of body armor, or a sash of office in the Klingon fashion? The Direidi had provided Kaden with an appropriate gold lamé one. Kaden decided he respected the locals. They displayed efficiency; their servitors worked well. Their customs were odd, but no odder than most humans exhibited.

And the plan of the Direidi Peet blak-Wood, to win enough honor to take his companion by right, that was cunning indeed. Wars of line-succession were to be avoided; they were long and expensive and as full of bitter fury as a Romulan caught stealing sweets.

The necktie (once a defense against strangling-wires and knives, Kaden supposed) resolved itself. Kaden smiled. There were things to take by force, and things to take by stealth. He thought that, if it were stated that way, Arizhel would agree.

Arizhel drew the single strap of her gown over her right shoulder, fastened it with a round bronze brooch bearing a bloodstone. She wore only a little jewelry: long, thin bronze earrings, a few golden bangles on her wrists. Charlotte had said that the local style of revel costume used little ornament, taking its impact from clean, dramatic lines. Rish looked into the mirror, decided that she liked the effect.

Her dress was of red silk, in two layers, a nearly transparent one shot with gold thread over an opaque, glossy one; as the fabrics shifted, the gown iridesced. It left her arms uncovered, and her shoulders except for the one broad strap, and was hemmed in what Charlotte called "handkerchief points," displaying more or less leg as she moved. The ambassador had proposed very strange shoes to accompany the gown. Arizhel had instead chosen soft flat slippers from the hotel's gift shop, a bright red, fastened with red satin ribbons around her ankles. Ambassador Sanchez had said, "Just so you don't go dancing off any balconies," and laughed, and thoroughly confused matters by trying to explain the joke. Rish had no such intention, of course, no matter how energetic the Princess D'di became tonight. Perhaps it was a superstitious phrase to draw away bad luck, like the admonitions to "break a limb," "tear a claw," or just "die well!"

Arizhel looked again into the mirror. She knew who would want to dance tonight, and not on balconies. Poor Kaden: he was in for a terrible surprise this night.

She wrapped a long scarf of red silk once around her neck, letting it trail down her spine. Klingons did not go out with their throats exposed. She went out of the room, walked to the bend of the V hall. There was an elevator shaft on the outside of the elbow, a broad, carpeted staircase on the inside.

Kaden was approaching, looking rather stiff in his *tuk'zedo*—but, Rish had to admit, quite elegant, quite noble, like a battlecruiser with a gleaming new hull.

They went down one floor. Kirk and Sanchez were there, Kirk in another of the black suits, Sanchez in dazzling white. Kirk held his elbow raised level, and the ambassador's hand rested lightly on it. Kaden looked briefly at Arizhel, and imitated the gesture. Rish took hold of his sleeve. It would be useful, she guessed, if one's party were hunting, and became lost in heavy fog.

They went downstairs to the dining room.

The captains and their companions were given the central table in the hotel restaurant, beneath a skylight that showed the moon just a little past full. Champagne was brought out in a huge silver bucket, and menus in Fed-Standard and Klingonese. There were five courses, with cold sorbets to clear the palate between. There were three wines. The quantities of everything were more than liberal, and by the time the desserts were brought the gibbous moon had sunk quite out of view.

"Would you like another bottle of champagne?" Kirk said.

Sanchez said, "Yes, it's really excellent." She said to the steward, "Is it a local product?"

"Yes, madame. Produced especially for the hotel."

Kaden said, "The texture is interesting. A good drink." He looked through his glass at the candles. "The gas is harmless?"

Sanchez giggled. "Depends on how you look at it. Some people find the bubbles the most dangerous part." She hiccuped. "See what I mean?"

Kaden said, "From what is it prepared? Fungi?"

"Grapes," Kirk said.

"And they do have grapes here," Sanchez said. "Estervy made that very clear. Lotsa grapes. But no lions."

The steward presented a new bottle, tore off the foil with an easy motion. "Actually, sir, the Klingon gentleman is correct. The sparkling wines of Direidi

200

are distilled from fungi." He rolled the bottle over to show Kirk the label, which read

CHAMPAGNE DES CHAMPIGNONS
MÉTHODE INCONNU

"Oh," Kirk said. "And the bubbles . . ."

"Carbon dioxide, of course, sir. If you would prefer a bottle of our Metheglin aux Méthane . . ."

"No, this is just fine, thanks."

The steward filled the long tulip glasses. Ambassador Sanchez raised hers toward the center of the table. "To Direidi," she said, "and to its peaceful and productive development. Whoever may do it."

"Whoever may," Kaden said, smiling with teeth, and they all touched glasses.

The last of the dishes were cleared. Kirk stood up. "Well," he said, sounding a bit rushed, "that was a perfectly magnificent dinner. My, look at the time, it's after midnight. Shall we . . . retire?"

"Retire? Now? I'm wide awake," Sanchez said. "And I'm told that there's a really terrific ice cream parlor in the hotel, open all night."

Kirk swallowed hard. "Ice . . . cream?"

Sanchez said dreamily, "It's been years since I've had an ice cream soda."

"Yeah," Kirk said, "me too."

Kaden said, "Is something stuck in your throat, Kirk?"

"No, I'm fine. Fine. And an ice . . . cream . . . soda sounds like just the thing after that . . . dinner."

Arizhel said, "The ambassador has told me of these *zhodas.*"

"She has?" Kirk squeaked. "I mean, she has?"

Rish said, "I should certainly like to try one."

Kaden said, "It was a very filling dinner."

Kirk said, "Oh, come on, Kaden, you don't want to break up the party so soon," and then more quietly, "You want a soda, friend. Believe me, you want one."

Kaden's eyes narrowed. Kirk nodded furiously. "Very well," Kaden said.

"Great," Ambassador Sanchez said. "I scream, you scream, we all scream for ice cream."

"Please tell me when I am supposed to scream," Rish said, as they left the dining room.

The ice cream parlor was up a broad, dim, fern-lined corridor from the dining room. It had stained-glass windows, bent-wire chairs, and a long chromium bar displaying forty-eight flavors. Above the door was a gilt sign reading GELATI DIREIDI. Kirk looked up at the sign, noticed that the last two letters hadn't been gilded, or had somehow had the leaf worn off. These old places, he thought, always having to replace things.

They sat down. A young man in a white uniform and a peaked paper cap said, "Evening, folks. What'll it be?"

"Four sodas," Kirk said. He pointed at himself, then at Sanchez. "Chocolate, chocolate . . ." He looked at the Klingons for a moment. "What the heck, four chocolates."

"Comin' right up."

Kaden said genially, "It was good of you to order all identical, but not necessary. After such a dinner, it would be absurd to choose to poison us now."

Sanchez giggled. Kirk said, "Oh, don't mention it."

The soda jerk appeared with four fluted glasses, heaped with ice cream and fizzing furiously. "You folks want seconds, I'll be here. All night long."

Sanchez tore the end from a wrapped straw, put it to her lips and blew the wrapper across the room. She laughed again. Kirk smiled, a little thinly, and put a straw in his own soda.

Kaden and Rish followed suit. Kaden took a sip. His eyes went wide and white. He took a long, long pull on his straw, released it, inhaled deeply, nodded. "Ahhh. Now *this* is a proper conclusion to a day."

"Yes, you're right," Kirk said. "Of course, it is very late, and we ought to be getting back to our rooms."

Kaden looked up. "Yes?"

"Yes, you know. Getting back. To our rooms."

"Of course you are right," Kaden said. "Back to our rooms, *that* is the proper conclusion to a day."

A boy in a brass-buttoned uniform came into the parlor. He looked around—which hardly seemed necessary, since there was only one occupied table.

"Call for Commander Arizhel," the boy said.

"Who calls me?" Rish said, then noticed Sanchez furtively shaking her head. "Very well, youth. I shall go." She stood up.

"Maybe I should go along," Sanchez said. "It might be for me, too."

Kirk said, "What?"

"Powder my nose," Sanchez said, patted Kirk's head and hurried after Rish.

The two captains watched the women go, and exchanged a look of mutual bewilderment.

"Captain Kirk, Captain Kaden," a low voice said.

Pete Blackwood came up to the captains' table, looking around nervously.

"Pete?" Kirk said. "What is it? Something wrong?"

"A lot. Zack's had an accident."

"He is dead?" Kaden said.

"No, not like that. He's twisted his ankle. He'll be all right, but he can't possibly play cat burglar."

Kirk said, "There's no one else you can ask?"

"Not that I'd trust with this, on this short notice."

"It'll have to be one of us, then," Kirk said, and thought a moment. "Rish is on the third floor. So the Black Cat needs to take her prisoner first, then come down to the second floor and get Charlotte, and finally take them both to the lobby. . . . It'll have to be me, then, so Kaden can be in Rish's room when I show up. Besides, Rish has fought alongside Kaden; she'd be more likely to recognize him in combat. That make sense to you, Kaden?"

"I think so. How will you become the robber, if you are with Ambassador Sanchez?"

"I'll find a way to get away from her." He half-smiled. "That'll be a switch. Okay, Pete. Where's the cat-burglar costume?"

"It'll be in the hotel basement, by the laundry. The sonic gun, too."

"That's it, then. Now you'd better get going before the girls come back."

"You're a fine man, Captain Kirk," Pete said. "And you too, Captain Kaden. You're both fine men."

"We are all warriors," Kaden said, and finished Rish's soda with a prolonged slurp.

Kirk said, "I'll go along with that. See you in the lobby, Pete."


"You are intoxicated," Arizhel said, quietly but firmly, as Sanchez caught up to her in the hallway.

"I'm no drunker than you are," Sanchez said. "This is an act for you-know-whose benefit."

"Yes? Yet Kirk is out of sight, and your walk is still unsteady."

"That's the shoes, damn it. That's exactly what these heels are supposed to . . . I'm not sure I can explain it."

"You do not need to," Rish said, adjusted the single strap of her gown, and laughed. "I understand that perfectly. Now, why have you come? Do you know who is calling me?"

"It can't be official, or they'd have called Captain Kaden. So it has to be Deedee."

"Too right," said a small, plaintive voice from a telephone booth on the wall, half-hidden by a potted plant. "Over here, quick."

The princess was sitting in the booth, head slumped. She wore a fur-collared cape over a Miskatonic University sweatshirt and jeans. One leg of the jeans was slit to make room for a bulky bandage around Deedee's ankle, and a pair of crutches was propped up next to her.

"What happened?" Sanchez said.

"I twisted my ankle," Deedee said grimly. "I can't be a slinky cat burglar like *this*."

"Okay, Commander," Sanchez said to Arizhel, "new plan?"

"Obviously one of us must wear the robber costume," Rish said. "But otherwise we need not change the plan at all. You were to be the one abducted, so I shall abduct you. After I have escaped, I shall return to my room and lock myself into the closet."

Deedee said, "But won't you have to, you know, fib about being put in the closet?"

"Not at all. I shall say that the kidnapper put me there. It will be the exact truth."

"You missed a wonderful career in diplomacy, Rish," Sanchez said with admiration. "Great, that's how we'll play it. Is the Black Cat outfit in my room, Deedee?"

"I put it there myself. Thank goodness for elevators."

Rish said, "And Peter will be present for the rescue?"

"I asked him to meet me in the ice cream parlor,

just like we'd planned." She smiled. "Now at least I don't have to stand him up, huh?"

Sanchez said, "That's the spirit, Deedee. Don't worry about a thing."

"I'm not worried," the princess said, and sniffed back a tear. "Both of you are just swell."

"We must return now, and start the plan," Rish said. "It is a pleasure and an honor to fight for you, Princess."

As they walked back to the ice cream parlor, Sanchez said, "We're going to have to figure out a way to get rid of our gentleman callers."

"You think they will try to follow us to our rooms?"

"Oh, I think they're gonna *try* to get us to follow *them*. But I'm not having that. You see my point."

"I see your point. Well. I shall find a way to send my captain away. And you?"

"Don't worry, honey. I know the drill."


They took the stairs up. At the second floor, Sanchez said, "Good night," and turned left toward her room. Kirk said, "Good night, Charlotte. And to you too, Kaden, Rish." He turned right.

The Klingons said, "And to you," and went on upstairs. When Kirk could no longer hear them, he turned around. Ambassador Sanchez was standing by the stairwell, arms crossed, leaning against the wall.

"Well," she said, "you gonna stand there all night?"


On the third-floor landing, Kaden said, "I wonder what is happening between the Federation pair."

"The Captain-strategist knows exactly what is happening," Arizhel said. "At least, his science officer knows. She knows what the Captain Kirk is thinking . . . and also the plans of the Captain Oparai."

Kaden was brought up short. "You know the plans . . . ?"

"It is an obvious plan," Arizhel said, "but sometimes obvious plans are cunning. If one knows the adversary well enough."

Kaden relaxed, taking Rish's meaning now. He held out his hand, and Rish extended hers to touch it, in the fashion of hunters prowling caves in the dark. They turned left and went down the hallway to 31, Rish's room.

Rish closed the door, pulled the coil of wire from her hair, letting it fall. Kaden began to sit down on the chair.

Rish said, "Does the Captain wish to sit alone now?"

Kaden tried to chuckle. It came out strangely. He sat down on the bed, and Rish sat next to him, as upright as any cadet.

Cadets did not have hair like that.

"Do I offend you with my presence?" Kaden said. "Do I dishonor you with my interest?"

"Not with your presence, nor your interest, nor your pursuit," Arizhel said, and put her fingertips on Kaden's forearm. "There is a scar there still, I think?"

"There is."

"I remember the taking of that scar. It was a bold thing."

"And there is a notch in your . . . left ear, from a Kinshaya bullet."

"You're sure it's the left ear?" she said, and covered her ears with her hands.

"Yes," Kaden said, grinning. "The left."

"Correct," she said, and laughed. Then more quietly she said, "What would we do, exactly, if we were to match our courses? Turn privateer?"

"We could," Kaden said thoughtfully. "Askade would be for it, surely. Maglus too, I think." He chuckled. "And of course Proke. I can hear the ship's name now: *Hailing Frequency of Terror*. . . . But it's not so easy as it was. The Thought Admirals counsel quiet borders, and they seem to have the Emperor's ear. Quiet borders mean at least a show of suppressing privateers."

"Thought Admirals all play double games. Sometimes more than double."

Kaden shrugged. *"Nil komerex, khesterex.* We are Klingon, we all play."

"So you are a believer in the Perpetual Game?"

Suddenly they both stiffened, and turned to look at the bedside clock.

Kaden said, "Excuse me a moment," and stood up. *"Ise krem zhoda* makes its way swiftly through the waveguides." He paused in the door of the disposal cubicle. "Though I think we could make our fortunes selling them on Klinzhai."

Arizhel laughed as Kaden shut the door. Then she stood up, careful not to make the bed creak, crept to the cubicle door, put her key in the lock and turned it. She coughed to cover the click.

She took a step toward the hallway door, two, then stopped still. There was no one to see the cat robber overpower and imprison her, but perhaps *seeing* was not what was called for.

"Who are you?" Rish shouted, and threw a pillow at the wall. "What do you want here?" She jumped up and down. "So, you will not speak? Then die silent!" She kicked the wall. "Dishonorable one, to attack an unarmed—" She tipped a lamp over. "I shall find you, thief, murderer," she said, panting as loudly as possible, "find you with my ship of the Black Fleet, and I shall hear your screams ten thousand times . . ."

She threw herself enthusiastically on the floor, groaned, and was still.

"Arizhel?" Kaden's voice came muffled through the disposal-chamber door. There were banging sounds. *"Arizhel?"*

Rish picked herself up, went to the closet. She jumped inside, landing with a whump and a jangle of hangers, and slammed the door shut. Then she opened it again, silently, went to the hall door and looked out. The hallway was clear. She went out and shut the door. From the hall she couldn't hear Kaden at all. Perfect. She went down the hall to the stairs and down to the second floor.

"How about a nightcap?" Kirk said.

"Nightcap? Sure. Just the thing after a five-course meal and an ice cream soda. Need a shot of something to remind my system it's not quitting time yet. Brandy's over there."

"Uh, yeah," Kirk said, "Brandy's fine." He picked up the bottle. He looked at the label, read VSOP GRAN RESERVE DIREIDOIS, then thought of the champagne and stopped reading. He uncorked it and poured two generous shots into small snifters, then picked up a glass in each hand and swirled the brown liquor.

"Clockwise and counterclockwise at once," Sanchez said. "That have something to do with warp-vee combat tactics?"

"Tactics," Kirk said absently. Thanks to Zack's little accident, he had to get out of here on the double.

"Yeah, you know, tactics. What you boys in the big ships do after us girls down in diplo screw everything up beyond all recognition."

There was a pause. They both looked at the bedside clock.

"Um," Kirk said, and held out one of the snifters. "Here's to, um, diplomacy."

They touched glasses. Suddenly Kirk's glass tipped backward. Sanchez's wobbled and lurched forward. Each lapel of Kirk's tuxedo jacket caught a shot of VSOP.

"Gee, what a mess," Sanchez said.

"Yes," Kirk said. "I ought to get this cleaned up right away."

"Uh . . . I guess that's right, you should."

"It'll stain if I don't. Grosgrain lapels, and all."

"Right," Sanchez said, looking at the double stain. "At least it's . . . very symmetrical."

"Yeah, that should . . . uh, I'd better go and, uh, do that."

"Here," Sanchez said, and handed Kirk the seltzer bottle from the bar. "Club soda's good on stains."

"Thanks. I mean that."

"Sure."

Kirk opened the door, seltzer bottle in hand. He took a step into the hall. He collided with a large canvas laundry basket.

"Sorry, sir," said a small, balding, beak-nosed man in a white linen jacket. "Just getting the linens from the empty rooms." He peered in at Sanchez. "This one isn't empty, is it?"

"No," Kirk said, terribly sorry that Zack had only minor injuries.

The laundryman looked at a clipboard. "You're right, sir, it's not. Sorry, sir. Good night."

"Good night."

The laundryman plucked at his lapels. "Club soda's just the thing for them, sir. Won't bleach like peroxide."

"Yes, thanks."

"They *are* nicely symmetrical, sir."

Kirk looked one last time at Sanchez, who shrugged and shut her door. Kirk hurried down the hall, toward the elevator. He got in, said, "Basement, please," then sighed and pressed the B button. The elevator descended.

Kaden banged again on the bathroom door. Stupid thing must have gotten stuck, he thought, stupid antique construction. And now he seemed to have missed the entire action outside.

He couldn't understand it. Of course Arizhel would not have betrayed his presence to an intruder. But Kirk *knew* he was here. Why had Kirk not let him out?

Obviously because Kirk did not consider Kaden necessary. Kirk was a glory-hunter, a selfish, swaggering, tin-plated . . .

Kaden took a deep breath. The air in the cubicle was chilly. There was a slight draft around the window.

He looked at the window, at the sign beside it: FIRE ESCAPE.

Kaden pushed the window open. The air was extremely cold by Klingon standards: no more than ten degrees above freezing, and nose-achingly dry. Kaden swore very mildly and climbed out onto the metal platform. It was extremely dark. Most of the hotel windows were unlit. There was a glow from the floor directly below him.

*Ah.* Kirk would have to go to the end of the hall, down the stairs, then down the lower hall to the ambassador's door, guarding Arizhel all the way. Kaden had only to climb down a short ladder. Kirk would have to fight Kaden after all, have to give Kaden his moment of honor before Rish.

Rish would be impressed, he thought as he stepped onto the ladder. Rish had *thathkek* better be—

211

Kaden brought his foot down hard on the ladder. It started to tilt backward, away from the building. Something went *clang,* and the ladder, with Kaden aboard, dropped. The two hit a thin wooden door, shot cleanly through it, and all was dark.

Kirk stepped out of the elevator into the hotel basement. It was badly lit, thick with dust (though not cobwebs—the Direidi had apparently decided not to import spiders), and smelled of paint remover, lumber, and industrial detergents. Kirk followed the detergent smell through the damp dimness until he found the leotard and mask, folded neatly beside a huge steel laundry bin. He put the seltzer bottle down and shook out the black suit. The sonic stunner was tucked inside the clothes. He examined the gun: cells unplugged, collimator pin pulled. Check.

He stripped to his skivvies, folded his tuxedo, and tugged on the leotard. It fit pretty well, except around the middle. Kirk picked up the stunner, practiced moving stealthily. It wasn't bad at all. And it didn't look like Federation issue . . . which reminded him; he took off his communicator, which certainly was a giveaway, and put it with the tuxedo and soda bottle.

He went to the elevator, pressed the 2 button, then thought better of it and hit DOOR OPEN. It didn't seem right at all for the Black Cat Bandit to be using the elevator. Kirk stepped out, turned.

There was a shuffling footstep ahead of him. Kirk stopped for a moment, then flattened himself against the basement wall, a shadow in shadow.

Someone walked by, then got into the elevator.

Kirk was pleased. He *was* invisible.

Somewhere around here there had to be an exit. He would take the fire escape up to Arizhel's window. He was supposed to surprise them while Kaden was in the bathroom: he would surprise Kaden, all right.

Rish paused on the stairs as someone approached, but whoever it was went into the elevator. She looked up the right-hand hallway toward Kirk's room: there was no one there. Surely Sanchez would have gotten him out by now.

She could not worry about it. She had a schedule to keep. If Kirk was still in the ambassador's room, they would get him out together. Arizhel turned left and went down the hall.

There was a laundry basket in front of the ambassador's room. Rish stepped around it, knocked three times lightly, rapidly.

Sanchez opened the door. "Thank god," she said.

From somewhere outside came a twanging sound, and a *crunch*.

"What was that?" Arizhel said.

Sanchez shrugged. "If it was a thunderbolt, he missed me. Come on, let's get you suited up."

Kaden shook his head. He stirred. Everything was dark and sideways and hurt like explosive decompression. The thought that he might be floating in space without a suit woke him up a good bit further. He pinched his nostrils shut.

No, wait, there was atmosphere. And gravity. Lots of gravity; he was lying on something extremely uncomfortable.

Finally he registered where he was and how he'd gotten there. He got up. He was in the midst of a pile that included several ancient mattresses and what looked like a broken piano. He wasn't sure which he'd landed on.

Kaden shook his head again. There was a schedule. Kirk had kidnapped Rish and was on his way to kidnap the ambassador. Kaden had to get there before Kirk got done kidnapping, so he could get shot and impress Rish.

Something like that.

Kaden stood up and wandered through the dark basement until he found the elevator. Someone was standing against the wall nearby; Kaden thought about killing him, just as a courtesy to his hosts, then remembered he was on a diplomatic mission, and he wasn't sure what the local rules were about trespassers. Kaden got into the elevator. Nothing happened. He looked at the panel, pulled out the DOOR OPEN button. The door closed. "Second floor," he said, and the lift took him up to 2.

He shuffled down the hall, dropping lint and wood shavings as he went. There seemed to be a piano wire caught in his coat, and it snagged at the carpeting and wallpaper.

There was a laundry basket in front of the ambassador's door. He stepped around it, raised his hand. What was the line? *Unhand that female,* that was it. Proke's sort of expression. *Unhand that female.* It had a ring to it.

He took a deep breath and pounded on the door.

There was a stirring from inside, but no answer. He knocked again, harder.

Sanchez smoothed Arizhel's red evening gown and hung it carefully in the closet, then went to help Rish squeeze into the cat-burglar suit. Squeeze was the word: the cat suit was sized for Deedee, who was about Rish's height but considerably skinnier. After some careful inhaling, muscular control, and tugging of zippers, however, they succeeded. At least the hood fit comfortably.

There was a heavy knock on the door.

Sanchez smacked a hand against her forehead. "Kirk," she muttered.

"I thought you had sent him away."

"Captains don't abandon ships, honey, Starfleet builds it into 'em."

Another knock.

"I have an idea," Sanchez said softly. "Did you see the basket in the hall?"

"Yes."

"Basket in hall. Jim in hall. Jim in basket." She illustrated with sweeping hand gestures.

"What then?"

Sanchez fought to control a laugh. "There's a laundry chute at the end of the hall. If *that* doesn't cool him off—"

The pounding got harder.

"That's it, he asked for this," Sanchez said. *"Now."* She flung the door open. Arizhel leapt, a fluid streak of black. The tuxedoed figure in the hall knocked hard on air, stumbled forward squarely into Arizhel's pivot-kick. He doubled over, fell backward and tumbled heels-over-head into the laundry basket. Sanchez dashed into the hall and slammed the lid on top of him. From within came only a faint rustling of linen and a whispered groan.

Arizhel caught Sanchez's arm. "We still need him as a witness."

"After his trip to the laundry," Sanchez said, overcome with the moment, and trundled the basket up the hall. The chute was a large panel in the wall of the left-hand corridor. Sanchez tipped the basket up and over, hearing terrycloth and cotton, linen and captain

and all, go tumble-tumble-bump down the chute.
Sanchez dusted off her hands and went back to her
room. She owed Jim Kirk a kick in the pants. He'd
just gotten it with eighteen years' worth of interest.

Rish said, "What now?"

"I'll wait for him in his room. Give him fifteen
minutes to get back upstairs, then come in and abduct
me. I'm sure he didn't see me here, and he ought to be
nicely primed to respond when he sees that black suit
again."

"Will I have to fight him again? I almost ripped this
costume apart."

"Between that shot you gave him, the trip
downstairs . . . and finding me waiting for him . . . I
don't think his system will take much more, honey."
She winked. "See you in fifteen."

Arizhel nodded, closed the door and turned
around, still adjusting the cat costume. The hip seams
were straining dangerously.

There was a noise in front of her. She looked up.


Kirk found the fire escape, began climbing the
ladder. It was iron, and creaky, and cold as Pluto's
posterior. The cat outfit wasn't very warm. He wondered if cat burglars wore thermal underwear on duty.

He paused at the second-floor platform, outside
Charlotte's room. There was a light through the
frosted glass of the bathroom window. Another light
filtered down from Arizhel's room directly above. He
reached for the ladder going up.

It wasn't there.

Kirk looked around, paced the platform. It was
dark, and the black iron fire escape was the nearest
thing to invisible (except, Kirk thought, for himself)
but the ladder *wasn't there.*

He thought for a moment. Well, this might not have stopped the real Black Cat Bandit, but there wasn't any way James T. Kirk was going to get up there without a ladder. And Charlotte was right inside the window in front of him, equally unsuspecting, nyaah *ha* ha ha, the villain chuckled to himself.

Kirk slid open the window and swung into the bathroom. He paused just a moment to check his mask in the mirror—wouldn't do to have Charlotte recognize him—held up the sonic stunner and took a long step, a catlike leap, into the bedroom.

He was standing face to face with somebody in a black leotard, mask, and hood.

Oh, boy, Kirk thought, of all the nights for the real Black Cat to show up . . .

The Bandit took a cautious-looking step toward him, then a dangerous-looking one. Kirk brought up his pistol and fired.

*Bweep* went the stunner. The Bandit froze, but didn't fall down.

*Oops,* Kirk thought.

Fluid shift of black-clad limbs, black foot in face, black everything.

Kaden was having another bad dream of deep space. He really seemed to be floating this time . . . but surely in a vacuum suit . . . yes, in a suit whose air filters needed changing something *fierce*. Someone in a black combat skin had kicked him out an airlock. . . .

The smell of ammonia roused him. He shook his head. Fabric rustled. He was lying on, in, and under an enormous heap of dirty laundry, a sock wrapping his nose. He clawed it away, thrashed around, trying to find some way out of the holding bin before the recyclers started and he wound up as a set of dress uniforms.

There was a hatch in the metal wall. Kaden got it open, emerged in a small cascade of regular-cycle cotton and linen. It wasn't a ship. He was in the hotel basement again.

Kaden's foot hit something hard. He looked down. There was a glass flask on the floor, next to a neatly folded tuxedo with nicely symmetrical brown stains on the lapels.

*Kirk,* Kaden thought. Kaden had opened the door to the ambassador's room, and Kirk, wearing the bandit outfit, had attacked him, and not with a deactivated sonic, either. That made twice Kirk had cheated Kaden out of his scene, the glory-mad, selfish, swaggering . . .

There was a Klingon proverb: *Fool me once, shame on you, fool me twice, prepare for doom.* Kaden's fingers closed around the flask. It felt good in his hand: hard, heavy. Kirk's head would soon discover how hard and heavy.

Kaden got into the elevator. The door closed. "Second floor," he said.

Nothing happened.

"Stupid human machinery," Kaden growled, and mashed the 2 button.

The door opened. Kaden saw a flutter of white disappearing down the stairs, but did not follow. Kirk was wearing black. Kaden grinned and hefted the flask. Black was a good color for him to be wearing. He went down the right-hand corridor, to Kirk's room. Behind him, soiled whites and a few odd socks trailed on a length of piano wire.

He stopped at Kirk's door. He held up the bottle, he held up his fist. He banged both against the wood.

* * *

Rish stood over the fallen enemy in black, raising her heel to kick-snap his neck. The true Cat robber should have chosen another night than this, she thought.

She heard, and felt, stitching give way. Black cloth peeled away from her right leg.

She paused, and had a better thought. Deedee had Pete waiting downstairs, to move him into the game of rescue. But they no longer needed the game. They had a real enemy for the young man to kill.

Capture. Capture. She had to keep remembering that. Crazy human customs.

Arizhel picked up the Cat robber and shoved him into the closet. She pressed the lock button, since Charlotte had the key, then shut the door, listening for the click. She heard the Cat stir within. That was disappointing; she must be out of practice.

She went toward the door. Stitches popped like bursts of gunfire. Instinctively she grabbed at the scraps of black as they fell away. It seemed to make things worse.

But she did not need the Cat costume any longer. She could simply change back into her dress . . .

Which was locked in the closet, behind the Cat.

Rish sighed. She felt a cold wind from the disposal cubicle. The window to the fire escape was open. That was a possible exit. In fact, it went directly up to her room. Very good. She crawled out.

It was cold, and she was wearing less by the second. Shivering, she reached for the ascending ladder.

No ladder.

Rish swore, climbed back into the room, and shut the window.

There was a white bathrobe, long and plush, hanging from a hook behind the cubicle door. She pulled off what was left of the leotard and put the robe on over her strapless undersuit. She looked in the mirror, pulled off the hood, looked again. Did humans go out dressed like this?

Yes, she thought, they did. She went back into the bedroom, ignoring the soft slow bumping from the closet, and opened the Index of Services folder. It said:

### HEATED SWIMMING POOL FOR OUR GUESTS

Rish chuckled triumphantly. She turbaned a towel around her hair and walked lightly out of the room, rolling her shoulders as if loosening up for a swim.

The elevator was coming up. Was it Kirk?

The door started to open. She saw a black trouser leg with a stripe, a dusty patent-leather shoe. Kirk indeed, fresh from his trip to the basement.

She clutched the robe around herself and ducked into the stairwell. It was the down staircase, and she was still entirely too visible. She kept going down until she reached the lobby.

"May I help you, madam?" a voice said. Rish whirled, hand raised to strike. The bell captain took a hasty step back.

"I am . . . on my way to the pool," she said.

"Oh," the man said. "I'm terribly sorry, madam, but the pool closes at ten P.M."

"Then open it!" Rish snapped, not in the mood for any of this from hotel servitors.

The bellman smiled, bowed slightly. "I think that can be arranged, madam. It'll just be a few minutes."

"Very well."

The servitor bowed again and went away. Rish noticed the desk clerk and several other persons in the lobby, trying to pretend they were not looking at her. She pretended she had not seen them, and ducked around the corner, toward the ice cream parlor. That was where Deedee and Pete were supposed to be waiting.

Except that they weren't. The parlor was dark, chairs stacked on tables. Rish tensed. Her feet were getting cold.

She turned around, walked by the bank of telephones. The one on the end was marked HOUSE PHONE. She went in, picked up the receiver.

"Front desk."

"I wish to speak to the officer in charge of laundry," Arizhel said, trying to sound commanding and unconcerned at once.

"One moment, madam."

There was a pause, a series of clicks. Then Rish heard the sound of humming machinery, and a gravelly male voice said, "Laundry Room."

"This is Commander Arizhel. You were given one of my uniforms for cleaning. I want it sent to—" She thought. Not her room, but where Sanchez was waiting. "Room 22. *Immediately.*"

"I'll see if it's done—"

"I said *immediately,*" she said, and slammed the phone onto its cradle.

"Ah, there you are, madam," said the bell captain, from barely a meter away. "We have the pool ready for you now."

"I've changed my mind," Rish said. "Close it at once."

She walked past the bellman, back to the lobby, straightened her shoulders and walked up the stairs.

Sanchez sat on the bed in Jim Kirk's room, wondering where the hell Kirk was. It wasn't *that* far to the basement. Unless they'd killed him by accident . . . ?

No.

Or the laundry recyclers had . . .

*Aack.*

There was a sudden pounding on the door. "You've got a hard knock, Jim," Sanchez said, took a step, then stopped still.

This was Kirk's room.

"Jim?" she said, in a tiny voice.

*"Kirk?"* Kaden's voice rumbled right through the door. "Kirk, we have a thing to settle!"

Several things ran rapidly through the ambassador's mind:

—An after-dinner drink with Jim Kirk in her room was one thing. Being found waiting for him in *his* room, without even a change of clothes handy, was something else again.

—Whatever Kaden wanted to discuss with Kirk, it wasn't going to be a friendly little chat.

—The door wasn't locked, and she didn't have the key to lock it.

This won't do, she thought finally, and as Kaden's blows shook the door in its frame, she turned and ran for the bathroom, closing the door behind her. It was purely psychological: she knew that a little thing like a bathroom door wasn't going to slow down an enraged Klingon officer for very long.

The words FIRE ESCAPE appeared before her eyes like a beacon in the fog. She pushed the bathroom window open, started to climb out, skidded on porcelain and nearly broke her neck on the shower rod. Evening slippers were no good at all for climbing on toilets while pursued by angry Klingons. She pulled off the shoes and tossed them out the window. (No point in incriminating Jim Kirk for something he *wasn't* guilty of.) She climbed up again, swung her feet onto the platform, and nearly yelled. The metal was

222

*cold.* Her skirt bunching and dragging, she fumbled for and grasped the ladder. She began to climb, (ancestral instinct to get to the top of the tree, she thought) heard the bathroom door slam open, a growl, a skid, a clattering crash.

The window slammed shut. Sanchez reached for the next rung, grabbed it and pulled like mad. Then she noticed the tug of her skirt, caught in the windowframe.

The zipper gave way, and the skirt slipped down, silk on nylon just like ice on ice, and fluttered away into the darkness below.

In her blouse and her stockings, Ambassador Sanchez dangled.

Kaden banged again on Kirk's door. He grasped the knob, ready to wrench the door off its hinges.

It swung wide, nearly tumbling him into the room. He looked around. No one was in sight. But the bathroom door was closed. "So, Kirk, we add 'cowardly' to our list of words for starship captains!" He booted the bathroom door open. There was a cold blast of air through the open window. Vaulting up on the toilet seat, he lunged for it.

The wire trailing from his suit caught on something, and his foot shot out from under him. Arms above his head, reaching for the window, he fell with a screeching thump into the bathtub, one hand just barely in the windowsill. The walls shook. The window slid shut on his fingertips.

He hung semi-suspended, spread-eagled, hand in window, hand on wall, foot in tub, foot in toilet. He could feel his right sock waterlogging. He groped with his free hand, found a handle, grasped it.

The shower came on, drenching him.

"Aaaah," Kaden said.

There was a knock at the hallway door.

Kaden twisted the shower handle off. He pulled his trapped fingers free of the window, and fell into the bathtub. Tugging his foot out of the toilet, he got to his feet, shook water off his shoulders, and walked with squelching tread to the door. On the way he snatched up the seltzer bottle, holding it aloft for maximum impact.

There was a short, bald man with a big nose standing in the doorway. "Good evening, sir," he said, "I was told to bring this up here right away." He held out a garment bag.

Kaden stared. The little man just stood there. Kaden lowered the bottle and took the bag.

The laundryman pointed at Kaden's demolished, sodden tuxedo. "I see you got the spots out, sir. I told you club soda was just the thing. Only you needn't have used so *much.*" He turned and went away up the hall.

Dazed, Kaden stepped back from the door. He looked at the objects in his hands. He put the bottle down and tore open the laundry bag.

He was holding Arizhel's dress uniform.

Delivered to *Kirk's* room . . .?

Kaden roared and ran up the hall.


Tatyana Trofimov, who once in the distant past had been the captain of a spaceship, shuffled from a dark tunnel into a dim basement, and paused, causing the two beings who used to be her crew to fall on top of her.

They untangled themselves, looked around. Whatever this place was, it had been made by intelligent beings. Messy, but intelligent.

"Look, Captain," Tellihu said, running his hands over a metal door. "A turbo-lift. Are we on the ship again, Captain?"

T'Vau made a low rumbling noise. "Computer," she said softly. "Computer, I am coming for you. I will unsolder you synapse by synapse . . ."

"No, Tellihu, we're not on the ship," Trofimov said. "There aren't any computers here, T'Vau, do you understand me?"

"Two raised to the power one one two one three, minus one, is prime," T'Vau said.

"Good, T'Vau, that's good. Hold that thought. Tellihu, press the call button for the lift."

"I smell fresh air," Tellihu said. "May I go outside and fly, Captain? Just a little bit?"

"First call the lift, please, Tellihu. Then we will all go outside and fly, all right, Tellihu?"

Tellihu beamed and pressed the call button.

T'Vau said, "Your kind exchanged the power of flight for intelligence. Have you found a way to reverse the trade?"

"I wonder how you would look falling from a very great height?" Tellihu asked T'Vau, in a friendly voice.

Trofimov noticed a man's formal suit, neatly folded. There were two stains on the lapels, nicely matched. She touched it, felt something heavy shift inside it. She pulled the object out. She looked at it once, twice, three times, turning it over in her hands, unable to believe it.

Captain Trofimov snapped open the Starfleet-issue communicator. It whistled. *"Enterprise,"* a voice said. It hissed and crackled, but it was a real voice, on a real communicator. "This is *Enterprise,* go ahead."

Captain Trofimov squared her shoulders, brushed

her hair back from her forehead. T'Vau and Tellihu huddled in close, Tellihu spreading his wings around them all. Tears ran down his face.

*"Enterprise,"* the captain said, "three to beam up."

"Aye," the crackling voice said, and there was golden light, beautiful twinkling golden light all around them.

Kirk bumped into something hard in front of him. Then he hit something solid to his left. And behind him. He felt to the right, lost his balance, and fell a few inches before striking another solid wall. Something was tangled around his feet. Something dangled against his shoulders. He bumped his head on a pole.

You're in a closet, dummy, he thought at once, and immediately recalled the battle with the Black Cat Bandit. I guess I lost.

It was not, truth to tell, the first time Kirk had ever been inside a closet. But that other time, he thought, he had been glad of a closet to hide in . . .

He pushed at the door. It was locked. He kicked at it. It wobbled but didn't open. He tried it again. It seemed to give a little further. He braced himself against the back of the closet, grabbed the clothes pole, picked up both feet and slammed them against the door.

It gave. So did fabric and stitching. With the natural instinct of all men in trousered societies, Kirk put his hand on his seat. Instinct was correct. The rip went most of the way up his spine.

Well, he thought, he didn't really want to go around dressed as a cat burglar, especially with the real thing on the loose. He exited the leotards through the new rear opening, stood there in undershirt and shorts. That wouldn't do for running around the hotel, either.

He looked into the closet he'd just vacated. The only clothing in there was a red evening gown, badly beaten up by Kirk's struggles to escape. It looked like the one Arizhel had worn at dinner. Kirk looked around: this still seemed to be Charlotte's room. He shrugged and put the dress on the bed.

He went into the bathroom. The hotel was supposed to provide bathrobes, but there wasn't one there. He took a long look at the red dress, was rather thankful it was so badly torn up, saving him a tough choice.

He opened the hallway door and peeked out. No one was in sight. He stepped carefully into the hall. He adjusted his boxers, jogged up and down in place. He began jogging down the hall, backpedaling, shadowboxing.

When he reached the stairs, he could hear someone coming from the direction of his room, coming fast by the sound of it. Kirk looked at himself, at the elevator —not there—and dashed up the stairs, out of sight.

On the third floor, he stopped to think. Kaden's room was 32, down the hall to the right. Kaden ought to have a shirt and pants he could borrow. He went down the hall, taking the occasional right cross at the paintings on the walls, to the door of 32. He reached for the knob.

Arizhel stepped from the stairwell onto the second floor, just in time to see a *tuk'zedo*-trousered leg stamp into view from the left-hand corridor, from Kirk's room. He was stomping like a stormwalker, with something in a plastic bag held almost in front of his face. He was bearing down on the elevator. His feet made a curious plop-squish sound.

Rish ducked back into the stairwell as Kirk swept

straight past her, into the elevator, banged a fist on the control buttons. Rish shook her head. The Federation Captain grumbled just like Kaden when he was angry.

The elevator went down, to the basement. Was Kirk going to complain to the laundry-*kuve* about their ridiculous and insubordinate service? No time to think about it now; she ran, robe flapping, up the hall to room 22.

The door was open. No one was there, certainly not the ambassador, and there was no sign of her uniform. Oblivion take all servitors! she thought, and sat down to wait, turning over in her mind suitable punishments for slow laundrymen.

Ambassador Sanchez dragged herself through the window into the bathroom of room 32. It was warm inside, unpleasantly hot after the cold outdoors. She looked at the array of interesting toilet articles on the cabinet and realized that this must be Kaden's room.

*Out of the frying pan,* she thought. But it was empty. And Rish's room was on this floor, just down the other hall. She reached for the handle of the hall door.

There was a sound up the hall. Kirk paused with his hand on the door of 32, turned to see what it was. The bald laundryman was pushing his basket down the other corridor. Kirk jogged after him.

The basket was stopped in front of room 31. The door was open.

Kirk reached the door, looked inside. The laundryman was coming out of the bathroom, holding a stack of towels in one hand and a passkey in the other. Arizhel was nowhere in sight. Kirk said, "Hey there! Just the fella I was looking for!"

"Sir?" the laundryman said, squinting up at him.

"I believe you've got a uniform of mine in the

laundry. If you'd send it up here, there'll be a nice tip in it for you."

"You want it sent up here, sir? This'll be your room now?"

"Well, I mean—"

"It's all the same to me, sir. The Klingon lady doesn't seem to be staying here anymore, so the room's marked down as empty. That's why I came up to change the linens."

"Sure," Kirk said, not having any idea what else to say. "I'd appreciate having that suit on the double."

The laundryman was crossing something out on his clipboard. "I'll do my best, sir."

"Fine. I'll be right here."

The little man looked Kirk up and down, from mussed hair to bare feet. "Too much water and wool barathea just don't mix, sir," he said sadly. "Next time, you'd better let me take care of it."

"Right," Kirk said, and closed the door. So Arizhel wasn't using this room any longer? Kirk breathed a small sigh of relief that he hadn't opened the door of Kaden's room. There were some surprises that weren't at all welcome.

Kaden stepped out of the elevator. It was dark. He looked around in confusion. He was in the basement again. Before he could turn, the elevator door had closed behind him, and the car started up. Hissing, he began walking around the basement, looking for a stairway up, and a better weapon than the seltzer flask in his hand.

He passed near the laundry. The little beak-nosed man was at work, muttering to himself.

Kaden paused to watch the laundryman. He made a sort of unconscious dance of his job, kicking one washing machine shut as he opened another, juggling packets of detergent, interrupting himself to pull the lever of a steam presser. "People can't make up their minds," he muttered to himself as he wrung out a cloth, cleaned a lint filter. "This room, that room, middle of the night, how do they expect me to get it straight?"

As he watched, Kaden's anger passed. Maybe he had misunderstood. Maybe the little man had just carried Rish's uniform up to the wrong room.

Thinking of Arizhel made him even calmer, and a little ashamed at what he'd been thinking. Rish and James Kirk? Kaden chuckled and turned away.

He saw Kirk's tuxedo, still folded up near the laundry bin. Kaden put down the seltzer bottle, pulled off his torn, stained, litter-bedecked jacket, and put Kirk's on. It was tight across the shoulders and it wouldn't button, but it was an improvement. He went back to the elevator, got in, and pushed the button for the third floor.

In Kaden's room, Sanchez paused with her hand on the doorknob. She tugged her blouse down over her hips. It wouldn't go very far.

She checked the bathroom. The plush bathrobe was damp, and scented with what smelled like Klingon Musk Aftershave. No, that wouldn't do.

She thought for a moment. This was a luxury hotel, hot and cold running bellhops. She got the Index of Services from the desk and flipped through it. The gift shop would probably have clothes, but it surely wasn't open at this hour—god, how late *was* it?

She thought of the laundryman with his basket. That was really what she needed. But she didn't have any clothes in the hotel laundry.

But Rish might, she thought. Surely Rish wouldn't

mind her borrowing an outfit, just for the stroll back to her room. It was the sort of thing friends did for each other.

Sanchez picked up the phone.

"Front desk."

"I am calling about the laundry for room 31," Sanchez said, in her best Klingon accent. "I wish a suit of clothes for 31 sent to room 32 instead."

"Yes, madam, immediately," the desk clerk said. His voice sounded unaccountably weary. It must be late for everyone.

She hung up and sat down to wait.

Arizhel was sick of waiting. The idiot laundry-*kuve* had obviously forgotten her, or gotten lost, or possibly destroyed the garment and feared reprisals. She had gotten this far in the bathrobe: she would go to her room, and anyone who saw her could find their own explanations.

Besides, she thought suddenly, Kaden was still locked in her room's disposal cubicle. She would have to think of an apology for that. She doubted that she would have to think terribly hard.

She opened the door and went out into the hall, toward the stairs and up them. There was a laundry basket parked outside her room. So, she thought, they had delivered the uniform to her room instead of Kirk's. Disobedient, but understandable, a minor offense. And Rish was in a forgiving mood now. She went inside. The shower was running; she didn't blame Kaden, this place was too cold, too dry. Steaming up the cubicle was the only way to get comfortable.

The water stopped. A grin wrinkled Rish's face. She would open the door for him now. And if he were

231

comfortable enough, she might not even need to explain.

She tapped on the door, reached for the handle.

Sanchez heard a knock on the door. It was a knock, so it wasn't Kaden; it was a light, polite knock, so it almost certainly wasn't Kirk. Sanchez picked up a heavy bookend, just for prudence's sake, went to the door, and said, "Yes?"

"Laundry," the gravelly voice said.

She tugged her blouse down again, then opened the door a crack, leaned around it, held out her hand. "Thanks a lot," she said. "There'll be a big tip for you in the morning."

"It's all right, ma'am," the little man said, and hung the laundrybag on the ambassador's hand. "I'm retiring in the morning."

Sanchez pulled the bag inside and shut the door. She pulled it open. She immediately recognized the contents as Starfleet Dress Uniform (Male).

"Any old port in a storm," she said heavily, and pulled the black trousers on. They were terribly loose around the waist, but she draped her white blouse artistically, and belted the outfit with one of Kaden's gold sashes. She checked the effect in a mirror: sort of Eclectic Revival. She still didn't have any shoes, but the hallways were all carpeted, and if anybody asked about it she'd tell them she was half-Japanese.

She went out into the hall, headed for Rish's room at the other end of the floor. Just a minute to check in, see what had happened in the lobby. She hadn't heard any commotion; then again, nobody could have had a night quite like hers had been.

Kaden got out of the elevator on the third floor, turned left toward Rish's room. He passed the laundryman, who was carrying a garment bag and mumbling. Kaden chuckled again. Misunderstandings: that was why one let the diplomats exist. Nothing was worse than a war over some stupid misunderstanding.

He stepped around the laundry basket in front of Rish's room, tapped lightly on the door and reached for the handle.

Kirk just heard the door click over the noise of the shower. His uniform was here right on time. That little fellow would get a huge tip in the morning. He toweled himself lightly, tossed on the bathrobe hanging on the door. He felt good.

There was a tap at the bathroom door. Of course; the laundryman would be expecting his tip now. Have to disappoint him, Kirk thought, but how do you explain you've left your wallet in your other pants, and your pants are in your other room?

He pulled the door open.

A pair of powerful arms pulled him into an embrace, one white bathrobe against another, and lips brushed his throat. Instinct took over for a moment, and then he pulled away just enough to look straight into Arizhel's face, her extremely wide eyes.

There was a knock from the hall and the door swung open. Kaden strode into the room, arms spread, mouth open in a big smile.

Nobody moved at all for a couple of seconds.

*"Ghrar,"* Kaden said. *"Ghrar ghrarar."* Kirk wasn't sure if it was Klingonese, but he understood it perfectly.

Kaden lunged. Kirk let go of Rish. Rish fell down. Kirk ducked into the bathroom, made for the window, the fire escape.

The entire back seam of Kaden's tight black jacket ripped apart. Kaden paused, groping behind himself.

233

From somewhere beyond the bathroom window came a long, fading scream.

Sanchez appeared in the doorway, in droopy blouse and floppy pants and Imperial Klingon Navy Officer's gold. "Rish?"

Arizhel scrambled to her feet, put her head down, her shoulder forward, and ran at Kaden, spearing him in the midsection, driving him back, back, out the door and into the hall. Kaden hit the laundry basket, tumbled, was swallowed. Sanchez slammed the lid without even thinking. "Rish—"

"*Chute,*" Rish yelled.

"Shoot *who?*"

"*Laundry* chute!" Sanchez nodded and took hold of the thrashing, bouncing basket, and the two women drove it up the hall just exactly like a bat out of hell, until they reached the wall panel and smashed the basket into it. It was all Newtonian mechanics after that, bodies in motion tending to stay in motion, rumble-bump-bump.

All was quiet on the third floor.

Sanchez and Arizhel leaned against the corridor wall, gasping. Rish looked at Charlotte, pointed at her clothes, and began to laugh out loud. Charlotte returned the gesture, and the laughter. They pointed at the chute, made *swoop* gestures, laughing too hard to speak.

A little distance away, at the entrance to the right-hand corridor, the bald laundryman was tossing towels through another wall panel.

After a few minutes of watching this, Sanchez got enough breath back to say, "Hey! Pal! What are you doing over there?"

The little man said, very patiently, "I'm putting laundry down the chute. That's my job for another . . . fifteen minutes."

"You have two laundry chutes five meters apart?" Arizhel asked.

"No, ma'am. The chutes zig-zag, y'see?" He waved his hands to illustrate. "That one I'm using is blue, for laundry. This one's red."

The two women were instantly silent. After a moment, Sanchez said, "And what's . . . red for?"

"Incinerator," the little man said.

Sanchez and Arizhel screamed with one voice and ran down the stairs.

James Kirk opened his eyes. Things jabbed at his back, and there were tinkling noises as he moved about.

I seem to be wearing a piano, he thought.

He sat up, looked around. He was in the hotel basement, sitting on a pile of junk, wearing a very distressed bathrobe and a towel around his neck. Cold air drafted down on him, and he looked up: through what was either a free-form skylight or a hole, he could see the sky just turning pink with dawn.

He stood up, walking carefully among spilled mattress stuffing and loose piano wires. He had left his tuxedo down here someplace, some while back. It seemed like about two thousand years.

After some hunting around, he found the tux trousers and shirt, and put them on. His patent-leather pumps were there too; they were most welcome. The jacket was gone, but it had been stained anyway. Very symmetrically. And the communicator—he'd have to remember to get that back. McCoy was still ragging him about the one they'd left in the gangster culture. The seltzer bottle was just where he'd left it. Kirk picked it up, idly wishing he had some brandy. Then again, if he had some brandy he wouldn't have cared about the soda.

He sniffed the air. In addition to the other basement smells, there was now a distinct aroma of burning.

*"Ghraaar,"* a very familiar voice said. Kirk looked up. Kaden was standing in front of him, smoldering. Literally. He was covered in soot, and smoke curled from his trousers and his jacket, which had stains on both lapels. *A smoking jacket,* Kirk thought uncontrollably, as the Klingon arched his fingers into claws and came at him.

Kirk raised the seltzer bottle. He pressed the trigger. Kaden hesitated. *"Ghrar?"* he said.

Nothing happened.

"It always works in the movies," Kirk said, and dropped the bottle and ran, Kaden barely arm's reach behind him.

Kirk could see a light up ahead. There was a tunnel, a ramp leading up. As long as it went somewhere, he thought, and made for it. Kaden wasn't giving up.

"Never a diplomat around when you need one," Kirk muttered, and ran for the light at the end of the tunnel.

# Chapter Ten

## *Dilithium Split*

CAPTAIN TROFIMOV, TELLIHU, and T'Vau materialized on a six-pad transporter stage. They looked around in genuine awe. There had been nothing like this aboard *Jefferson Randolph Smith*. There hadn't been any *rooms* this big aboard *Smith*. And just ahead, coming around the console, was a person in Starfleet uniform. A real live Starfleet person coming to welcome them aboard a real live Starfleet ship.

"Hello there," Captain Trofimov said, and saluted.

"Just hold it right there," the crewman said, and reached for a wall panel. "Whoever the heck you are, Security'll have to figure out what to do with you."

*"Non sequitur,"* T'Vau said calmly. *"Post hoc ergo propter hoc."* She reached out and grasped the crewman's collarbone.

"Ooolgh," the crewman said, and fell down.

*"Quod erat demonstrandum,"* T'Vau said.

*"Sic semper tyrannis,"* Tellihu added.

"Shhh," said Trofimov. "We don't want to wake him. We'd better get some uniforms, so that doesn't happen again."

They tiptoed to the turbolift. "Laundry room," Trofimov said, and they all hesitated, huddling slightly against a shower of god knew what. But the lift just closed and whisked them away.

Moving slowly and carefully, learning by degrees how to manage the cargo unit—since even an object with zero net weight still has mass and inertia—Thed and Orvy got their loot to the transporter stage.

"Now what?" Orvy said.

"This is the easy part. We put it on the teleporter and down we go."

"Really? Do you know how to work a teleporter?"

"Sure. You push the handle down to go up, and up to go down. It's easy."

"O-o-okay. *Who* pushes the handle?"

"Well, I do, of course. Unless you just want to."

"So how do *you* get down?"

Thed chewed her lip. Then a voice said, "Excuse me," and she nearly bit it through.

There were three aliens right behind them. One had wings, one pointy ears, just like the three on the planet; but these were wearing crisp new uniforms. A commando team, Thed thought, of course.

The humanest-looking one of the three said, "May we give you some assistance?"

"We, waa, woo," Thed said, and stood in front of the cargo unit as if trying to hide it behind herself. "That is, we, well . . ."

*"We want to get out of here,"* Orvy blurted out.

"Right," Thed said. "On the, ah, teleporter. Thing. Here."

"This is not difficult," the pointy-eared one said.

The human said, "You're new aboard this ship? Cadet crew?"

"Yeah," Thed said, putting her hand casually over one of the TOP SECRET labels. "We're cadets, and we're supposed to get this . . . really ordinary cargo off the ship. Funny that they told . . . ordinary cadets like us to do that. You know?"

"You don't need to tell us about stupid assignments," the human said, and the winged one whistled very loudly and flapped his red wings. "Tell you what, we'll trade you. We can run the transporter, if you'll tell us where the nearest messroom is." She smiled in a crooked sort of way. "Funny us not knowing where that is, isn't it?"

"Sure," Thed said, relaxing. "There's one right that way."

The winged one chirped. The pointy-eared one looked ready to sprint. The human held up a hand and said firmly, "Our friends here have a job to do. We can wait. We *are* still in Starfleet, after all. For at least another couple of days . . ." She shook her head. "Let's get you two dirtside."

Thed and Orvy maneuvered the cargo box onto the transport stage. The pointy-eared alien did something with the controls (Orvy elbowed Thed) and pushed the levers up (Thed returned the gesture).

Light swallowed them, and the ship vanished.

"I do not trust this most recent set of directions," T'Vau said. "These were only cadets, and highly inexperienced ones by all evidence."

"They looked familiar to me," Tellihu said.

Trofimov turned the corner. "It's a messroom."

They walked slowly, slowly, to the slots. Captain Trofimov cleared her throat, said very clearly, "I would like a large glass of orange juice, please."

*Pleep.*

*Pling.*

The tray slot opened. There stood a third-liter tumbler of liquid. Bright blue liquid.

Trofimov reached out a trembling hand and took the glass. She tasted it. Orange, vividly orange, with pulp in her teeth.

As her crew rushed to place their orders, Captain Tatyana Trofimov wept tears of pure joy.

Fortified, they moved on through the cargo bays. One large door stood open, and beyond it rested—an impossibility.

Seven-C, read the signs, and beyond them sat the escape pod from *Jefferson Randolph Smith.*

For a moment they thought it was some illusion, or another pod of like shape; but the door was missing, the interior was pink and smelled of peppermint and spoiled milk.

Without a word, the *Smith* crew climbed into the pod, and lay down on the still-damp couches. Starfleet would come for them. Starfleet took care of its own.

They closed their eyes, and in a moment all three, even the Vulcan, were asleep, dreaming happy dreams.

Kaden was gaining on Kirk, and the end of the tunnel seemed a long way away. Suddenly the gentle downslope of the tunnel floor seemed to steepen. It was the surface, Kirk realized. It was coated with something slicker than vacuum lube. He tried to keep his balance, skated on it for a moment, then tumbled and skidded, unable to stop, even to slow down. Behind him, there was a great Klingonese oath and an even greater thud, and Kaden was sliding too.

Up ahead, the end of the tunnel loomed large: and beyond it Kirk could see an expanse of glass overhead. Somehow or another, they were headed for the glass-roofed banquet hall.

Rish and Sanchez were neck-and-neck down the stairs. When they reached the lobby, Rish seized the desk man by the throat and shouted, "Which way to the basement?"

The clerk's eyes bulged. He pointed. The women ran.

TO BASEMENT, a sign said. They followed, down a flight of slippery wooden steps.

The steps folded flat, into a polished hardwood chute that ejected them both into the glass-roofed Great Hall. All around them were tables, piled high with something under white cloth drapes.

From another side of the room, captains Kirk and Kaden tumbled through a doorway, bouncing over each other.

Kirk slid into a table, used it to pull himself out of Kaden's way. He staggered to his feet, watched Kaden keep rolling another half-dozen meters. The banquet hall was full of white-covered tables . . . and Charlotte, and Rish, both stumbling as Kirk was, both at least as peculiarly dressed.

There was a crash from the far wall, and a shower of lath and foam crumbs. Dr. McCoy, Lieutenant Sulu (sword in hand, oh God, not again, Kirk thought) came directly through the wall, accompanied by two of the Klingons. What next? Kirk thought, and there was a splintering, tinkling sound from the windows along the near wall: Ensign Chekov had just come through the glass, wielding what appeared to be a sword of his own. An even louder crash followed, and a Klingon with *two* swords came through to stand next to Chekov.

*"Kirrrrrk!"* Kaden roared, and took two very heavy and extremely uncertain steps toward Kirk. Instinctively Kirk reached for his phaser.

It wasn't there. Of course not, this was a diplomatic mission. But there was something suddenly in his hand, something flat and not too heavy. Without any thought at all, Kirk threw it; he wasn't even aware what it had been until it hit Kaden squarely in the face with a great white *splat*.

The Klingon captain stood still for a moment, half-smothered in whipped cream, custard streaming down his boiled shirt front. There was a maraschino cherry in the middle of his forehead. Kaden reached up, slowly scraped his eyes clear. Someone dressed all in white linen dashed past, and then, like magic, there was a pie in Kaden's hand.

Blueberry, Kirk thought instead of ducking.

*Splat.*

Blueberry it was.

The drapes fell away from the tables, and more pies were revealed. Kirk grabbed one and flung it at Kaden, who ducked. The pie hit Engineer Askade: strawberry cream on impact. Askade grabbed a pie and threw it. It took off Chekov's tam o'shanter, not neatly. Chekov got a pie, got Ambasador Sanchez. Good old Chekov, Kirk thought. Force Leader Memeth had a pie in each hand, and double-shotted Montgomery Scott with laser-guidance precision. Bones McCoy had the look of a man on whom the gods have smiled as he raised a lemon meringue and delivered it on Memeth.

There were plenty of pies. There was plenty of good old-fashioned hostility. *"To hell with the Organians,"* someone shouted; no one would ever recall who or what race. The moment was all.

\* \* \*

Thed and Orvy had gotten to within sight of town when the gravity unit started to fail. The box started to acquire weight, several hundred kilos of it. This made it first difficult, then impossible to handle.

"Before you say anything," Thed said, almost calmly, "We did get it this far."

"I wasn't going to say a thing."

"Maybe we should bury it," Thed said.

"Take a pretty big hole. Especially without a shovel."

"Yeah."

"So what *do* we do with it?"

"I thought you weren't going to say that."

Orvy just put his head in his hands.

Thed stood straight. "We open it, that's what we do. Maybe it's hand disintegrators, and we can use them ourselves ... And before you ask, yes, I know how to open it. Right here's the handle." She pointed at the red-striped, recessed grip at the end.

"I still haven't said anything."

Thed grabbed the handle. It wouldn't turn. She pushed in, and there was a click, and the grip rotated easily. Red lights began flashing. Thed looked very hard at the red lights. "I think maybe we better get away from this," she said.

"There is a certain logic in your position," Orvy said, as they sprinted for shelter.

The box blew open with a great deal of sound but not much fury. Inside was a mass of folded, blue silver material. The lump began to swell. A blob extended itself on a shaft, like the neck of some prehistoric monster emerging from its egg. Legs—no, wings—began to spread.

Scarcely half-inflated against the push of atmosphere, no more than an overgrown kite, the Klingon battlecruiser drifted on the morning breeze.

Most of the walls and floor of the Great Hall, and everyone in it, were coated thickly with fruit and syrup and cream, with rimes of flaky brown crust. There seemed to be an army of snowmen at war.

Captain Kaden was stalking Captain Kirk, a banana-cream held at port arms. Kirk held a cherry custard, twin to the first shot fired, in both hands, ready to attack or defend as the moment dictated.

Kaden threw. Kirk threw. It was mutual annihilation. They looked around; the tables had become depleted, and they were out of reach of ammunition —but not of each other. They fell into a clutch that might have been deadly had it been possible to get a grip on anything.

"You," Kirk said, "do you know just how tired I am of—"

Charlotte Sanchez pushed Kirk aside, not hard since Kirk's shoes were frictionless. He bumped against a table, reloaded and fired. The chocolate custard landed top-down on Sanchez's head and remained there, the crust tilted rakishly.

"Stay out of this, Jim," the ambassador said. "You don't have any authority here anyway." She planted a hand directly on Kaden's chest. "I am sick of you," she said at absolute top volume, "sick of this crazy planet, sick, sick, *sick,* and I don't ever want to see *any* of you again!"

"In this at least we are in agreement," Kaden yelled right back. "We would leave this world to shiver in the dry dark!"

"Dry dock?" Scott said.

"Dark, dark," Maglus growled, and dropped another blueberry on Scott.

"I'm *busy*, dagnabbit," Dr. McCoy said, shoving a coconut custard down Maglus's trousers.

There was an abrupt silence. Then Estervy's voice called out, "Cut, *print!* Okay, everybody, that's a wrap!"

A metal platform drifted down from above: two video and two film cameras were mounted on the anti-grav unit. Pete Blackwood waved from the cameraman's chair, while Princess Deedee flew the crane.

"Smile," Estervy said, with all the primness gone from her voice. "You're on Candid Diplomacy."

There was a shaft of twinkling golden light in the Great Hall. First Officer Spock materialized, looked around at the cream-covered crew.

"Captain Kirk," he said, almost indifferently.

"Spock," Kirk said, "Spock." Then, from the heart, *"Spock."* He held out his arms. "Somebody give the captain a *pie!"*

At least twelve pies intersected on Kirk.

A shadow fell across them all. Through the huge glass skylight, the silhouette of a Klingon battlecruiser blotted out the sun.

Kaden was screaming in Klingonese. Arizhel took a firm grip on his arm, said calmly, "It's a bit low to be ours. And a bit limp."

The boom was indeed flopping badly, the wings folding up. As everyone watched from below, the Deployable Practice Target [Prototype, Klingon] draped itself over the Great Hall of Direidi.

Blackout.

The Federation, Imperial, and Direidi principals, showered and freshly dressed, sat in the hotel lobby. Uhura and Aperokei, fortified with strong tea after stun-weapon recovery, sat propped up on pillows. A shadow passed the skylight as the anti-grav camera crane peeled the Klingon cruiser from the Great Hall roof.

"Time for us to introduce our principals . . . and our principals, if you take my meaning," Estervy said. "This is Ross Goch Flyter, also known as Ross Red."

"Oh, only when I'm writing," Flyter said. "And *this* is Esther Vicinanzo, late of—"

"Starfleet Academy College of Humanities," Lieutenant Sulu said suddenly. "You were head of the drama department before Dr. Slaff."

Estervy bowed politely. "Always happy to be recognized. You studied under Dr. Horvendile, didn't you, Mr. Sulu? I taught him that high-prime parry business."

Ambassador Sanchez said, "Starfleet Academy has a drama department?"

The officers all stared at her.

"Oh, my dear," Estervy said quietly, "we're not *all* swaggering, tin-plated, toot-toot, prepare to board, sir, types."

Sanchez said, "Touché." Kirk's face tightened, but his lips stayed straight as a steel rule.

Gladiola appeared to prove she wasn't a pile of dust somewhere, and the stunt teams took cautious bows and promised to send best wishes to those who weren't up and walking yet. Estervy hit one of the "dilithium statues" with a hammer, shattering the plastic resin. The street magician who had switched noisemakers for Uhura's and Proke's communicators returned the genuine articles. Rik, the mechanical effects specialist, showed off the artillery simulators and spring-metal collapsing swords—Memeth grunted in what might have been approval—and Ilen the Magian obligingly drank the ginger beer in the little flask.

"To understand our particular mode of . . .

approach to this situation," Flyter said, "you simply have to understand the principles that Direidi was founded on."

Kirk said, "Which are?"

"If I could explain them, I'd be wrong," Flyter said happily. "We're not anarchists. Or maybe we are, but we're not nihilists. There is a strong Dada element, I confess. Or maybe—"

"The constant factor," Estervy said, "is that we came a long way out here in order to *not be part* of Federations or Empires or Anything Elses more structured than a game of contract bridge."

"Unfortunately," Flyter said, "what we thought was space noise, that would isolate us from all of you, turned out to be Hecht radiation. If we hadn't bought this cheap second-hand sensor gear—"

Estervy kicked him politely.

"Ahem," Flyter said. "At any rate, our little paradise turned out to be the biggest dilithium lode for a kiloparsec around. Sooner or later, we were going to be discovered, by one or more of you."

Ambassador Sanchez said, "You knew about the Organian Treaty."

Estervy said, "The Organian Treaty automatically hands over the planet to the most efficient finder. Efficiency is another thing we were running away from."

Flyter said, "There wasn't any hope of arming ourselves against you . . . *either* of you. So we determined just what our most potent available weapons were. We started working on Plan C."

Arizhel said, "What happened to A and B?"

Estervy said, "Not C as in alphabetical order. C as in Comedy."

"Or Con game," Flyter said. "Or Cream-pie Chorale."

Kirk said, "You can't run a society based on . . . *comedy routines.*"

"You can't?" Flyter said, almost innocently. "I thought it was rather a common thing. Not under that name, of course."

Sanchez was trying, and failing, to conceal her giggles.

"And what will you do when true enemies come?" Kaden said, not very fiercely at all. "With what will you meet the armed one?"

"With the thing none can stand against," Estervy replied, in perfect Klingonese. "Being laughed at."

"It is," Spock said mildly, "a most credible threat. Which is all that one can ask of a weapons system."

"You see?" said Flyter. "Vulcans are the greatest straight men in the galaxy."

"That's all very nice," Aperokei said, "but who's got the Black Bird?"

Kaden said, "What are you talking about *this* time, Lieutenant?"

"Oh, I know what he means," Estervy said. "Who gets the dilithium?"

"You understand, we don't want any part of any of you," Flyter said, a serious undertone creeping into his voice. "I mean that very sincerely. But what we're sitting on is so valuable, you'll find some way of getting it, no matter what we do. And besides," he said more lightly, "your languages both have a word for 'being laughed at.' But somewhere out there, there might be someone who doesn't. I'd be very afraid of them."

Estervy said, "What we propose is to join the Federation—"the Klingons, except for Proke and Arizhel, tensed—"on a provisional basis, of course, *and* contingent on the Federation's contracting out all

Direidi dilithium mining to the Klingon Empire. The percentages of commerce, percentages of trade—" she sang the words—"we'll leave to your Empires' legal minds, who'd get hold of it anyway."

Flyter said, "You're going to have to watch each others' backs. If we don't like the way one of you behaves, the other had better get it fixed . . . or else. And you've seen our 'or else.' "

Charlotte Sanchez was helpless with laughter. Kirk said, "You're joking."

"Just this once, we're not."

After a long pause, Estervy said, "It even saves time for everyone. Ambassador Sanchez is already here . . . as is the Klingon mining expedition, am I correct, Force Leader Memeth?"

Memeth nodded. He was smiling. There actually seemed to be some warmth in it.

"And we'd also like to invite Lieutenant Aperokei to remain, as . . . Special Cultural Liaison. If that's acceptable."

Proke said quietly, "I am still subject to my captain's orders."

Kaden said, "I have long considered the many ways that I might be rid of you, *Zan* Aperokei, but I admit I never thought it would be to a command of your own. *Kai* Proke!"

Pam, in toque and apron, appeared in the doorway, wooden spoon held high. "The Great Hall having been scrubbed, first call to dinner is issued. And *this* time, there will be no strange noises from the kitchen."

They stood. Kirk offered Ambassador Sanchez his arm. "No, uhm, hard feelings?" he said.

"It was in a good cause," Sanchez said. "Besides, every comedy needs a *hieros gamos.*"

"A—"

"Tell you later," Sanchez said.

The landing parties were gathered outside the Hotel. Good-byes were said, and Estervy distributed small packages. Uhura found the silver harp in hers, none the worse for its adventures. Sulu and Memeth received trick swords, Askade a tabletop sculpture of *faux* dilithium. Chekov and Korth were awarded the Direidi Cluster for Valor Under Par. Scott and Maglus got heavy cylinders that gurgled when tilted. McCoy was given a cryostore cube filled with frozen ham steaks, biscuit dough, and red-eye gravy, along with Pam's recipes for all of them. Kirk and Kaden received small brown-wrapped parcels, with strict instructions to open them later. And Estervy gave Arizhel a leather-bound Shakespeare, pointing out the marked passages in *As You Like It, Much Ado About Nothing,* and *The Merry Wives of Windsor*.

The departing crews started for the small platforms, still draped with the wrong empires' flags. In the glass streetcar pavilion, the band struck up the same tune they had played on the visitors' arrival, and the Direidi chorus sang:

> We hope that you've enjoyed your stay
>   Although the good times don't last
>     Forever, it's true
> We're sorry that you're on your way
>   And hope that pleasant memories
>     Accompany you
> And now you're all packed up, and
> Your visit's complete
> We're gonna count the silver
> And burn all the sheets

So until you come again someday
We hope that you've enjoyed your stay

We hope that you've enjoyed your stay
  We're gonna miss you sorely
    And hang down our heads
This really is a sad, sad day
  We're gonna draw the blinds and
    Check under the beds
You know you're welcome here
As sumac in leaf
So here's a hearty wave and
A sigh of relief
Although we'll miss you anyway
We hope that you've enjoyed your stay

As she walked away from the hotel, Uhura paused. She turned to look at Proke. They held the pose for a long moment. Then Uhura said, "Here's lookin' at you, kid."

Aperokei's face froze. Slowly he said, "If you can stand it, I can stand it . . . say it, Uhura."

"Good-bye, Proke."

He nodded. She turned away, went to join the *Enterprise* crew.

Both stages were illuminated, and the landing parties vanished.

Kirk had locked the door of his cabin and activated the privacy circuits. He tore the paper from his parting gift. As he had feared, it was a videocassette. Sweating just slightly, he popped it into the desktop player, and watched from above as pies were thrown. The sound was recorded live. Everyone involved was clearly identifiable.

When the fight was over, the tape went suddenly from color and sound to scratchy black and white and tinny organ music. Flyter and Estervy were on the screen, wearing dark suits, white shirts, narrow neckties . . . and round derby hats.

Flyter smiled fussily and flapped his tie at the camera. Estervy blinked, raised her hat, and spoke, though there was no sound. Instead the screen went black, except for an ornate white border and fancy lettering:

CAPTAIN KADEN HAS ONE TOO.

The two figures reappeared, waving, tipping their hats. An organ chord played, and another title card appeared:

THE END

Kirk took the cassette from the player. Now what was the combination of his personal safe . . .?

On Cargo Deck C, three figures approached the deck officer, who looked up from her reading. The three wore Starfleet uniforms, but stained with something like paint, and smelling to high heaven. The one in the middle looked human. The one on the right had wings. The one on the left had pointed eyebrows. The ensign, who was well-read and not overly superstitious, thought of Faust escorted by good and bad angels, or maybe a William Blake illustration.

"Pardon me," said the one with wings, "but we'd like directions to—"

"No, that's all right," said the middle one, "quite all right, *entirely* all right. We'll just find our own way, thanks very much."

"I sing the hypotenuse," said the arch-eyed one, "sweeping square of other sides! Pythagoras led boldly, on his great gold thigh!"

The trio walked on up the corridor.

The ensign looked after them for a moment. She supposed that there was someone she ought to say something to about whatever had just happened.

But whom? she thought. What? And most importantly, *why?*

She picked up her book.

*Enterprise* sailed on.

For more information regarding

# STAR TREK®
## THE OFFICIAL FAN CLUB

please call or write to:
STAR TREK: THE OFFICIAL FAN CLUB
P.O. Box 111000
Aurora, CO 80011

# THE
## STAR TREK
### PHENOMENON

_____ ENTROPY EFFECT
66499/$3.95

_____ KLINGON GAMBIT
66342/$3.95

_____ PROMETHEUS DESIGN
67435/$3.95

_____ ABODE OF LIFE
66149/$3.95

_____ BLACK FIRE
65747/$3.95

_____ TRIANGLE
66251/$3.95

_____ WEB OF THE ROMULANS
66501/$3.95

_____ YESTERDAY'S SON
66110/$3.95

_____ WOUNDED SKY
66735/$3.95

_____ CORONA
66341/$3.95

_____ MY ENEMY, MY ALLY
65866/$3.95

_____ VULCAN ACADEMY
MURDERS
64744/$3.95

_____ UHURA'S SONG
65227/$3.95

_____ SHADOW LORD
66087/$3.95

_____ ISHMAEL
66089/$3.95

_____ KILLING TIME
65921/$3.95

_____ DWELLERS IN THE
CRUCIBLE
66088/$3.95

_____ PAWNS AND SYMBOLS
66497/$3.95

_____ THE FINAL REFLECTION
67075/$3.95

_____ MINDSHADOW
66090/$3.95

_____ CRISIS ON CENTAURUS
65753/$3.95

_____ DREADNOUGHT
66500/$3.95

_____ DEMONS
66150/$3.95

_____ BATTLESTATIONS!
66201/$3.95

_____ CHAIN OF ATTACK
66658/$3.95

_____ DEEP DOMAIN
67077/$3.95

_____ DREAMS OF THE RAVEN
67794/$3.95

_____ ROMULAN WAY
68085/$3.95

_____ HOW MUCH FOR JUST
THE PLANET?
62998/$3.95

_____ BLOODTHIRST
64489/$3.95

_____ ENTERPRISE
65912/$4.50

_____ STRANGERS FROM
THE SKY
65241/$3.95

_____ FINAL FRONTIER
64752/$4.50

_____ IDIC EPIDEMIC
63574/$3.95

_____ THE TEARS OF THE
SINGERS
67076/$3.95

_____ THE COVENANT OF
THE CROWN
67072/$3.95

_____ MUTINY ON
THE ENTERPRISE
67073/$3.95

_____ THE TRELLISANE
CONFRONTATION
67074/$3.95

# THE

## ⟍STAR TREK⟍

### PHENOMENON

_____ **STAR TREK– THE MOTION PICTURE**
67795/$3.95

_____ **STAR TREK II– THE WRATH OF KHAN**
67426/$3.95

_____ **STAR TREK III–THE SEARCH FOR SPOCK**
67198/$3.95

_____ **STAR TREK IV– THE VOYAGE HOME**
63266/$3.95

_____ **STAR TREK: THE NEXT GENERATION:
ENCOUNTER AT FARPOIINT**
65241/$3.95

_____ **STAR TREK: THE KLINGON DICTIONARY**
66648/$4.95

_____ **STAR TREK COMPENDIUM REVISED**
62726/$9.95

_____ **MR. SCOTT'S GUIDE TO
THE ENTERPRISE**
63576/$10.95

_____ **THE STAR TREK INTERVIEW BOOK**
61794/$7.95

_____ **STAR TREK:
THE NEXT GENERATION:
GHOST SHIP** 66579/$3.95

_____ **STAR TREK: THE NEXT GENERATION:
THE PEACEKEEPERS**
66929/$3.95

_____ **STAR TREK: THE NEXT GENERATION:
THE CHILDREN OF HAMLIN**
67319/$3.95

**POCKET
B O O K S**

**Simon & Schuster Mail Order Dept. STP
200 Old Tappan Rd., Old Tappan, N.J. 07675**

Please send me the books I have checked above. I am enclosing $_____ (please add 75¢ to cover
postage and handling for each order. N.Y.S. and N.Y.C. residents please add appropriate sales tax). Send
check or money order—no cash or C.O.D.'s please. Allow up to six weeks for delivery. For purchases over
$10.00 you may use VISA: card number, expiration date and customer signature must be included.

Name_____

Address_____

City_____ State/Zip_____

VISA Card No._____ Exp. Date_____

Signature _____ 118-09